The Case of the Missing Pug

A Laura Boxford Mystery

by

Nicky Stratton

Speart House Publishing
Billesley House
Elgin Gardens
Stratford-upon-Avon
Warwickshire CV37 7BG

Copyright © Nicky Stratton

Nicola Stratton has asserted her right under the Copyright, Designs and Patents Act 1988 to be identified as the author of this work.

All rights reserved. No part of this publication may be reproduced, stored in a retrieval system, or transmitted, in any form or by any means without the prior written permission of the publisher, nor be otherwise circulated in any form of binding or cover other than that in which it is published and without a similar condition being imposed on the subsequent purchaser.

This book is a work of fiction and any resemblance to actual persons, living or dead, is purely coincidental.

ISBN: 978-1-911323-18-1

Acknowledgements

I'd like to thank Paul Budd and Mary Durndell at Speart House Publishing.
Tony G and Debs for the cover design and the Ellenden writing group for their continued support.

Chapter 1

Laura let Parker off the lead for his evening constitutional. The pug was keen and trotted off in the dark and rain of a cold October night. She could hear him snuffling hog-like in his search for calling cards charged with hidden meaning and the intoxicating aromas that exude from rotting matter. It was a calculated risk to let him go. If he rolled in something she would have to put him in the shower when they got back and that always ended in a mess of sodden towels on the bathroom floor.

Waiting on the path that led through the rose garden, Laura stared through the gloom, straining to follow his outline before he disappeared into the dense mass of sprawling shrubs that ran in a wide semi-circle beyond the formal gardens. In one direction it stretched almost to the old stable yard of the former somewhat dilapidated Chipping Wellworth Manor, where she had spent most of her adult life. Taken over, transformed and rebranded as Wellworth Lawns by her grand-daughter Victoria's husband Vince Outhwaite, it had risen phoenix-like as the five star residential care home where at the age of eighty-six, she continued to live.

At the other end of the shrubbery was a pond. Parker was careful to avoid it on account of having once mistaken duckweed for terra firma while chasing a mallard. She could see the disgust on his face as he sneezed and shook himself down after she had pulled him out. Apart from this episode, Laura never knew exactly where he went on his nocturnal rambles, but he was never gone for long.

Sheltering under a corporate umbrella she'd taken from the stand in the hall, she felt the therapeutic effects of fresh air. She had been to The Blue Dolphin fish and chip shop in the local town of Woldham earlier that evening. The result was a hint of indigestion. She took some deep breaths, thankful not to have suffered a case of full-blown heartburn.

Minutes passed. Now mildly irritated by Parker's continued absence, she called him.

She thought she heard rustling in the bushes. Why didn't he get a move on? He knew a scampi tail was waiting for him back in the warmth of her apartment. She always saved an extra morsel for when he came in.

'Parker,' she called again.

There was no sound. She checked her watch, but couldn't see the dial, so she took a small torch from the pocket of her puffer jacket. The faint light flickered. It was nearly ten.

'I'm going to miss the news,' she said to herself, as the light died. Returning it to her pocket, she walked back towards the house, deciding to skirt round the side to see if he wasn't at the rear of the building.

She passed the main entrance and turned the corner into almost total darkness. Her eyes were drawn to a chink of light shining out from where the dining room curtains had not been fully closed. She froze. Was it the outline of a figure illuminated? It was gone before she had time to work out who it might have been.

The sound of rain pattered louder on the umbrella. It was disconcerting and despite her cautious steps, she tripped on the slippery flagstones. Trying to save herself, she dropped the umbrella as she fell to her knees. A hot flush of shock came over her. She knew the consequences of taking a tumble in one's later years. She had once attended a Fall Prevention class in the Recreation Room. These meetings were high on the agenda of activities available. Her dear friend Venetia Hobbs, who lived in the room next to Laura's, said she was on grade eight, in itself curious, but doubly so as she'd fractured her wrist during a demonstration on tying shoelaces safely. Now Laura took a moment to gather her senses. Relieved she could feel no pain, she was wiping her hands down the sides of her jeans when ahead of her a light came on.

Alfredo the chef stood outside the kitchen complex stretching his arms above his head.

She called to him and he ran over.

'Holy tortelloni Lady B, what you doin' out here this time of night?' he asked, helping her to her feet.

'I can't find Parker.' Her voice was shaky. 'It's so unlike him not to come back.' Unable to stop herself, Laura felt tears bubble in the corners of her eyes, as the swarthy Italian held her steady.

'Hold on one sec, I got an idea.' Alfredo looked down at her, his dark eyes twinkling. 'Maybe he is smelling my shepherd's pie for tomorrow's lunch. We can go and check?'

Together they searched the kitchen and the pantry, the larder and the staff room. They even searched the cold store, but there was no sign of Parker. Reluctantly they continued down the passage to the heavy swing doors that led to the public areas.

In the bar, Mimi the Bulgarian maid, was doubling up her duties by serving nightcaps to a handful of stalwart residents.

'Lady B, she lost the pug,' Alfredo said.

'I come finding him.' Mimi pulled her long dark ponytail taut. 'I shutting bar right now.' She replaced a bottle of Cointreau on the shelf behind her.

Seated at a table, Reggie Hawkesmore jumped up. 'Count me in,' he said, standing to attention.

Beside him Crawford Tuthill remained slouched in his chair, his hands resting on his corpulent belly. ''Fraid I'll have to sit this one out.' He leant forward with a wince and rubbed his knee.

'Don't worry old chap,' Reggie said. 'I'll go and stop the film in the Recreation Room. It's Casablanca again. Full house I should imagine; nothing like the wide screen to pack 'em in. Should be able to muster a decent search party.'

As people gathered in the hall, the new manageress, Jayne Harcourt came out of her office to see what the commotion was about. Having apprised herself of the situation she took control.

'All those fit enough, form yourselves into groups of three or four. Stick together. No mobility scooters on the lawns if you don't mind.'

They set off, and soon the sound of Parker's name resounded through the darkened grounds. Lights came on in upstairs windows. Alfredo and Laura went back inside to make sure he hadn't snuck upstairs unnoticed.

But there was no sign of him, and it was gone midnight when Jayne called off the search.

'Try not to fret Lady Boxford,' she said, pressing her hand on Laura's shoulder. 'I'm sure he'll turn up in the morning.'

Laura returned to her apartment. She sat down on the sitting room sofa clasping her silver and turquoise Navajo bracelet and stared at Parker's empty basket. Not that he ever used it, preferring as he did, to sit with her.

In her mind she pictured him. His shining saucer eyes and damp coal-black nose; his curly tail like a French pastry and his soft furry brow furrowed in an expression of quizzical indignation at her imagined question.

'Why didn't you come back when I called you?'

Beside her was his blanket. She picked it up and clutched it to her chest, but the familiar aroma gave her no comfort.

She must have dozed off because she woke with a start. On the mantelpiece she saw the minute hand on the clock align with the hour hand. It was six in the morning. Parker had been missing for over eight hours.

With a crack of her knees, she stood up. Even though she was still wearing her jacket, a shiver ran through her stiffened limbs. Alone in the bitter cold, Parker had no coat on.

She must get back outside.

Her hands went to the jacket pockets. In one she felt her mobile. In the other the torch and the molded plastic of his retractable lead.

At least he was wearing his collar with his lucky silver charm and the metal tag with her phone number on it.

'Just stay where you are,' she said, hurrying to the hallway. 'I'll find you.'

She swapped her slippers for a pair of boots, grabbed her shepherd's crook and Parker's blue fleece lined mac that hung on the coat peg on the back of the door. Then, picking up her keys she set off, shutting the door behind her.

The night-lights were still on in the passage as she passed the lift and took the stairs to the ground floor. She could hear the sound of a vacuum cleaner coming from the direction of the dining room as she passed the empty reception desk on her way to the glass doors of the main entrance. Twice she took a step back then forward in frustration, before remembering the out-of-hour keypad. She pressed the numbers, heard the buzz and then the smooth swoosh as the doors slid open.

Outside a bleak grey dawn was breaking. She hurried back through the rose garden. Calling Parker's name, she crossed the grass and headed into the shrubbery where she had first lost sight of him. She pulled a laurel branch to one side peering into the dark interior. Drips of last night's rain slid off the shiny leaves down her sleeve. She backed out, carrying on down the rough paths that meandered through more laurel, rhododendron and yew. Her feet squelched on the soft ground. She stopped, listening for his familiar yap.

The silence was broken by a couple of wood pigeons that flapped and cooed overhead.

Silence again. Then further afield, the clarion two-tone crow of a cock pheasant.

She walked on down to the pond before cutting back under the high red brick wall of the old kitchen garden. Turning right, she joined the tarmac drive and passed through the pillars that formed the entrance to Mulberry Close. It was a small development of mainly bungalows. They were privately owned but affiliated to Wellworth Lawns and had taken the place of the cultivated land and greenhouses. A few espaliered pear trees were all that remained as testament to its bygone productivity.

There was no one about, so she headed back to the shrubbery. Planting her stick in the ground she checked the time. It was now nearly eight o'clock. Should she call the RSPCA? She looked at her watch again. A minute had passed. No one would be in their offices yet, anyway he really hadn't been gone that long. She was overreacting. He would turn up… he must. Mustn't he?

She pushed her way into the bushes once more. Disorientated amongst the leaves and branches she felt a sense of confusion. It was so out of character. Parker always came back. He was never truly defiant…well, only that one time in the car park at Hidcote Gardens when he had followed a toddler's dripping ice cream and scrambled into the foot well of the family car as they strapped the sticky child into its booster seat. Apart from that he was her utterly loyal companion.

'Parker! Where are you?' she shouted, from the far side of the undergrowth, as she scanned the grassy hill ahead. From behind her she heard the faint sound of someone call her name.

'Laura dear.' It was Venetia.

Laura walked back to meet her.

Venetia's Zimmer frame was hampering her progress as she made her way along the track. 'No sign of him?' She leant on the aluminium support to catch her breath. 'Mimi told me when she brought me my breakfast. I must have slept through it all. Why didn't you come and find me?'

'I didn't want to disturb you. Then I kept thinking he'd come back, or someone would bring him to reception.'

Venetia let go of the frame and held out her arms to Laura. 'You mustn't worry. I'm sure he'll turn up, but now I think we should go in and get warm. I don't suppose you've had anything to eat?' She gave the Zimmer a tug. 'The rubber bits have fallen off its feet. They've sunk like pastry cutters.' She gave it another ineffectual yank. 'It's well and truly stuck.'

'Stuck?' Laura's eyes lit up. 'That's it … Oh my poor boy.' She looked back in the direction of the small wood that nestled half way up the hill.

'He'll have gone up to the old fox earth in the larch spinney.'

'Stuck down a fox hole?'

'The foxes moved out years ago. A colony of rabbits have appropriated it. Parker is forever trying to catch one. He wouldn't know what to do if he ever did, but only the other day he caused a mini landslide with all his quarrying.' Laura gave a short high-pitched laugh. 'I had to pull him out by his collar.'

'He's a sensible fellow,' Venetia said. 'He'll curl up nice and warm and wait. It could be a tight squeeze though.'

'Are you saying Parker's fat?'

'Well covered perhaps? He does get a lot of extras…'

Laura knew she spoiled him. She felt herself well up. 'He never got to have that last scampi.' She could see him now, leaping and twirling, his toenails clattering on the kitchen floor beside her as he anticipated the treat.

'You mean you went to The Blue Dolphin?' Venetia said.

'I'm sorry. I meant to ask you, but you'd said it was the final episode of Love Island and I knew you wouldn't want to miss it.' Laura yanked at the frame to no avail. 'Listen,' she said. 'I'm going up to the wood. Can you get yourself back to the house if I give you my stick?' She handed Venetia the shepherd's crook.

Venetia looked doubtful. 'It might take me a while.'

'Go as quickly as you can.' Laura stroked Venetia's frail hand. 'Find Alfredo. Tell him to get a spade and meet me up beyond the old stable block, where he picks the wild garlic. We'll have to dig Parker out.'

Laura climbed the hill. With Alfredo's help, they would get Parker safely home. She had heard so many stories about dogs being trapped, sometimes for days, but they always ended happily. She would get the naughty pug checked over by the vet. He would probably have to have an extra dose of flea powder, but he would be right as rain after a good lathering with his tea tree shampoo.

As she reached the tree line, her yearning to be reunited with him was intensified by the knowledge of where she was standing. How many memories were contained within that circle of larch? For years a glade in the centre of the wood had been the final resting place for the family pets of Chipping Wellworth Manor, each one commemorated with its name carved on a small individual Portland headstone. Few of the residents of the care home ventured up the hill, so it remained almost exclusively Laura's private space.

In the shelter of the wood, she consoled herself recalling another occasion there with Parker. Sitting on a tree stump surrounded by evidence of rabbits; little piles of droppings and flattened earth, she had chatted with him about one of his predecessors as he continued his excavations behind her. Unbeknown to him, a rabbit had popped out at her feet and hopped off, disappearing down another hole.

She crossed over to the stump. Its roots splayed out into the sandy soil like the fossilised tentacles of some primordial deep-sea creature. She knelt down, smelling the warm damp soil and called Parker's name into the entrance to the disused fox earth. She put her ear to the ground, but there was no sound, so she pulled herself up with the aid of a root and returned to the edge of the wood to wait for Alfredo.

Trying to stop imagining Parker in the bowels of the earth, she was reassured when at last she saw the chef striding up the hill, still in his uniform kitchen whites, a spade resting on one shoulder.

'Faking hell,' he said, reaching her. 'Excuse my French but these Crocs ain't no good in the wet.'

Laura looked at his muddy yellow plastic clogs. 'It's drier amongst the trees,' she said.

The Crocs weren't much good for digging either. Alfredo's foot kept slipping on the spade as the edges of the hole caved in. Laura was fearful they were making matters worse.

'You've done your best,' she told him. 'But we haven't got the right equipment, and we must keep an air channel open so Parker can smell us. What I really need is the terrierman.'

Alfredo wiped his brow. 'I never heard this,"Terrierman." I got the can of Lynx back home for attracting the ladies, that any good? Parker smelling it and start his yapping?'

'No, it's a man. The hunt employ him...' How could she explain the main purpose of the job in a few short sentences? 'He has Jack Russells to help him,' she volunteered.

'Excuse myself Lady B, but why this Jack Russoles fella needed? I get my lace up boots, and we're cooking on gas. No time at all.'

'I agree, but you have lunch to make ...' Laura's anxiety level was rising. 'And I can't wait until you've finished your shift.'

Every minute that ticked by was putting Parker in more danger. What if he was getting short of oxygen down there? She was beginning to panic at the thought of his continued entrapment. 'We have to get back. I must speak with the huntsman,' she called out, as she ran from the wood and down the hill.

Chapter 2

From behind her desk, Jayne Harcourt looked askance at Laura. 'I've rung the dog warden in Woldham for you Lady Boxford, but I'm not sure I see how bringing in the local fox hunt is going to help find Parker. He may be bold, but I wouldn't rate his chances with those dogs.'

Exasperated, Laura tried to interrupt 'I don't…'

'I've seen the size of them,' Jayne carried on regardless. 'They're huge and we all know why the sport was banned.' She tapped the computer keyboard with her pink lacquered fingernails. 'Still, I can find you the number if you must.'

Laura thanked her. 'It's not the hounds I want,' she explained. 'It's the old hunt terrierman. I can't remember his name, but he'll be able to dig Parker out. They'll have his number at the kennels.'

'I see… Perhaps I should speak with them as it's going to involve groundwork on the estate. I don't want to upset the farmer who rents the park for his sheep.' Jayne picked up the phone, her lack of urgency agonizing.

'Hello.' She introduced herself. 'We require the services of your…' She gazed wide-eyed at Laura as she spoke. 'Senior terrierperson? You see I have Lady Boxford with me. Her pug has gone missing down a fox's hole here at Wellworth Lawns.'

Jayne put her hand over the receiver. 'It's a huntsperson. He wants to speak to you. He says your friend has retired.' She passed the phone to Laura.

The huntsman remembered Laura. 'Those were the days,' he said. 'When people knew how to behave and you and Sir Tony held the lawn meet at the Manor. Helluva craic that always was. Proper drop of tawny port.'

'That's very kind,' Laura said, remembering her late husband. 'But about my dog…'

'Chap called Kaminski's the one you want. There's not a lot Stan doesn't know about the "old ways"…' He cleared his throat '… If you get my drift. Lays us a mean trail, fantastic secret recipe; fox urine – never ask where he gets it from. Hounds go mad for it. He's a first rate shot too. Spanish over and unders; Sir Tony would have turned in his grave, but that's the fashion nowadays. Anyhow, Stan's got a couple of dogs. Little one's a fantastic ratter. They should flush your pug out, no problem.'

Laura rang Stan Kaminski. He said he couldn't get there before two o'clock. She didn't know what to do. It was an age. She went to see Venetia who suggested Laura take a bath to calm her nerves.

Lying in the warm water seemed like an unbearable waste of time and she was getting out when the phone rang. It was her friend Strudel Black who lived with her partner, Jervis Willingdale in one of the houses in Mulberry Close.

'We're downstairs in the lounge sitting.' Strudel had never quite managed to lose the grammatical vestiges of her Bavarian childhood.

Laura rushed to pull on a pair of clean jeans and a jumper. In the hall she picked up her coat, a scarf and pair of cashmere mittens. It was on the tip of her tongue to call for Parker. She gave a short, choked intake of breath as she closed the door behind her.

Strudel and Jervis were seated at a table in one of the bay windows overlooking the drive. Jervis stood up to greet Laura, straightening his silk tie.

'We've posted on the Ancient Eros Facebook page that Parker is missing,' he said, as Laura sat down next to Strudel.

'This could be most useful,' Strudel said. 'We have literally hundreds of followers now and many are of the local vicinity. They will spread the word.'

Laura wondered if Strudel and Jervis's commercial enterprise, the dating agency Ancient Eros, was really the right platform for missing dogs. 'It's alright, I know where he is,' she said.

'The Neighbourhood Watch website might be a good one too,' Jervis said. 'I don't think we need go national yet. He can't be far away I wouldn't have thought.'

'I know where he is,' Laura repeated.

'And I've told our Ballroom Dancing WhatsApp group.' Strudel offered her a biscuit from the plate on the table.

'Probably not so much help as most of our pupils are residents here.' Jervis leant across and took a chocolate digestive.

'I'm sure he's in the wood,' Laura said.

'We'll get some posters mocked up for shop windows,' Jervis continued.

'Stop.' Laura raised her hands in mock surrender. She explained about the fox earth. It seemed to have no effect on Jervis's way of thinking.

'I'm sorry Laura, but what if he's not there? Of course, we hope it won't be necessary, but we want to be prepared. Speed is everything in these situations. Sightings are key.'

Sightings? A worm of doubt slid into Laura's brain.

'Have you got a photo of him?' Jervis asked.

'I'll find one.' Laura thought of the leather-bound album that her grand- daughter had given her one Christmas. In a typical act of generosity Victoria had asked the well-known Bond Street supplier to emboss the cover in gold leaf with the words, 'Parker's Scrap Book.' It was now filled with photos, from puppydom to his successes in the show ring and recently his latest exploit as an ageing lothario, fathering a litter of three Dachshund crosses.

The thought of him with his delightful offspring made her heart palpitate. Jervis's doubt was infectious. What if he was right and she had been wasting all this time when she should be back outside searching?

She leapt to her feet. Her blood pressure dropped. She steadied herself on the back of Strudel's chair. 'I'm going to walk through the village.'

It was not something that she and Parker often did, as the grounds of Wellworth Lawns were so extensive. They mostly drove straight through the village on their way to Woldham to do some shopping ... Or buy fish and chips ... Laura's mouth went dry.

'I'll join you,' Jervis examined his black patent leather shoes. 'I'm sure Strudel is more than capable of taking the class on her own.' He turned to her. 'You can, can't you, my love?'

'I will concentrate on the waltz.' Strudel smoothed her figure-hugging green Lycra dress.

'No, really Jervis, your shoes will get ruined in the mud,' Laura said. 'I'll be fine on my own. I'm only filling in time until Stan Kaminski arrives.' She hoped she sounded more confident than she felt.

Pulling on her mittens, she set off down the main drive and through the wrought iron gates that led to Chipping Wellworth. The village consisted of the church, the Old Rectory, a rambling Tudor house and a dozen or so cottages that huddled in twos and threes on either side of the road leading to Woldham five miles away.

Laura walked down the empty street calling Parker's name. She rounded the bend beyond the cottages and passed the present-day ecclesiastical residence. Unimaginatively named The Rectory, it was the epitome of all that was wrong with 1970's architecture. Built from reconstituted stone, it had large single pane windows and a porchless half glazed front door painted dark blue. The only good thing about it was that since the latest cutbacks, there had been no incumbent to tidy up the grounds so that the house was now partially hidden from view by overgrown hedging and brambles.

With time still to spare, Laura decided to continue as far as the main road. Reaching the T-junction, she heard a car approaching. As it passed, an image of

Parker rushing out in front of the vehicle set her heart racing. Even though she was sure he would never venture this far alone, she felt unsettled and turned for home.

Retracing her steps she noticed three randomly deposited wheelie bins beside the gateway of The Rectory that she had somehow missed from the other direction. Yet another eyesore; the observation calmed her nerves. She stopped, as from behind the bushes she heard footsteps on the thin gravel of the driveway.

'Step on it Prendergast,' came a gruff voice. 'Prendy, do get a move on. There's nothing to be frightened of.'

Laura peered round the gatepost and saw the stooped rear of a woman in a pleated skirt and mackintosh. On the end of the taut white lead she was holding, a white miniature poodle shook its head. The woman gave the lead a tweak. The dog crouched low and growled. The woman straightened herself; tall, not overweight but well built. She readdressed the dog. 'I can see I shall have to be firm. Come Prendy… Now.'

'Hello,' Laura said.

The woman's body stiffened. She turned. Her long manly face, accentuated by short straight grey hair and a bluntly cropped fringe, held a tense expression. 'You shouldn't creep up on people like that,' she said.

'I'm…' Laura dithered. 'I do apologise.'

The woman's cadaverous cheeks were gaining colour. 'I was on the verge of a breakthrough,' she snapped.

Laura was about to move on, but then the woman seemed to relax.

She sighed. 'Oh, I suppose it's not your fault.'

'You have to be very patient with dog training,' Laura said.

'You don't have to tell me that, it's my profession. But most of my clients are from London. They don't understand how a small thing like gravel can set the programme back.'

Laura thought for a moment. The Rectory had sometimes been rented out. It hadn't been that popular, but since Covid you could pretty much refurbish a windowless garage and get a good income from it as an Airbnb.

'Are you new to the village?' she asked.

'Actually, I've been here on and off for some weeks now.'

'That's nice,' Laura said. She wasn't sure it was that nice, but with Jervis's words about sightings ringing in her ears, she needed to cut to the chase in a civilized manner. She introduced herself.

'Dr. Gwendoline Shackleton.' The woman said in reply, as if Laura should recognise the name.

'So, you know your way around, Gwendoline?' Laura continued, 'I don't suppose you've seen a fawn-coloured pug, have you?'

'A pug?' Gwendoline tutted. 'Such terrible brachycephalic malfunctions, have you mislaid one?'

She gave Laura a look of disdain that reminded her of her primary school maths teacher, a man who's name she had erased from her memory on account of the trouble she'd had with the seven times table.

'Well no, not really,' Laura said. She wanted to say that Parker wasn't one of those sad pugs whose squashed noses had been so over emphasized through in-breeding. 'I expect he's back at Wellworth Lawns right now.'

'I hope so for your sake,' Gwendoline said. 'Don't get me wrong, but I shouldn't waste any more time chattering if I were you. If a dog finds freedom, breaks the chains of a mundane existence, it's nigh on impossible to turn the clock back.'

Laura felt her face flush. 'Thinking about it, I'm pretty sure I know where he is.' She gave a nervous laugh and retreated.

Hurrying back down the street, she checked her watch. It was nearly two and she didn't want to be late. She quickened her pace further, almost running up the drive.

Parked on the gravel outside the house Laura saw a sleek dark blue car. She didn't take much interest in cars, but she knew the Maserati logo. The driver's door opened, and a large black hound sprang out. Another small, light chestnut coloured dog followed it. Its coat was short and on the end of its wagging tail was a soft cream pompom of hair that looked like it could be useful for dusting. It scurried after its friend into the bushes.

A slim youngish man in muddy dark green overalls and a ribbed grey beanie got out of the car. He didn't see Laura as he shouted after the dogs, 'Baloo, Kuko.'

After a moment he put his thumb and middle finger to his mouth and gave a short sharp whistle. Within seconds both dogs had returned and were sitting at his feet, staring up at him.

He pointed at the open door.

They bolted in. He slammed it shut and walked smartly to the main entrance. Laura didn't usually like to make assumptions, but on this occasion she did wonder what a man like him with dogs like that was doing with a two-door sports car.

She followed him to the house and by the time she caught up, he was leaning against the reception desk talking to Mimi.

'I said I'd meet her here at two,' he said, pulling off his hat to reveal a mop of dark disheveled hair.

'I thinking any moment...' Mimi said.

Laura waved and caught her eye.

Mimi smiled. 'But here, I seeing Lady Boxford coming now.'

The man turned.

Laura was generally suspicious of people with eyes a little close together. His were dark brown, almost black. They gave him the look of intensity of a hypnotist, forcing Laura to lower her gaze momentarily. He was unshaven and had a sallow complexion, as if he was lacking the vitamin D of a naturally sunnier climate.

'Mr. Kaminski?' She held out her hand.

He didn't reciprocate, but said, 'Call me Stan. Are you ready?'

His throaty intonation reminded her of Russia. She nodded and followed him back outside. He opened the car and let the dogs out again. As they milled around him, he took out a green waterproof jacket and a shiny wooden handled spade from the boot.

'This dog of yours valuable?' he asked, pressing the lid down.

Laura recoiled. How could she put a price on Parker? 'Why do you ask?'

He bent down, checking the laces of his expensive looking leather boots. 'No reason.'

'Well, he's not,' she said.

'No matter.' He pulled on his coat. 'Badger's sett in the wood at the top of the hill I suppose you're thinking,' he called out, as he strode off towards the shrubbery.

'You know the area?' Laura was trying to keep up. 'I thought the larch spinney half way up. There's a rabbit warren.'

'He won't be there.'

It was hard to follow his voice as the dogs crashed through the bushes, zigzagging either side of her. She heard him whistle and managed to catch up with him in the strip of open ground that divided the gardens from the parkland. The dogs were already at heel as he reached the gate into the park. Without bothering to open it, he vaulted over. The hound followed suit as the small dog squeezed itself under the bottom bar.

'I meant to say…' Laura coughed, short of breath. 'It's an old fox earth.'

'I said if he's stuck, it won't be there. We shouldn't waste time.'

It occurred to Laura that he might not wait for her. He did, but she had only just managed to shut the gate behind her before he was striding off up the hill.

'Stan,' she called out. 'That's the little wood on your left. I did think…'

He turned to look at her, then whistled again and veered sharply back into the spinney.

By the time she caught up he was on his way out again.

'I told you,' he said, passing her. 'If he's stuck, he'll be in the badger's sett at the top.'

Laura hurried behind him, as the grassy slope got steeper. A bitter wind was making her ears ache, and she was glad when they reached the main wood. She had to trust what he was saying. Parker must be there.

They reached a boggy rutted track. She slowed her pace on the rough terrain. Surely it wouldn't be long before they found him?

Then the track petered out and she realized she had lost sight of him.

The dogs were barking somewhere up ahead.

She climbed higher, brushing past dead nettles and low scrubby hawthorn saplings, until the undergrowth thinned, as the trees grew denser. She could no longer feel the wind. Even at this time of year it was warm and dry amongst the trees. Her feet crunched into a carpet of leaves that had accumulated over previous seasons. She stopped to listen. The dogs were silent. Stan must have started digging. As she pulled off her mittens, untied the scarf around her neck and stuffed them in her pocket, she felt a surge of relief.

Ahead of her, in the middle of an extended area of flattened reddish-brown earth that delineated the badger's sett, Stan stood with his hands on his hips. His spade was sunk deep into the ground, a mound of freshly dug earth beside it.

'He's not here.'

Laura frowned as she made a last effort to reach the summit. Beads of sweat were forming on her brow as she grasped a low branch. She hauled herself up until she was standing on the periphery of the sett.

'How do you know?' She looked at a huge hole in front of her. The sides, patted smooth by nocturnal traffic, led into who knows what kind of dark subterranean maze.

'Kuko's been down.' Stan gestured to the little dog that sat panting beside Baloo as they both stared at another entrance to the sett some yards away.

'But surely you can't tell just like that. Shouldn't we try digging in another area?' She called to the dogs, patting her thighs in encouragement. They jumped up to join her, their ears pricked. The little dog's pompom tail wagging.

'What about here?' Laura kicked some earth at the mouth of another hole. The little dog gave a discontented whimper.

'No point,' Stan said.

'Why not?' Laura tried to keep the tenor of her voice even. Why had she put her trust in this complete stranger?

'There's one sow down there, probably got a cub. Either way she'd have killed your dog.'

'Killed him?' Laura's cheeks were burning. 'How can you be so certain?' she snapped.

'My dog Kuko; look at her. She's only trying to please you, but she's no fool. She'd no more go back down there than take a train to Athens.'

'But Parker's not a hunter like her. He's not aggressive. How could he have been after the amount of battered fish he'd eaten for goodness' sake?'

Stan laughed. 'So that's why you thought he was stuck.'

'What I mean is, he could no more have started a fight than...'

'Didn't need to. If he'd got stuck or not, he was still in the sow's territory. She'd have ripped his throat out.'

Laura felt her knees buckle. She sank to the ground. The two dogs began to nuzzle her, Kuko licking her salty face with a warm abrasive tongue.

'You want my opinion?' Stan said, his voice less harsh.

She took a fistful of earth in each hand, as if she needed to add substance to herself. 'What?'

'There's no sign of blood.' He pulled the spade out of the ground.

She clenched her fists as he walked towards her.

He held out a hand. 'I don't believe he was ever here.'

Laura let the dry soil slip through her fingers. She didn't want to, but she took his hand. As he pulled her to her feet, his words sank in.

So, if Parker wasn't here, where was he?

Chapter 3

As they walked back down the hill Laura kept one step in front of Stan, her head lowered. It had started raining again. She was cold and dejected. Parker can't have simply vanished. The awful realization that she had no idea of his whereabouts hit her with a fearful force.

'If I was you, I'd put it on Facebook,' Stan said. 'Make some posters for footpaths, pubs, local shops, that sort of thing. Widen the range if he doesn't show up in a couple of days. Have you got someone who can help you?' He opened the gate into the gardens for her and they walked back through to the drive.

His words haunted her as she remembered her offhand response to Jervis's offer. It was unthinkable Parker would be gone that long.

He bleeped the car door. 'I'll take the dogs out again tomorrow if you tell me where you'd like me to look.'

Laura glanced at him. She had felt suspicious of his confidence. His extensive knowledge of the locality, the land that had once been hers, had made her think of him as somehow arrogant, but this was an unexpected act of kindness.

'I haven't thought beyond where we've just been,' she said.

'Was he ever a stud dog? Had he any lady friends nearby?'

'Not that I know of.' She felt like the mother of a teenager, hopelessly out of touch.

'There are many new dogs around now. New houses. People working from home.' He opened the boot and took out an old striped towel. Leaning down he picked up Kuko and dried her off before putting her in the car. He reached out to Baloo, but the hound dodged him, jumping into the car beside Kuko. Stan shook his head in resignation as he got in. He shut the door and opened the window. Already steam was fugging up the windscreen. 'I'll have a wander round,' he said. 'Maybe nearer to Woldham. Perhaps he was chasing something? Went further afield and now he can't find his way back. I'm sure he'll turn up. I'll ring you if I see anything.'

Laura was comforted. 'That's very kind,' she said. 'But how much do I owe you?'

He raised a hand. 'It's nothing.'

The sound of scattering gravel as Stan drove away masked the approaching footsteps of Canon Frank Holiday and Laura was startled by his familiar deep voice beside her.

'Have you got a fancy man?' he asked. ''Fraid my old Audi's never going to compete with a Maserati. Ah well, I am patient in my tribulation.'

Laura was used to these little Biblical references, but the large black umbrella he was holding over his head reminded her of being at a funeral. She shivered.

Oblivious, he continued, 'I thought, as you hadn't called me back last night, I'd better come and check up on you.'

Laura recalled their telephone conversation. He'd wanted her to think on his marriage proposal again. Her latest objection, that she considered him, in his late eighties, an unnecessary risk, had not gone down well. It was the reason why she'd abandoned the plan to have dinner with him, but instead had taken Parker to The Blue Dolphin. Arguing at their age was exhausting, but as usual Frank hadn't taken it to heart.

'Don't worry, I'm not going to embarrass you by getting down on one knee,' he said with a cheeky smile. He nodded his head in the direction of the house. 'Mind you, it might cause a bit of a stir with all those net curtain twitchers.'

'Don't joke, Frank.'

His wry perceptions were often amusing, but now Laura realized that he didn't know what had happened. 'Parker's missing,' she said. 'He didn't come back last night when I took him out.'

Frank's face fell.

'That so-called, "fancy man" was trying to help me find him. But as you can see, we haven't,' she added unnecessarily.

'This is terrible, what can I do?'

'Help search of course.'

Strudel rang, inviting them for supper. She said Jervis was already making one of his plans of action. In the meantime, Laura asked Frank to call the RSPCA while she made a pot of tea.

By the time she had brought the tray in, Frank was busy giving them a description of Parker. 'I believe he is ...' He put his hand over the receiver and asked Laura Parker's age.

'I think he's nine,' she whispered.

Frank relayed the message, his voice resonant and commanding from years in the pulpit. Laura had to admit he cut a fine figure with his snow-white locks and jet-black eyebrows above piercing blue eyes. A smart shirt and tie had replaced the dog collar since his retirement, but he still wore the well-cut black serge suit made by the famous ecclesiastic tailoring house of Gammarelli. As her gaze travelled down to his elegantly crossed legs it seemed even the tasseled black loafers, that ordinarily she might have deemed a little camp, accentuated an air of dignified gravitas.

'Yes, I believe he's grey all over,' he was saying.

'No, he's not, he's fawn and he's got black ears.' Laura handed him a cup. 'You pour. I'd better talk to them.' She took the phone from him. 'He's also got a black muzzle and a little white patch on his chest ... and he's got a scar on his shoulder, though you can't really see it now.'

Finishing the conversation, she put the phone down and recalled the incident. He'd become over familiar with a Pekingese bitch at Crufts and she'd gone for him. A vivid picture came to Laura. Blood everywhere and the show vet none too handy with the stitching. Oh Parker... In her mind she reached out to stroke the roll of fat around his neck.

The sound of the phone woke her from the reverie. It was Venetia.

'I'm still waiting for someone to fetch my Zimmer frame,' she said.

Laura went next door to see her.

When she returned Frank was reading the paper. Something in his inactivity and the timing of it – it was about now that she would have fed Parker – brought on a fresh round of agitation. She suggested they go and search outside again.

'Now?' He folded the paper. 'But it's nearly six.'

The significance of the hour was lost on him. She sat down heavily next to him and crossed her arms.

'But, if you like … if I'd known I'd have put some wellingtons in the car.'

'How could you have known?' Laura's frustration grew as, for the second time that day she watched a man inspect his footwear. Frank was making small circling movements in the air with one foot, admiring the shine of his shoe.

'Of course, what we really need is a drone,' he said.

She put thoughts of his vanity aside. It was an inspired idea.

'Brilliant,' she said. 'I'll call Victoria.'

One of the many benefits of Laura's life was the fact that her granddaughter Victoria's husband owned Wellworth Lawns. Vince Outhwaite, the Leeds business magnate and proprietor of the underwear giant Foundation Rocks had saved Laura from bankruptcy when he bought the house and had it converted.

Allowing Laura the best suite of rooms was a most generous act on Vince's part. Albeit there had been a delicate conversation regarding profit margins, but Victoria had stepped in, nestled her pretty nose into her husband's neck and in no time the deal was done.

As usual Victoria quickly took stock of the situation. 'I'll send the company helicopter,' she said. 'The pilot – you remember Robin? He's recceing a logistics shed near Milton Keynes tomorrow. Online underwear sales have gone mad ever since lockdown. It shouldn't take him long, then he can come on to you. He's got a drone on board. Don't worry Granny, we'll have Parker located in no time.'

Laura put the phone down with a feeling of temporary relief, but time was still weighing heavy as she thought of Parker's empty bowl in the kitchen. She hurried to the sitting room window, looking frantically to left and right.

'I tell you what,' Frank said. 'We'll walk round the rest of Mulberry Close on our way to Jervis and Strudel's. Knock on some doors. You never know, perhaps he's lost his collar and some new person's taken him in. Those bungalows in particular are always changing hands.'

Laura looked at him. The implication was not lost on either of them. It was a fact that turnover in the care sector was always going to be high, but it was another grim moment in what was already a dark day.

Chapter 4

It had stopped raining, but the air was cold and dank as they walked to Mulberry Close.

Crawford Tuthill's wife, Melissa, was waiting outside the open front door of their bungalow as her French bulldog, Elodie, shuffled at a snail's pace towards her.

Stan's words about a lady friend came back to Laura. She was certain Parker would no longer waste his time on Elodie as he once had. The tragic creature wasn't very old but had developed a hip disorder. Laura had been present when the condition first became apparent. She and Parker had been on their way to see Strudel and Jervis when Elodie had bounded out of the Tuthill's to meet them. Excited by her approach, Parker had engaged playfully with her. Perhaps he had been a little over exuberant? Or possibly their interaction had exacerbated the underlying complaint, because Elodie fell and by the time Melissa called her back, it was plain the dog was unsound. That looks expensive Laura had thought at the time, thinking of the vet's fees.

Now, as they drew near, Melissa called out, 'No sign of Parker?'

'Not yet.' Laura tried to smile.

'Shame,' Melissa said. She had one of those long-suffering faces that could have once been pretty, but years of domestic unhappiness had ingrained an expression of melancholy onto her features.

'Crawford told me last night when he came in. I've been asking around for you, but no one's seen him here I'm afraid.'

As Melissa stood there, her arms folded tight under her flat chest with Elodie lying at her feet, Laura felt a dart of envy. At least Melissa still had her dog. 'That's kind of you,' she managed to say. 'Especially as you've got your hands full with Elodie so lame and now Crawford too.'

'Crawford?'

'His knee?'

'Oh. He never tells me anything. That's men for you.' Melissa put her hand to her mouth and giggled nervously. 'Begging your pardon Canon.'

'No offense taken.' Frank took Laura's arm and began to steer her on down the road. 'We're just off to see how Jervis is getting on with the publicity.'

'Publicity?'

Laura stopped. 'For Parker, on Facebook,' she said. 'We'll be doing some flyers too.'

'That's a coincidence. A man delivered a flyer earlier today. Let me get it for you. It might be useful; it was to do with dogs.' Melissa went indoors, leaving Elodie lying on the doorstep. She returned with a piece of paper that she handed to Laura. On it was a photo of an elderly black Labrador, an old-fashioned nurse's cap on its head. Below the letters "PICS" were printed in pink followed by a strap line, "The charity for Pooches in the Care Sector." It didn't appear to bear any relevance to the situation with Parker, but Melissa insisted Laura keep it.

'Well, I'd better get on,' she clicked her fingers at Elodie who heaved herself into a sitting position. 'Crawford likes dinner to be punctual.'

As they walked on the few paces to Strudel and Jervis's house, Laura folded the piece of paper and put it in her bag.

Strudel answered the door and ushered them into the sitting room where Jervis was asleep in a chair beside the gas fire. Tapping him on the shoulder, he woke with a start.

'We must check for updates; Parker has still not returned,' Strudel said.

'Oh, bloody hell, no sign of him?' Jervis headed for the cocktail trolley. 'Action stations it is then. Spirits up; A Negroni?'

'Nectar of the gods, but not for me,' Frank said.

'Are you sure? Not on the wagon I hope?'

'Driving; have to be careful.'

Jervis nodded in commiseration, his bottom lip jutting forward. 'You can guinea pig a mocktail.' He picked up a small black and yellow bottle. 'Pina Colada? I found it in Lidl.' He shook the thick contents into a glass and handed it to Frank.

'We've made some progress,' Laura said. 'Victoria's sending Vince's helicopter and a drone tomorrow.'

'Good show.' Jervis took ice from the bucket and added the alcoholic ingredients to the shaker. 'But I think we should continue with the social media, don't you?' He poured the drinks then rubbed his stomach. 'Christ Strudel, I'm ravenous. I could eat a horse.'

'Jervis,' Strudel scolded, 'I am sure Laura is not feeling like this eating of large mammals at the present time. I have prepared a more delicate collation for us.' She turned to Laura. 'Would this be acceptable?'

Laura nodded. 'I really couldn't face the dining room at Wellworth tonight.'

As Strudel disappeared to the kitchen, Laura and Frank sat down on the sofa.

From behind his desk, Jervis took a large slug of Negroni and started tapping the keyboard of his computer. 'Did you get a photo?' he asked. 'I've prepared the copy for the posters. Did he have a collar on? We should describe it.'

'It's leather with Masai beadwork.' Laura put her glass down on the table beside her, feeling faint. 'It's got a small round metal tag with my mobile number on and his silver charm.' She remembered the tinkling sound that the two pieces of metal made when he shook his head. 'It's in the shape of a pug...' She could feel tears welling. She reached for her drink. It didn't seem like much of a good luck charm now. 'Vince gave it to him on his fifth birthday.' She took a sip. 'He had it made specially...' She finished the glass. 'At Asprey's.'

Frank squeezed her hand, and Laura was relieved as Strudel popped her head round the door to say the food was ready.

They followed her to the kitchen where even the sight of Strudel's favourite, pickled herrings laid out on a platter surrounded by cocktail onions could not elicit in Laura the usual feeling of dread. She felt numb as they helped themselves to the bread and butter Strudel handed out.

'I think we should return to last night.' Jervis unscrewed the top from a bottle of Riesling. 'Where precisely did you see Parker last, Laura?

'In the bushes beyond the rose garden.' Laura squashed a piece of bread and butter between her forefinger and thumb.

'In which direction was he going?' Jervis continued.

Laura put the bread down uneaten on her plate. 'I don't know.'

'Do you remember anything out of the ordinary? Who did you see when you took him out that last time?'

Laura stared at the flaccid fish on her plate. There was something so final about Jervis's words.

'I thought I saw something moving outside the dining room before I fell. I couldn't be sure.' She took a sip of wine, casting her mind back. 'But I did see someone earlier when I was setting out with Parker. It was more of a silhouette really, but a man, I think. He had his head down. I've no idea who it was, there are people coming and going all the time.'

'Whereabouts was he?' Frank asked.

'He was coming from this direction. Mulberry Close. I was standing in the drive, about to put my umbrella up.'

'Good.' Jervis leant forward. 'Where was Parker at the time?'

'He was beside me, still on his lead.'

'Where did the man go?' Frank asked.

'He went back in the direction he had come from.'

Jervis's brow creased. 'Back to Mulberry Close?'

Strudel leant forward. 'What did he look like?'

'I don't know,' Laura said. But there was something about the figure, almost as if when he'd seen her, it had made him change his mind about where he was going.

She remembered the click of the umbrella catch as she raised it over her head, then him turning away. Perhaps it was the recollection of the sound the umbrella made that reminded her of Melissa clicking her fingers at poor Elodie. And that in turn sparked something else in Laura's mind.

'He might have had a limp,' she said.

Jervis broke a moment's silence while they took this in.

'I thought we were on to something there,' he said. 'But a limp… The chap must have been a resident if he was lame. Did he have a walking frame or a stick?'

'I don't think so.'

'Perhaps he was visiting someone here in Mulberry Close,' Jervis said. 'Forgot something and had to go back. The Fanshaws in number eight are always having people round at strange times of the day and night. He's a Rotarian, you know.'

'Rotarians.' Strudel tossed her head and snorted. 'Such people are not all they may appear you know.'

Laura put the comment down to teething problems with the Fanshaws who had bought the bungalow from Strudel and Jervis when they had up-sized to one of the few two storey houses in Mulberry Close.

'Was there anyone else?' Jervis carried on.

'I saw Mimi arriving for her evening shift. She waved to me. There was a van parked in the drive, an Amazon delivery probably. They come and go like an army convoy since that new woman Lulu Vandermoss arrived.'

'But tell me, what can she be ordering?' Strudel asked.

'Books Mimi says. I saw her in the hall on my way out to The Blue Dolphin. Come to think of it, she had a package in her hand then.'

'You went to the chip shop?' Frank said.

Laura realized she hadn't told him.

'That's the one in the dead end off Sheep Street, isn't it?' Jervis said. 'Tileman's Road. We must ask to put a flyer in the window.'

'It's not exactly a dead end, but it's blocked off by concrete bollards,' Laura pointed out.

Jervis nodded. 'Excellent fare at The Blue Dolphin, when we're allowed.'

'I don't know what you mean?' Strudel huffed.

'Parker and I have been going there forever.'

'So it was just you and Parker?' Frank said.

Laura was too tired to work out if he was hurt. 'Actually, I asked Lulu if she'd like to join us as she was hanging about in the hall. She always looks half starved. At first she was eager to join me. Then she changed her mind. Something about the cholesterol.'

'Idiotic. She's practically anorexic.' Strudel reverted to rolling her 'r's' in the Teutonic way she had when slightly drunk.

'Hopeless trying to teach her ballroom; nothing to get hold of,' Jervis agreed.

'So what about when you got to the chip shop?' Frank asked. 'Did you take Parker in with you?'

'Of course I did.' Laura's thoughts were stuck on dancing. She had a perfect vision of Parker doing a sort of Cha Cha Cha on his short back legs as the smells of frying coming from behind the counter sent him increasingly wild; his little front paws bouncing up and down as he tried to retain his balance. 'But actually he became quite cross,' she said.

'Parker?' Strudel frowned. 'Why?'

'I gave Sally Bowman a lift to her sister's, so it took longer to get home and he had to sit on the back seat.'

'Who's Sally?' Jervis asked.

'She's married to Bryan Bowman. They own The Blue Dolphin. Sally's sister is Val Farmer. She works as a carer here at Wellworth Lawns. She lives in one of the cottages in the village.'

'I know this sister,' Strudel said. 'Custard hair with liquorice roots.'

'Delicious.' Jervis licked his lips.

'Well, Sally and Val often have supper together. As Sally doesn't drive, me taking her saved Val a journey.'

'So you dropped Sally off with her sister. Then what?' Jervis asked.

'Parker and I went home and had our supper.' Laura could feel tears again. 'I should go home,' she said, looking up at the cuckoo clock on the wall. 'What if he's returned and I'm not there?' She turned to Frank. 'You stay. I'll be fine on my own.'

He looked taken aback. 'Of course I'll come with you.'

'Good show.' Jervis broke the moment of tension. 'I'll finish the flyer and print some off. We can add a photo when you've found one. Strudel and I will start distributing them tomorrow morning. What d'you think Frank, pubs and restaurants; Woldham library; the school?'

'I'll join you,' Frank said. 'I can put one on the church noticeboard.'

Outside a chilly mist had descended. Frank took Laura's arm and with the aid of a torch Strudel had lent them, they detoured through the gardens calling Parker's name.

Laura felt that Frank's arm, instead of offering support, was weighing her down. They were out of step. She supposed it was a combination of the mud sticking to his leather shoes and her tiredness. As they crossed another sodden path, he asked her if she could remember anything else about the man she had seen.

Looking up at him in the darkness, she could still make out his jet-black eyebrows as they perched like a couple of ravens acting as gatekeepers to the bridge of his nose.

'He may have been wearing a hat,' she offered, realizing she didn't really have a clue what the man looked like.

They turned out of the shrubbery and headed towards the main house.

'Or a hoodie possibly; something pulled low that hid his face.'

'That puts him in a younger category than the average resident at Wellworth Lawns. I'd say he was an outsider.'

'He could have been staff, but how does that help find Parker? And please don't say The Lord works in mysterious ways.' What prompted such facetiousness? It was unkind, but all she felt was creeping exhaustion.

'I wasn't going to say that, no, and I can't be sure myself right now, but we should certainly put our efforts into identifying him. Either way, I believe things will be clearer after a good night's rest. '

'How can I rest?'

'You must try not to worry too much. These small breeds are most resilient.'

'You're right.' Laura felt herself begin to crumble again. He meant well, but Frank was not a natural dog lover.

As they climbed the steps to the house, she remembered the last time the three of them had been together in her sitting room. Frank was trying to get Parker to sit on his lap. Parker was as usual refusing, knowing full well that Laura would invite him up when she was ready. After endless exhortations of encouragement, Frank had tried tempting him with a mint from his pocket to which Parker had reacted with the utmost disdain.

'I'll meet Jervis first thing,' Frank said, as he left her at the front door. 'Then I'll give you a call. We can go out again before the helicopter arrives, that is of course if there are no developments overnight.'

Developments… The word was ominous. He gave her a peck on the cheek and somehow his nose prodded her in the eye. She leaned away as graciously as she could. She yearned for her bed, but more than that she yearned for Parker to be sharing it with her.

Chapter 5

Laura tossed and turned, desperate for the night to end. As soon as the kitchen staff were on duty, she rang down to cancel her breakfast. She got up and set off to resume her search. The mist was lifting. It was dry and still as she patrolled the grounds, hunting for unlikely places in which he might have become trapped. She checked the outbuildings before returning up the hill to the pet cemetery.

The place was empty.

As she came out from the trees, a pale ray of sunlight broke through the clouds. At least it would be a good day for the helicopter. Hoping she wasn't missing a call from Victoria she hurried back to the house. The reception desk was still unmanned, but Laura could hear the clink of china coming from the dining room and decided to get a cappuccino. Of the few residents that made it down to breakfast, no one ever spoke much. In fact, people tended to studiously ignore one another, as if they were all complete strangers, until pre-lunch sherry, whereupon they all became the best of friends. She was on her way to the white clothed table that displayed all the necessary accouterments for tea and coffee making, when she noticed Lulu Vandermoss. She was sitting on the edge of her chair like a Giacometti sculpture, staring out of the window onto the drive. A book lay on the table beside a plate of untouched pastries and a pot of tea. Laura walked over.

'Hello Lulu,' she said. 'Are you expecting someone?'

Lulu looked up, startled. 'I saw you in the garden earlier. No sign of your little dog?'

'No, but I was wondering, the night before last when I met you in the hall, were you waiting for a delivery... From Amazon possibly?'

'Me? Why? I don't think so.' Lulu's goose white hand reached for the lump of polished agate hanging from a gold chain that rested on her chest.

'It's nothing personal. I'm trying to find out about a man I saw, and I thought it could have been a delivery driver who didn't know his way around. But you didn't see anyone?'

'No. I'm sorry.'

'What's that you're reading?' Laura saw the title, 'The Secrets of Plastic Surgery.'

Lulu reached for the book. 'Just some research I'm doing.' She got up and put the book in a canvas bag that she had been sitting on. 'Well, good luck, I hope you find him.'

Laura returned to the coffee machine. She watched as Lulu wove her way around the tables and out through the door that led to the recreation room.

She could hear the telephone ringing as she put the key in her door. She rushed in, spilling coffee on the carpet in her haste.

'The helicopter should be there about eleven,' Victoria said. 'I've spoken with Jayne Harcourt. She's making sure everyone's indoors so it can land on the lawn.'

Laura was wiping the coffee stain with a damp cloth when the phone rang again. It was Frank.

'I'll be there,' he said.

The wait was increasing Laura's anxiety level. She went to see Venetia.

'I missed you last night,' Venetia said, 'I wasn't going to go downstairs, but Mimi brought my Zimmer frame back.' She was sitting with her legs tucked beneath her on an old green wingback chair a couple of feet away from the massive screen of her TV, a pile of mail on her lap. Laura wondered how Venetia's tiny brittle boned legs didn't snap into pieces in such a position.

'I'm sorry.' She sat down beside her. 'Frank and I went to see Strudel and Jervis. He's printing posters.'

Letters fluttered to the floor as Venetia leant forward and clasped Laura's wrist.

'What are all those?' Laura asked.

'We won't worry about them now dear. I had a very interesting evening with Reggie Hawkesmore,' she said, ignoring the mess. 'We spent most of the meal listening in to Melissa and Crawford Tuthill having a row on the table opposite. They obviously thought we were deaf.'

'Funny, I bumped into Melissa in Mulberry Close, I'm sure she said she had to go and cook Crawford's dinner.'

'She can't cook to save her life according to Reggie. Crawford was complaining about her to him.'

'How disloyal. So what was the row about?' Laura wondered how Venetia could be so preoccupied by such insignificant gossip when Parker was still missing.

'Melissa wanted pudding and Crawford wouldn't let her.'

'Poor thing, she needs cheering up. How mean of him.'

'The point was that she wasn't drinking, but Crawford was, and she said that was unfair.'

'I quite agree.'

'Reggie told me Lulu Vandermoss told him they're short of money. I don't know how she knows so much about them, she's only been here two seconds.'

'They shouldn't have dinner in the dining room so often then,' Laura said. 'It's expensive if you're not a resident, especially if you have wine.'

'That's just what I said to Reggie. As if Crawford wasn't fat enough already. But there was something else I meant to tell you... They both had starters too... But what's that whirring noise?'

'It's Vince's helicopter.'

They went to the window.

'Looks like it's come from that old TV series MASH,' Venetia said of the small bubble on skis that was parked on the lawn, its rotors slowing.

It was not Vince's normal sleek white Agusta, that was for sure.

'I hope it takes our weight,' Laura said. 'You'll have to finish the story later. I must go.'

Laura bumped into Frank in the passage. Together they went downstairs and out to where Jayne Harcourt was waiting with the pilot.

Jayne started introductions, but he and Laura recognized one another.

'Robin, how nice to see you,' Laura said.

'Ladies day at Ascot last year wasn't it Lady B?'

Laura always found the occasion faintly ridiculous. All that dressing up, but then Vince so loved buying Victoria and her a hat.

'Yes, but I hardly recognize you out of your uniform.'

Robin was wearing baggy cargo pants and a T-shirt with MENSA, Brain Champ written on it.

'The thing was Vince agreed that my little Bell 47 here's got far better visibility than the Agusta. So I swapped over at the airfield where I keep her. The uniform just didn't seem right for the Bell somehow. I hope you don't mind?'

'Of course not,' Laura said.

'So here's my plan,' Robin continued.' We'll do a localized circuit. If we spot anything that looks like it could use closer inspection, I'll get the drone onto it. To be honest I think the drone's going to be more useful, but there's no harm in taking a recce first.'

'Alfredo our chef here is all geared up to help with the search. He wants to get a team together after his shift.' Jayne said.

'Top man.' Robin nodded in approval as he held the passenger door for Laura and Frank. 'And he's doing me some lunch.' He turned to Jayne. 'No offence, I spoke with him earlier. We didn't want to bother you with the minutiae.'

Laura felt giddy as they lifted off the ground and swung suspended. Robin was right. She marveled at the visibility below. The slate roofs of the house, the chimneys and lead lined gullies all in pristine order. They banked over the village. Then further afield the familiar landscape stretched out in a disorder of shape and hue. But how would they ever see a small dog? Black thoughts began to overtake her as the sound of the engine throbbed. What if he was entangled in a strand of barbed wire; caught in a poacher's trap or cowering in a ditch, lost and alone?

Through the headphones Robin said, 'we'll keep a tight radius. No more than six miles.' He pointed to his left. 'There's Woldham coming up.'

The gradual sprawl of houses became denser. Laura could see the spire of the church, the Town Hall and the main street. Then the houses straggled out again to a matrix of gardens and sheds that were the allotments. She recognised the hospital, the school with its playing fields. A game of football was in progress. Figures ran back and forth, but if she couldn't see the ball how would she ever see Parker?

They flew lower as they passed on into open countryside. The river came into view, silently flowing through the landscape almost at her feet. It should have been so beautiful, but to Laura it was a malevolent thing, waiting to lure a poor swimmer into its murky depths.

They gained height for a pair of riders. These were fields and hills Laura had ridden over; taken hedges and ditches; tiger traps and walls; galloped over meadows and skirted plough.

They came in lower again. She recognized a village pub. She could see cars, cyclists and pedestrians. At this height she saw people walking their dogs, but none were Parker.

Then Frank pointed to the railway track. Laura's heart sank further.

'We'll just look at those woods.' Robin's voice broke through her increasingly despondent thoughts.

They banked away again.

Below them lay an avenue of grey poplar trees that looked like it should have lined a drive, except there was no house at the end of it. It was less than a mile from Wellworth Lawns as the crow flew, but Laura hadn't been there for years. She remembered the only access was at least four miles away down a lane that led off the road to Cheltenham. The poplars converged into some dark green conifers beyond which the brown of a deciduous wood lay in a random pattern. It was so much bigger from the air than Laura remembered. They hovered over a horseshoe shaped clearing on the far side from where she could see the tops of two white vans. She could see a little girl running from one to the other. The child craned her neck, waving up at them.

'There's some barns ahead,' Robin said. 'We'll check them out. Then I think we're about done.'

As they circled the cluster of decaying buildings, Laura saw the main barn roof was bowed. Mossy slates were clinging on as if the gusting from the helicopter might be enough to dislodge them, sending them crashing to the ground. To her amazement, a barn owl flew out from a single wooden door, huge and angled precariously on one hinge, the remains of its pair lying flat on the ground.

The courtyard had been concreted, but tufts of grass and nettles sprouted out amongst pools of stagnant slime that glinted in the light. Beside a pile of rubble and some rusting farm machinery a row of red brick sheds extended, their roofs patched with rusting corrugated iron sheets. Laura could remember the complex as a working farmyard. It had stood for centuries housing cattle and sheep and storing bales of hay and straw. How could it have fallen into such a state of disrepair?

They came into land. Robin said he'd have his lunch then take the drone out. 'I shouldn't be more than a couple of hours.'

Frank said he'd go and join Strudel and Jervis who, with a team of ballroom dancers, were setting off to distribute posters.

He suggested that while she waited, Laura should choose the photo of Parker for the second printing.

Having dropped in on Venetia, she settled herself on the sofa with Parker's photo album. She kept changing her mind, but in the end opted for a picture she thought did justice to his appealingly alert expression. She remembered the occasion she had taken the snapshot. They were picnicking in Norfolk where Vince and Victoria had taken a house one summer. Parker was looking in her direction; ears pricked; nose glossy as he sniffed the air. It was not so much that she was encouraging him, but because right behind her Vince had been eating a crab salad. Parker always went wild at the merest hint of seafood.

She took the picture down to the office where Jayne Harcourt made her a copy. They were emailing it to Jervis when Robin returned.

'No sign of him I'm afraid,' he said. 'And right now I've got to get back to Leeds to pick up Vince for a meeting in London this evening. I'll send you over a full report with images tomorrow. There are a few places I couldn't get a good view of that you should check out – that last lot of barns we saw for one. But if you want my advice, I'd prioritise those two vans in the wood. Looked suspicious to me. Make sure you take the Canon with you.'

Laura's mind was racing. Who else was with the little girl she'd seen waving up at them?

Chapter 6

Laura took a gamble trying Frank on his mobile. Invariably he didn't have it on him, or it wasn't charged even though she'd reproached him on the subject, so she was surprised when he answered. He said he was in the middle of delivering posters.

'I want to finish this section of Woldham. Then I'm afraid I've got a church meeting.'

'But you've got to come with me. They might move on.'

'It's too late today,' he said. 'We'll go first thing tomorrow.'

'But I must go now,' she pleaded.

'I'm sorry. It's almost dark. Have you checked with the dog warden again? Then what about Parker's microchip?'

It was not what she wanted to hear, but she knew he was right. She made the calls. The warden said he was on the case. The vet said they would tell the microchip company and spread the word amongst their own community. It made Laura feel marginally better. With all these people looking out for him, Parker must turn up.

She decided to see if Venetia would join her for supper upstairs. She hated the idea of making extra work for Mimi or whoever was on duty, but knew she couldn't face breaking up the convivial atmosphere of the dining room that her appearance would inevitably cause. The comfort of her friend was what she needed.

Walking the few paces to Venetia's room, she let herself in.

Venetia was, as usual, engrossed in a TV programme, but uncharacteristically she snatched up the remote and flicked the TV off just as Laura saw what looked like an Alsatian dog. It appeared to be anesthetized on an operating table.

'What are you watching?' she asked.

'I thought it was something else…' Venetia, pink in the face, her lapis drop earrings swaying from her sagging lobes, the only giveaway of her age in an otherwise remarkably unlined face. 'At least I thought it might have some practical advice that might be useful,' she continued. 'But it was all about medical interventions. I got hooked, I'm afraid.' Venetia straightened herself up on the chair. 'But tell me, is there any news?'

'Nothing certain, and now I'll have to wait until morning. The wait is driving me mad. I wondered if you'd have supper on a tray with me?'

'Oh yes, I'm longing to get away from all of this.' Venetia leant forward and picked up a handful of junk mail from a pile on the carpet in front of her. 'It's to do with my daughter, I guarantee it.'

'Angel? But she's still in prison, isn't she?'

'Yes, but I can only think she must have sold my address to all these people as a way of making money.'

'I'm sure we can sort them out.' Laura sat down beside her. 'Let me look.'

Venetia lifted the skirt of the chair revealing a hoard of more envelopes. She picked up a wad and handed them to Laura.

'It started with victim support charities,' she said. 'Worthy causes I know, but where do you draw the line? I mean do mis-sold PPI claimants need, "grief therapy"?' She gave Laura a wide-eyed stare. 'Then it was for people with age related problems – as if I haven't got enough of those. I wouldn't mind a bit of post traumatic hip replacement stress if it meant I was the beneficiary of some top-up money for a cruise around the Adriatic.' Venetia rubbed her thighs. 'Just recently it seems the animal welfare lot have got me on their radar.'

Laura riffled through the pile. 'Looks like Angel's told them about her job with the donkey sanctuary.' She held up an all too obvious envelope.

'Oh, I know and cats. I've given money to them as well.'

'How much?' Laura knew Venetia's resources were limited.

'I've no idea.' Her friend shrugged her shoulders. 'But at least they come with prepaid envelopes.'

'We must be the only age group who still use cheques.' Laura picked up another pile from the floor. 'You must stop. You've no reason to feel guilty. I'm sure you've more than done your bit.' She took the uppermost envelope in her hand. On it was printed the picture of a Shetland pony. She tore it open and scrutinised the contents. The letter, written from an address in France was asking for donations of unwanted ponies to take into schools as therapy for disruptive pupils. It was badly translated, and an error flagged up the possibility that it was not a bona fide charity. 'We can pay all shipping costs in our tranquilised stables of full air conditioning,' Laura read, and then further down the page, 'a lot is at steak for these young people whose needs we aim to meat.'

'Throw them all away.' Laura considered the pile. 'On second thoughts I'll go and get a bin liner from the kitchen. I'll see what's for supper while I'm there.'

'Anything for me except pork,' Venetia said. 'But I must finish telling you about last night before I forget… Oh yes and then this afternoon…'

'It will have to wait,' Laura said. 'I won't be long.'

As she made her way down to the kitchens it seemed to Laura that she had been thoroughly waylaid by Venetia's problems. On the other hand it was filling the emptiness of Parker's absence.

She pushed open the swing door to the kitchens and found Alfredo intent upon the job of garnishing ramekin dishes with tiny pansy flowers with the aid of a pair of tweezers. It was a delicate operation for someone more often found tenderising sides of beef with a hefty wooden mallet.

'There you are Alfredo,' she said.

The tweezers tinkled onto the side of the dish and fell to the floor. 'Fak, Lady B. Excuse my French, but you didn't half give me a fright.'

The chef wiped his brow with the dishcloth slung over his shoulder. 'Still no sign of my old compadre?' He retrieved the tweezers. 'Robin said something about some vans in a wood. I can go with you tomorrow if you wish?'

'You're too kind Alfredo, but the Canon's going to come with me. Anyway, you've got far too much to do here. It looks like you're short staffed again.'

'Andy's got the night off but Harriet's keeping me on my toes with all this flower arranging. To be honest, these work experience kids scare the living daylights out of me. She's gone out to get her blow-torch for the crème brulée.' Alfredo wiped the rim of a ramekin dish with his finger.

'They look lovely. What are they?'

'Smoked eel paté, you want try one?' The chef brought his fingers to his pursed lips and kissed them. 'Bellissimo. Then we got a nice coq au vin for mains.'

Laura remembered the times she had come down to the kitchens looking for a treat for Parker. Alfredo would often save him a fresh chicken winglet since she had told him of the vet's recommendation. 'I'm having supper upstairs with Mrs. Hobbs,' she said. 'I hope I'm not too late to put the order in?'

Alfredo checked the clock on the wall. 'Holy roasting Charlottes!' He ran over to a bank of ovens and pulled out a tray of sizzling potatoes.

It was some minutes later, after she had assisted him in filling cream jugs for the dessert, that Laura asked him if he could spare her a bin bag.

'I was all in favour of animal charities,' she said, explaining what it was for. 'Until I saw the mountain of requests poor Mrs. Hobbs has had.'

She followed him out to a storeroom in the yard where the deliveries arrived. A row of wheelie bins stood against the wall to one side. As Alfredo unlocked the door, Laura lifted the lid of one of them.

The chef was aghast. 'What you doin' in there Lady B?'

Laura put the lid down. She didn't really know herself, but she knew it was not a good idea to dwell on it.

'But hold on, this reminds me,' Alfredo continued. 'I found a Gitano woman looking in the bins a coupla' days ago.' He took a sheaf of rubbish sacks from a shelf and peeled a couple off. 'Couldn't hardly understand a word she said except "council," and "Health and Safety." Except she saying "heaf and safely". I'm telling you Lady B, I'm not a racist.' He handed her the sack. 'Poco Dio I'm a wop myself for goodness sake, but since when's the council employing gypsies in management positions?'

'A traveller?'

'Traveller, Romany call 'em what you like, but people in Health and Safety all covered in dangly gold necklace bits jangling about in people's bins like some incense swinging Catholic priest, that can't be right.'

'Perhaps you should mention it to Jayne Harcourt,' Laura suggested as they walked back to the kitchen.

There was no one at the reception desk so Laura went back upstairs and telephoned down the dinner order to Mimi who answered from the bar. As they waited, Laura and Venetia stuffed the bin bag full of junk mail. They took it to Laura's apartment and opened a bottle of Merlot from the drinks cupboard in her small kitchen.

Venetia was recapping on the Tuthill's row in the dining room the night before when Mimi brought their supper in.

'Are you short staffed in the dining room too?' Laura asked.

'Few people's off,' Mimi said. 'Is no big problem.' She left the white damask covered trolley and wished them 'bon apeti.'

It was not until they were eating their meal that Laura reminded Venetia to continue her story.

'So, what happened this afternoon?' she asked, putting her knife and fork together after a few mouthfuls. She had chosen the chicken for both of them, but she hadn't the stomach for it. Without Parker there to share, the meal had a sense of desolate deficiency.

'I'll finish telling you my story about the Tuthill's dog first.' Venetia scraped her plate clean. 'It's got health issues you see. That's how I got started on the TV programme.'

Much as she loved her, Laura wondered how long she could listen to Venetia's tittle-tattle. 'Elodie's got a hip problem, I know.'

Venetia looked up from her tray. 'Who hasn't? But it means she can't have puppies. Some time ago, according to Reggie, Crawford had been bragging about how much he could make from breeding from Elodie.' Venetia poked at a scrap of food lodged between her front teeth with her fingernail. 'I'm afraid it's the reason Crawford doesn't like you.'

Laura frowned. 'What do you mean?'

'He's jealous and who knows where that could lead …'

'What?' Was Venetia being deliberately obtuse?

'Well, you know how Parker had those puppies last year with Sybil Thorndike.' Venetia wiped her mouth with a napkin.

How could Laura forget the late actor Sir Repton Willowby and his long-haired Dachshund named after the great actress? Not least because Sir Repton had met his untimely end at the hands of Venetia's daughter Angel, but that was another story. Now Laura felt a lump in her throat. The coupling of Sybil Thorndike and Parker had been a mistake. Parker had proved a terrible father, taking no interest in his offspring, but the Dachshund proved a wonderful mother and the three "Pughund" puppies were utterly adorable.

'Well,' Venetia continued, 'Crawford told Reggie those sort of cross breeds can go for thousands of pounds. What's more, he had the idea you'd engineered the whole thing deliberately to make a fast buck.'

'You mean Crawford Tuthill thought I was making money from the puppies? That's too unfair. They weren't even mine. When Repton died so unexpectedly, they went to his heir, Ned Stocking. Everybody knows that.' Laura could feel a tremor in her voice. She clamped her lips tight shut.

'Anyhow,' Venetia was saying, 'It's probably all a lot of idle gossip. Let's change the subject. I haven't told you about the meeting this afternoon.'

'What meeting's this?'

'I can see you're not interested.'

Laura hadn't meant to snap. 'Let me put the trolley out and make us some mint tea,' she said. 'Then you can tell me about it.'

As she put the kettle on, her thoughts were still on Crawford Tuthill. She supposed it must have been galling that Elodie couldn't breed, but to take it personally against her and Parker was ridiculous. Downright hurtful. On the other hand, it did account for Crawford's reluctance to come out and help with the search for Parker, using the excuse of his knee injury. The injury Melissa wasn't even aware of.

She took the tea into the sitting room, handing Venetia a cup. 'Here we are,' she said, sitting next to her. 'Now, tell me all.'

'Well, I feel this could lead to something important.' The cup wobbled precariously as Venetia tucked her legs under her on the sofa. 'I went to a talk in the Recreation Room. It was by a chap called Harry Constantine. Such an attractive young man, most presentable and such lovely manners, not like those people who give the tax planning seminars in their shiny black suits.' She put the cup down leaning forward, one elbow resting on the arm of the sofa. 'He told us all about the charity he runs. Now what did he say it was called?' Venetia ran her fingers over her lips as she tried to remember. 'Pocks … Picts… Scots… What was it? Anyway, it raises money to look after dogs whose owners have died.'

Laura recalled the piece of paper Melissa Tuthill had given her. "PICS?" she suggested.

'I don't think so… Another of those silly acronyms anyway.'

'So, what happens to all these…' Laura was about to say pooches, but she didn't want to spoil Venetia's story. 'Dogs?'

'They get re-homed within the care sector, to people like us.'

'To more old people you mean?' Suddenly Laura didn't care about secondhand dogs. She wanted Parker back. 'And then those old people die …' She couldn't stop herself. 'What a mad idea.'

'Don't be like that Laura. It's a chance for dogs that no one else might want to find a loving home. Don't forget, most old people don't want a puppy. Even if it isn't forever, it's still a good thing to try. But more to the point it got me thinking. There are other reasons old people might want another dog.'

'Like what?'

'Theft for one, I'm often reading about it. Handbag sized dogs are particularly vulnerable.' Venetia reached out her hand to Laura. 'I don't think Parker could be described as a miniature, but he'd fit in a largish tote.'

Chapter 7

Why had Laura not thought of theft? Questions tumbled round her head as she endured another sleepless night. Parker in a carrier bag? No, the idea was ridiculous. Who would want a dog like him? She could almost feel his warm breath puffing at her – how could she love something that smelled so bad? And then the racket of his snoring…

She had come to the conclusion that Venetia was suffering from a charming delusion when the doorbell rang. Mimi came in carrying a tray.

'You getting up for it Lady B? I take into lounge area?'

Laura threw back the bedclothes and followed her through to the sitting room as Mimi placed the tray on her desk.

'I bringing this from Ms. Holloway.' Mimi handed Laura a large brown envelope she was clutching under her arm. 'She printing drone pictures for you.'

Almost the first image Laura saw was of the two vans in the wood. She looked at it with a new clarity of thought. If Parker had been chasing something, it was not impossible that he had gone in that direction.

Could the people in the vans have seen him? Even caught him…Perhaps he'd lost his collar? She must get to them. Why hadn't Frank rung?

Terrified she was already too late, she called and agreed to meet him outside in the car park.

On her way down, Laura took the black bag full of Venetia's junk mail to the recycling bin in the yard outside the kitchens. As she was leaving, she bumped into Alfredo. Ignoring what appeared to be a bundle of dirty aprons that was trailing at his feet, she lied, telling him how much she had enjoyed dinner.

'This is good,' he said. 'I was thinking you maybe have lost your appetite. But now maybe you bring Canon Frank to lunch after you been out? He's waiting in the car park. I seen him driving up here on my way in. He ask me if I want a lift. I told him, holy drumsticks no. He sure wouldn't want this in his car.' Alfredo lifted the bundle an inch or two off the ground from where Laura could smell pungent odour.

'What's in that thing?' she asked.

'Last night chicken carcasses. I been laying a trail. If Parker catches a whiff, he'll follow it back here for sure. I know how that dog goes wild for the prawns, so I added some. Kept 'em out overnight so they got a bit of the Mediterranean drain about 'em.' As the chef opened the food waste bin and tossed the bundle in, a blue whippet ran into the yard and careered towards Alfredo.

'That's Hilda Frampton's dog Toyboy if I'm not mistaken,' Laura said. 'He must have slipped his collar again.'

Alfredo grabbed the dog, lifting it into his arms. 'I'll see to him.'

From outside the yard, they heard the beeping of a reversing vehicle. 'That's my potatoes,' Alfredo said, as a dark blue lorry neared. 'You come and find me later if you want me to go out again.'

Laura thanked him. As she carried on past the lorry the driver stuck his head out of the cab window. He had a ruddy face and bulging pock marked nose, a pale blue cotton cap too small on his head.

Ahead she could see Frank leaning on the bonnet of his car parked next to hers. He waved and went to open his passenger door.

'I think mine's better for rough terrain,' Laura said, getting out her key. They had bickered about their respective vehicles before. Laura's invariable response was that hers was automatic and a nicer colour. In reality there was not much to distinguish between their two old Audi hatchbacks.

'I've just filled mine up,' he said.

Laura pacified him by suggesting that as neither had satnav, he would be the better map-reader. He conceded. Equilibrium was restored. As it was Laura knew exactly where she was going.

'It's better than being driven by Jervis, I have to admit,' Frank said, as they turned onto the main road. 'He rang earlier offering to take us in his Mercedes.' Laura put her hands over her eyes in mock terror.

'Look where you're going,' Frank shouted. They laughed. It was a small moment of levity in the bleak circumstances.

'I put him off,' Frank continued. 'He was fine about it. Said he and Strudel had plenty to do since Strudel posted on the Neighbourhood WhatsApp group. They've linked up with some missing dog groups. I believe there've been a few sightings reported.'

Laura gasped. 'Where?'

'I'm afraid none of them fit the bill. Extraordinary how you can say it's a pug that's missing near Woldham and someone pipes up that they've seen a collie in Sheffield.'

Laura glanced at Frank, his glasses resting on the end of his nose. He had taken the map out of his old canvas rucksack and was intent upon it, his finger pressed down on Woldham.

She indicated left. He should have turned the page.

Frank looked up from the map. 'I suggested to Jervis that I put a note about Parker on the Parish website,' he said.

'That's good.' She wondered who read the Parish newsletter.

'And I know who owns the wood.'

Laura checked the road before turning to him. 'Who?'

'It was a late parishioner of mine. I don't believe there will be any trouble about trespass. We may have to pretend we are potential buyers though.'

'What?'

'The family came to see me about turning it into a natural burial site. I had to put them straight about tree roots amongst other things, so they decided to sell it through a company that parcels off plots of woodland for recreational use.'

'Good detective work,' Laura said. 'So the van owners might be there legitimately?'

'Not according to Jervis, he's checked. It's not yet on the market.'

'Oh no.' Laura pressed her foot on the accelerator.

'Steady,' Frank said. 'Whoever's in those vans, they are officially trespassing.' He closed the map, dropping it by his feet. 'You know the way don't you.'

Laura turned down a track newly filled with hard core, flanked by the line of poplar trees they had seen from the air. The sun filtered through the almost bare branches as they swayed in a light breeze. The flickering light made it hard to see. Laura leant across and took a pair of sunglasses from the glove compartment.

'We're only going to ask if they've spotted Parker, aren't we?' she said, putting them on.

'I believe it may require a certain amount of tact. We don't know how many of them there may be. Harmless as a dove and all that.' Frank gave Laura a knowing look.

'Don't worry, I'll leave the talking to you.' She smiled at him. It seemed an age since she had used the muscles around her cheeks.

Ahead of them the track divided. 'This should lead us to the middle of the wood,' Laura said, taking the left-hand fork.

Frank nudged her arm with his elbow. 'Look,' he whispered, pointing through the windscreen.

The two white vans were parked in the clearing some yards in front of them, one parked at an angle adjacent to the other. Laura drew up a few yards away.

Outside the nearest one a tall dark-haired man in a checked shirt, tattered jeans and thick leather boots was sawing through what looked like the door of a kitchen cupboard. It was resting on two plastic trestles. He was using one knee to keep it in place, the sleeves of his shirt rolled up as he worked. He stopped what he was doing as Laura and Frank got out of the car.

'Good morning,' Frank called out.

Beside the man, sitting on a wooden camping stool a woman was painting a small cabinet in a dirty off-white colour. Her black hair was partly covered in a red and green floral scarf. She had on a tabard like a housewife from the 1950's. Now paint spattered, it might once have been bright but was faded through years of washing. She turned to them and Laura caught the glint of gold around her neck as her jewelry caught the light.

The man put down the saw. He wiped his brow with his sleeve, nodded at them.

The passenger door of the second van creaked open. A little girl got out. Laura was not good at telling the age of children, but she supposed she might be about ten. Her long dark hair was tied in two ponytails. She was wearing a thin blue cotton dress. It was too short for her and too thin for the time of year. She slammed the door shut and stood beside the van kicking at the grass with one trainer.

'I hope we are not intruding,' Frank said.

'You don't need an appointment.' The man's East European accent held a hint of irony that Laura had not been expecting.

'We're looking for a missing dog; a light-coloured pug, do you know the breed?' Frank asked.

'My mistake, I thought you were coming to buy my furniture.' The man gave a gruff laugh. 'But I know this kind of dog; Percy in the Disney movie I remember.' He paused. 'But I have not seen one here.'

'Do you like dogs?' Laura directed the question to the little girl. She watched for a reaction.

'Oh yes.' The girl beamed and skipped back towards the van. 'Papa, can I…?'

'Camilla!' The woman pointed the paintbrush at the girl and started shouting in her native language. The girl's face fell. She turned her back.

The man started speaking to the woman, also in their native tongue. Laura studied his profile. His long straight nose and jutting jaw reminded her of an Emperor on a Roman coin. Whatever it was he said made no difference to the little girl. She opened the van door. A large hound with a sleek dark coat jumped out. It knocked the girl over. As she lay on the ground it licked her face. It was evidently a bitch that had recently borne a litter, but it was in good shape. Although not a breed that Laura could put a name to, she had seen one like it before, recently in fact.

'Oh Truda,' the little girl shouted at the dog, pushing it off.

The woman called out again. The girl, picking herself up, took the dog by the collar and pulled it back to the van. The dog jumped back in, followed by the girl who slammed the door behind her.

'Don't mind them,' the man said.

'How many puppies did the dog have?' Laura asked.

'Five. We have one left. A friend is looking after it. I can get it sent here if you like?'

'I'm sure it's a lovely dog, but much too big for me.'

'We can get you smaller one. Nice orange coat. Pure Kukoni. From my home country.'

'That's very kind,' Laura said. 'But, no thank you.'

'You wait a bit I sure I am finding you a pug,' the man continued. 'Maybe like in the movie Men in Black?'

'No, really,' Laura said. 'I want my own one back.'

The man nodded in assent.

'So, you like what I am making?' he asked changing the subject. He pointed to the cabinet. 'My wife can make any colour you like. I can make table, chairs, all same styling.' He walked to the van where he had been working and opened the rear doors. Inside Laura could see old bits of furniture in different shades of greys and taupes. It was hard to tell what anything was as it was stacked tightly up to the roof. With open arms, the man gestured expansively at it. 'Plenty of choice. Very honest prices.'

The smell of gloss paint was making Laura's head spin. Parker wasn't there. She wanted to leave.

'I'm sorry, we don't have much room for furniture in the old people's home, I'm afraid,' she said.

Frank took out a piece of paper from his coat pocket and wrote down his number. 'Please call us if you see the pug,' he said.

Chapter 8

As they jolted back down the track, Laura turned to Frank in desperation. 'Should I have agreed to him getting me a pug? If only to see what he came up with. Have I missed an opportunity?'

'I don't believe so. They didn't look dishonest.'

'How can you be sure? There was something odd about the whole set up. The little girl should have been at school surely? And that big dog, it was the spit of the one Stan Kaminski has. I've never seen one before. Then to see two in such a short space of time…And the man had the same accent as Stan.'

'There's probably some perfectly rational reason. Perhaps they come from the same country – even the same area. That sort of dog could be two a penny wherever that may be. A bit like Norfolk terriers in Hunstanton; you can't move for them.'

'But then the smaller dog he was trying to sell sounded like Stan's other one.'

'A Kukoni,' Frank said. 'Not a breed I've ever heard of. Orange coat? Most alarming.'

'Don't be so literal. He meant a tan colour. He didn't mention the feather duster tail, but then why would he necessarily? But the thing is, Stan's is called Kuko, quite a coincidence wouldn't you say?'

They had reached the end of the track. 'I must find Stan.' Laura said. 'There's something suspicious about this.' She turned the car in the direction of Woldham.

'I thought you said you liked Stan? Trusted him.'

'I could be wrong. What if he's connected to those people? Oh, I don't know, but Parker could have been in the back of that other van for all I know.'

'Why would they want Parker?'

'Oh, I don't know, but I wish we'd looked all the same.'

'We could hardly break in, could we?' Frank gave a dry laugh. 'But at least you said "we".'

Laura felt her face redden. 'But what if they leave. We might never find them again.'

'They'll be there for a day or two. They'll have to wait for the paint to dry for a start. Anyway, I made a note of the registration plates, both UK. Now, how about we get something to eat in that new café on Sheep Street? You can call Stan from there.'

Laura backed into a parking spot outside the cafe. As she waited for Frank to feed the meter, she could see a poster in the window. In bold lettering she read 'Missing,' and underneath, 'Have You Seen This Dog?' Centred below was the photo of Parker. She walked over to read the small print.

'Jervis is doing sterling work,' Frank said, as he put the ticket on the dashboard.

Of course he was right but seeing Parker's name in print and then his dear picture made Laura wince in pain.

They went and sat in the café. While they waited for their order to arrive Laura tried Stan's number. It went to answerphone. There was no point leaving a message, it was all too complicated.

Crude pottery bowls filled to the brim with steaming minestrone arrived. She took a spoonful, trying to avoid the squares of potato that were bobbing about on the surface.

'This is so awful,' she said.

Frank stirred his soup. 'It's not that bad.'

'I mean not knowing what direction to take.'

He leant across the table and took her hand. 'I believe we must follow the leads we have. Carry on searching and hope that any one of the agencies we've informed hear something.' He returned to the meal and as he tore a hunk of bread in two, Laura found herself unhelpfully reminded of the holy sacraments.

'I'll call Phil Sandfield again,' Frank was saying.

'Phil Sandfield? You didn't tell me you'd rung him.' Laura had a chequered history with the Woldham Police Inspector. Things had not always gone smoothly in their relations with one another. 'He won't be in the slightest bit interested in Parker,' she said.

'He hasn't returned my call, it's true. Rather rude considering I confirmed his daughter some years ago.'

'I can't see that carrying much weight.'

'Under normal circumstances no, but I had to conduct a private service on account of her exclusion from school for being rather heavily pregnant by the time of the confirmation. She was a mere thirteen.'

'That certainly does add some weight.'

'I thought you'd see my point. I had to get a special dispensation from the Bishop.' Frank layered his bread with butter. 'We'll go and look at that abandoned farmyard next,' he continued. 'Then I suggest we catch up with Strudel and Jervis. I'd still like to identify the man with the limp.'

Laura pushed her bowl to one side. 'Strudel agreed with me. He'll just have been another passing delivery driver.'

Frank gave a small sigh of resignation. 'Well, to the barns then?'

'Before that, can we stop at The Blue Dolphin? It's only round the corner. I was thinking, it's a long shot, but Sally Bowman might have seen something while she was at her sister's that night.'

The windows of The Blue Dolphin were steamed up. As they entered the shop the aroma of chip fat was mixed with a smell of cleaning fluid. With her back to the door, Sally Bowman plunged a floor mop into a bucket. She was humming to herself and swaying from the hips. She looked like she needed the exercise as a couple of inches of pale flesh wobbled between the top of her jeans and her top.

'Hello,' Laura said.

Oblivious, Sally continued pumping the mop to dry the excess water. Laura tapped her on the shoulder.

Sally swiveled round. 'Lady Boxford,' she said, pulling out her earplugs. 'My goodness you didn't half give me a fright.'

Her dyed blond hair was tied back from her face so that the dark roots framed the perspiring forehead of her round face. Laura remembered Strudel's description of Val Farmer's hair. The sisters were certainly alike in that respect.

Laura thought about formally introducing Frank, but Sally gave a quick nod of recognition in his direction and walked round to the other side of the counter. 'Fryers are off, I'm afraid. Lunchtimes can be slow and if Bryan's expecting a delivery we tend to shut early. Spuds should be here any time. We must be the only chip shop still using fresh not frozen.'

'That's what makes yours so delicious,' Laura said. 'But actually, we didn't want anything to eat.'

Sally frowned. 'Thanks for the lift the other night by the way,' she said, walking to the door that separated the shop from the back of the building. She opened it an inch, listened, then shut it again. 'I think that's the lorry now.'

'It's about my dog,' Laura continued. 'You remember Parker?' Even saying his name made her throat constrict.

'Who could forget him? Pug with a seafood habit like him. Not many dogs eat scampi round here.'

'You see he went missing...' Laura could hear a scuffling noise coming from the other side of the door behind the counter. 'It was on the evening I dropped you at your sister's.'

'Missing? Oh no, that's terrible.'

'I wondered if you or your sister saw him? Maybe later when Val took you home.' The scuffling was getting louder and now Laura was sure she could hear whining.

'No,' Sally said. 'We never saw him.'

Laura's mind started to race. 'Have you got a dog back there?' she asked.

'It'll be...' Sally walked back to the door and opened it an inch. 'Bryan,' she shouted. 'I've got Lady Boxford here, don't let Bailey in.' She slammed the door turning back to Laura and Frank. 'It'll be my brother's collie. He lets him out of the truck when he gets here.'

'Your brother?' Frank asked.

'From Lincolnshire, he's a potato farmer.'

'I thought Sally was behaving very oddly,' Laura said. 'And I'm sure the whining started when I said Parker's name.'

She and Frank were on their way to the farmyard, bumping their way down another stony track.

'Sally explained what the noise was,' Frank said.

'It sounded so familiar though. We should have demanded to see the dog.'

'Whining dogs all sound the same. I'm sure you are imagining it. We can go back, but think about it, what would Sally want with Parker?'

'I know it's irrational, but I can't help it. I'm suspicious of everything and everyone.'

'I understand but try to be patient. I'm sure Parker will turn up,' Frank exhorted, as Laura parked outside the farm buildings.

'So, you think he'll be here?'

Frank sighed. 'I don't know. Let's take a look though.'

It was somehow even more depressing on the ground than from the air. The rattle of the corrugated iron roofs in the wind gave it a desolate air. They checked every ramshackle building, their dry earth floors covered in rat droppings and bird feathers, but there was no sign of Parker. Then, as the light began to fade, Laura insisted they cross a field to look in the fisherman's hut she remembered had stood near a small, disused quarry that had been flooded and stocked with carp.

The hut was empty, a brightly striped fibreglass float lying on the floor, the only indication of its purpose.

It started to rain. Great droplets broke the surface of the still dark water.

They left the cheerless scene and returned to the car, cold and muddy.

'That was a waste of time,' Laura said.

'Early days.'

Frank's words were little consolation. They drove back to Wellworth Lawns in silence. In the car park he took his leave, sensitive as ever, saying he would drop in on Strudel and Jervis for an update and would call her in the morning.

Laura went to see Venetia. They agreed it would be better if Laura made an appearance in the dining room for dinner.

'You've got to face the music,' Venetia said. 'I know it might be difficult, but everyone is rooting for you, honestly they are.'

Unconvinced, Laura returned to her apartment. She made herself a gin and tonic before sitting down to try Stan Kaminski again.

This time he picked up straight away. She asked him if he knew about the travellers in the wood.

'They can't have been there long. I was there only a few days ago myself.'

Laura didn't ask why. It was probably some business for the hunt. 'They've got a big dog just like yours,' she said. 'It had recently had puppies.'

She could hear Stan's tongue click against his top teeth as he tutted. 'Sounds like they were Lithuanians, Baloo's a Lithuanian Hound. I brought him with me eight years ago and I swear he was the only dog like it, but now people are coming over all the time with them, and other foreign breeds. They'll sell anything they think looks new. It's fashion and the Covid effect.'

Laura was surprised at his volubility.

'They were making furniture too,' she said.

'Furniture?' Stan was silent for a moment. 'As I said, they'll try anything.'   'The man tried to sell me another dog. It sounded a bit like your Koko.'

'You're joking. A Kukoni? That's crazy. I think I better pay them a visit.'

'If you do, could you ask them about Parker again; I'm not sure they understood how important he is to me.'

'Sure, of course, although I don't think he'd have strayed that far, but I'll call you if I find out anything.'

As Laura waited for Venetia, she thought about Stan's story. What was it that didn't ring true?

Chapter 9

The general buzz of conversation died as Laura and Venetia walked into the dining room.

'Any news?' Gladys Freemantle asked from where she was sitting with Reggie Hawkesmore.

'Not yet.' Laura tried to keep her voice steady.

'I'm sure he'll turn up soon,' Gladys continued.

'Let us know if there's anything we can do,' Reggie offered.

A murmuring of agreement followed from around the room. Laura had been dreading this kind of bonhomie and when Mimi tried to seat them in the middle of the room, she said they'd prefer to take a table near a window at the side.

They sat down to study the menus that were placed on starched white napkins in front of them.

'I might have two starters. At our age it's really all we need,' Venetia said. 'I do love Alfredo's garlic prawns...Do you think I could have them twice?'

It was meant to be a joke, but to Laura it was like a stiletto wound reminding her of Parker's love of seafood. She thought of the trail Alfredo had set. It had proved futile. Parker hadn't taken the bait.

'Are you sure?' she said. 'What about having the guinea fowl terrine, followed by the prawns?'

'What a good idea,' Venetia agreed.

Mimi giggled when Venetia explained her logic.

'You so funny, Mrs. Hobb. We all having sometimes wind you know. Big portion keeping you strong too,' she said. 'But you telling that to Mr Tutt.' She nodded her head in the direction of the swing doors to the kitchens near which the Tuthill's were seated. 'Him always saying me, "is this all?" when I serving.'

Venetia raised her already arched eyebrows – she could be heavy handed in her make-up application. 'Melissa and Crawford having dinner here again?'

Fearful Crawford had noticed her staring, Laura turned away. She saw Lulu Vandermoss sitting alone, waif-like at a table not far away. Lulu had the menu in her hands, but was taking scant interest in it, preferring also to stare at the Tuthills.

'Lulu's a strange one, bit of a loner,' Laura said. 'She doesn't seem to go in for company. Do we know anything about her?'

'Not much,' Venetia said. 'As you say, she keeps herself to herself. I tried to get her to join me for the bingo. She said it brought about bad memories. I'm not sure what kind of bad memories bingo could bring on... But that's enough of her. Tell me how you've got on today.'

It wasn't the end of Lulu though. Laura was in the middle of relating the events of her day when she noticed her wafting in their direction.

She stopped at their table and addressed Laura. 'When you asked about the delivery driver the other night,' she said. 'I remembered later that I had had a parcel. I'd received a notification that it would be arriving, but it was a woman who I took it from. I think that's what put me off my stride, because as I recall it was a man you were interested in.' She sighed as if the monologue had exhausted her. 'There is one other thing though…'

'Yes?' Laura waited, as Lulu appeared to gather her strength.

'Well, I did see Crawford Tuthill wandering about outside that evening. I don't know if that's of any interest?'

'I don't know, but thank you anyway,' Laura said. 'But look, would you like to join us? I'm sure Mimi could lay another place.'

'No thank you. I've lost my appetite.' Lulu gave an enigmatic smile. 'I'm going to retire to my bed if you don't mind.'

As she wandered trance like out of the dining room, Laura asked Venetia if she thought Lulu might be somewhat deranged.

'I think it's her nerves.'

'Well, d'you think she might be on the wrong medication then? With sudden weight loss, one might need to adjust the dose?'

'I haven't come across it on 'Embarrassing Bodies'. But anyway, she's had anorexia for years. Then her best friend being murdered must have brought on added complications.' Venetia pasted terrine on to a piece of Melba toast. It cracked into pieces on the plate.

'How do you know all this? Are you sure?'

Venetia mashed the toast and guinea fowl mixture into a ball with her fingers. 'I'm fairly certain she told me on the bus on our way to the theatre in Stratford.'

Venetia hadn't been to the theatre for some years. Not since she'd got so upset by the see-through costume of the protagonist in the trans gender production of Salome. It was hard when those close to one could no longer be considered entirely reliable in their recollections. Laura changed the subject, but Lulu's behaviour was still niggling her when, as they finished eating, Gladys Freemantle came over. She asked if they would join her and Reggie for a nightcap.

Laura was about to refuse, but Venetia said it would be a lovely idea.

They followed Gladys and Reggie out and found a place by the fire in the bar from where the ever-adaptable Mimi was serving drinks.

'My accountant once lost her Bedlington Terrier,' Reggie was saying, as the four of them nursed whiskeys. 'It was gone for nine days before they found it. Thin as a bloody rake it was and a bit bonkers. Mind you it was like that before it got lost.'

'A bit like Lulu Vandermoss,' Venetia said.

'Bonkers?' Reggie scratched his ear.

'Skeletal,' Venetia said. 'The dog I mean, not your accountant.'

'Yes, she is a vulnerable looking creature,' Gladys agreed.

'Let's hope she recovers completely; the Bedlington certainly did,' Reggie continued. 'Bloody miracle.'

'So, you mustn't give up hope Laura,' Gladys said.

Out of the corner of her eye, Laura saw the Tuthills come in. They were making their way over to the bar when Melissa called out, 'No you certainly mustn't.'

She's got good hearing, Laura thought.

'If you want my opinion …' Crawford's voice was uncomfortably loud. He took a few paces nearer to their
table. 'I should think that dog of yours has been in an accident.'

Laura stared at him in horror. His bald head was shining, as if Melissa had polished it with beeswax. Above his creased grey flannel trousers, he wore a white shirt. The top three buttons were undone, revealing his fat sagging neck and curly white-haired chest.

'Oh Crawford, don't be silly,' Melissa gave a nervous titter.

'I suppose he had his collar on,' Crawford carried on regardless. 'Bloody dangerous. Could have got caught up in something.' He put his hands to his throat and started gurgling.

'Christ man,' Reggie said. 'You're drunk.'

'Take him home Melissa,' Gladys implored.

Melissa's face pulsed red. She was pulling at her husband's jacket sleeve when Jayne Harcourt walked in from the hall.

'Ah, Mr. and Mrs. Tuthill,' Jayne said. 'Just the people I wanted to see. Good dinner? I wonder if I could have a quick word in my office?'

'What a horrible man,' Laura said, as she and Venetia made their way upstairs. 'I knew it was a mistake going down to dinner.'

An image of Parker strangled by his own collar flashed intermittently in her head leaving her feeling increasingly grim. She yearned for him. His funny face and the sound of his expectant high-pitched yap as she opened the tin of his favourite treats.

Crawford had acted with cruel vindictiveness, as if he really hated her. A moment of paranoia overcame her. Could it be that she had that effect on people? She asked Venetia her opinion.

'Don't worry, it's one silly man.' Whisky fumes filled the air as Venetia hiccupped. 'It's bound to happen in the hothouse environment we live in.'

Her words were of little consolation as another night alone without Parker loomed.

Chapter 10

Mimi's ponytail swung forwards as she placed the breakfast tray on the table in Laura's sitting room.

'Oh silly me, my hair so clumsy.' She giggled briefly as she rearranged the toast that had fallen out of its rack. Then her expression changed to one of seriousness.

'Oh, Lady B I thinking, no Parker very bad. You having any ideas finding him for today?'

Laura could feel her bottom lip start to quiver. She had gone into every step so far with a conviction that she would find him, but like a solitary church bell, the list of disappointments tolled; Stan and the badger sett; Vince's helicopter and the drone; the travellers; the farmyard. All these lines she had been sure would lead to his return. But they had come to nothing.

'I'm sure the Canon will join me to resume the search,' she said.

'This is best thing.' Mimi poured coffee from the pot, handing it to Laura. 'My English teacher saying a worry halved is a worried shed. I go out looking Woldham side after my lesson later.'

'You're so kind.' Laura smiled, but when Mimi had gone, she stared silently at the crust-less triangles of toast. She was alone with a full rack and no one to share it with.

Abandoning the tray she went to ring Frank. There was no answer. She tried Venetia.

'I'm going out with Gladys in her car. We didn't bother you, as we were sure you'd have other plans. We've got a poster from Jervis. We thought we'd stop and chat with people. Try to jog their memory.'

Laura put down the phone. So much kindness; she was filled with guilt. How could she have lost him? She picked up the phone again, this time to try Strudel and Jervis, but there was no answer from them either. Her guilt increased. How long could she rely on the goodwill of her friends?

Friends? Doubts from the night before crept back. What if Venetia was being kind and was covering up the fact that Laura was unpopular?

She seized the coffee pot. 'No, surely it was just Crawford Tuthill. She poured herself another cup. But what if Crawford hated her so much...Her hand was shaking as she drank it down. ... Hated her enough to take Parker from her out of sheer spite?
The caffeine hit home.

Why had he referred to Parker having an accident?

The cup fell from her grasp, and clinked, unbroken onto the tray. But what would Crawford have done with him?

A feeling of disquiet overtook her. Where was Frank when she needed him? Jervis would know what to do, but where were he and Strudel? Laura looked at her watch. By the time she had walked over to Mulberry Close they might be back.

The weather was blustery, but bright and clear as Laura set out. She passed one of the gardeners on a ride-on mower trying to make the grass look tidy in an ever-increasing autumnal scene. The breeze was sending leaves flying in all directions. It was the kind of day that gave Parker a spring in his stride. He would rush ahead of her, turn, rush back and then just before he reached her, bark a provocative, 'catch me if you can' at her.

The gardener, intent upon his stripes, was oblivious to her as she rounded the corner into Mulberry Close. She could see Strudel and Jervis' house ahead and almost missed a young lad, bending down beside the path leading to the Tuthill's front door.

'Hello,' she said. 'Have you lost something?'

As he stood up, two pebbles dropped from his hand. They landed with a clatter on the paving slabs and rolled into a low lavender hedge. He looked down at them, then at Laura.

'Or are you up to a bit of what my children used to call, "pranking"?' Laura asked.

'Pranking, that's hilarious.' The boy laughed, running his fingers through his long blond fringe. With the hair swept back he had a sort of old fashioned, almost Edwardian look. His strong blue eyes were widely set, his skin clear of the usual outbreak of pubescent spots.

'In fact, I'm doing my Duke of Edinburgh Gold Award. Working for a charity.'

Laura hadn't seen the plastic container at his feet. He picked it up and held it out.

'Let me see.' Laura walked a few steps closer. The boy was tall. She could have felt intimidated, but as it was, when she drew nearer, he seemed to lose his nerve, and his eyes started blinking rapidly.

'It's called Guide Dog Rehab.' He pointed to the picture wrapped around the container. It was of a yellow Lurcher in a high viz harness. 'They get stressed out doing all that work guiding people around. You know, Zebra crossings; loose curbstones; trip hazards. Must do their heads in. They need a bit of R&R. Rest and relaxation, that is.'

'Poor things; that sounds like a very good idea,' Laura said. 'But there are quite a few canine charities around at the moment. Have you collected much?'

He shook the container. Their eyes met. The clank of coins was not encouraging.

'Notes mostly,' he said, covering himself. 'People are very generous round here.'

'You've been here before?'

'No.' He paused. 'I mean not since last hols.'

'Shouldn't you be at school now?' Laura asked.

'I'm … I'm off sick. Broke a load of bones in my hand during judo training. Meant I couldn't even use a keyboard.' He wriggled his free hand. 'It's much better now. I'll be going back next week.'

Laura thought about getting out her purse. The transparency of a youthful lie always rather appealed to her, but on this occasion, she wished him luck and carried on to Strudel and Jervis's.

As she rang the bell, she saw the boy saunter off, his job apparently complete. She rang the bell again. It was unusual for one of them not to be in. Jervis normally did the shopping on his own as Strudel liked to have him out of the way when choosing her outfit for the day's dance classes.

Laura was about to phone them when she realized she hadn't charged her mobile. Feeling a brief moment of shame as she remembered admonishing Frank for the very same thing, she walked round to the kitchen window and peered in. All the surfaces were immaculate, a cloth folded neatly on the empty draining board.

She returned to the front door. This time she knocked. Then took a few steps back, looking up at the bedroom windows. Was that the flutter of one of Strudel's nets? Did a vague shadow pass behind the curtains? She knew that Strudel tended to fling clothes around before making a decision on her daily attire. Perhaps she had bought herself a set of headphones and was practicing a waltz? There was nothing for it but to return to her apartment.

Laura had not long got back when Strudel rang. Frank and Jervis had been out leafleting in Woldham when Jervis had got a call from the local rescue centre.

'He had given them his own number when he called on them earlier,' Strudel was saying. 'And they rang to say…'

Laura felt her heart surge. She dropped the phone. She could still hear Strudel's voice as the receiver landed on a cushion beside her. A pug had been brought in that matched Parker's description.

Chapter 11

It was a fawn pug, that much was true. But it wasn't Parker.

'We were so sure,' the girl at the rescue centre said. 'He fitted the description perfectly.' Compassion emanated from her as she held the dog in her arms under the glare of an old-fashioned strip light. The poor creature was grossly overweight and even from where Laura stood on the heavily disinfected rubber matting, she could smell its panting breath. Parker's was never good, but this was putrid. Beneath bleary eyes a thick fold of balding skin sat on the bridge of its nose and its coat had nothing of the sheen of Parker's. Laura felt as if her heart had been broken. A wave of tiredness swept over her as she looked at Frank beside her, his shoulders sagging in disappointment.

They walked back through the inner sanctum of cages filled with sleeping cats. Then down another corridor of smaller dogs pitifully curled up on blankets, an ear pricked here or there, but mostly with their heads tucked deep between front legs as if the light was a terrible reminder of their plight.

The girl pushed open another door that led to a further row of kennels containing what appeared to Laura to be never ending German Shepherds and Bullterriers, all barking wildly from behind the bars. Finally, they made it out into fresh air and the afternoon sunshine. They walked slowly across the tarmac. As Frank held the car door open for her, without thinking she hugged him. He seemed surprised but reciprocated.

She could feel his Adam's apple touching her hair. 'We'd better ring Strudel and Jervis,' he said.

She sat beside him in the passenger seat of his car listening only vaguely as he spoke on the phone. She had been so sure that he should drive so that on their return she could have had Parker on her lap.

'Right.' Frank put the phone back in his breast pocket and started up the engine. 'I agree with Jervis. We must go further afield with the posters.'

On the drive home they discussed the villages they thought would be good for coverage in an attempt to divert their despondency. Frank took a back route avoiding the centre of Woldham and they were almost through Chipping Wellworth village when Laura saw a woman sweeping leaves on the path in front of one of the cottages.

'Hang on,' she said. 'That's Val Farmer, Sally Bowman's sister.'

Frank braked and stopped a few houses further up the village street.

Laura got out and ran back.

'Hello Lady B,' Val said, stopping her work to lean on the broom. 'Sorry to hear about your dog, Alfredo told me he's gone missing. Still no sign of him?'

'Not yet... But how are you keeping?' It was a mistake to ask such a question. Val's ailments necessitated lengthy description. Eventually Laura halted the medical monologue and managed to change the subject. She asked Val if she remembered seeing anything unusual the night Laura had dropped her sister off.

'As a matter of fact, I do,' Val said. 'After we'd eaten and had a catch up over a couple of shandies, I dropped Sally back in Woldham. Then I came home. I'd just parked up when I saw a man wandering down the road. He looked a bit unsteady on his pins. I thought he might be drunk, so I waited 'til he'd passed before I got out of the car.'

'Did you see what he looked like?' Laura asked.

'It was dark. I couldn't see much, and he had a hat on.'

Laura was about to ask if Val could remember what the hat was like when they heard the sound of a buzzer coming from inside the cottage.

'That'll be my chocolate sponge.' Val glanced anxiously behind her. 'Sorry not to be more help,' she said.

Laura was about to return to the car when she saw another figure she recognized. Coming down the road in the opposite direction was Gwendoline Shackleton towing a small white Shih Tzu. The dog saw Laura. It gave a series of short high-pitched yaps, running towards her. Despite its diminutive stature, its bold approach caught Gwendoline off guard, and she let go of the lead.

The dog stopped at Laura's feet and snarled. Laura knew the signs. Her ankle was in a position of extreme vulnerability. She put her foot out, nudging the dog to one side before it had time to sink its teeth in. It rolled over on its back, gave an imploring mewl and stared up at her with adoring eyes and wagging tail. Laura bent down and let it sniff her outstretched hand.

'I saw that, you kicked her,' Gwendoline shouted as she ran up. 'Zaza, what have I told you about nasty strangers.'

'You could hardly call it a kick, but anyway she was going to bite me for goodness sake.' Laura stood up to face Gwendoline. 'Anyway, I'm not a stranger, we've met before.' It was a more strident response than she might have wished, but then what did it matter?

Gwendoline stooped to pick up the dog's lead, then raised herself to her full height, peering at Laura through watery grey green eyes. 'I may have made your acquaintance, but Zaza has no idea who you are.' Her gaze travelled over Laura's shoulder. 'And who's this? Your husband I presume.' She pulled the dog aside. 'Zaza, stay clear.'

Frank, bored of waiting in the car was walking up the road to join them.

'No, he's not my husband,' Laura said. 'This is Canon Frank Holliday.'

Laura noted a grey-lashed flutter of Gwendoline's eyes as she shook Frank's hand. The two of them stood at roughly the same height. Laura was struck with the idea that if Gwendoline greased back her short fringe and blackened her eyebrows, they might almost be related.

'Have you told Miss Shackleton about Parker?' Frank asked.

Gwendoline gripped Frank's arm with her free hand and gave him an unbecoming leery smile. 'Who is Parker?' she asked with misplaced coquettishness.

'Lady Boxford's pug. He's gone missing.' Frank extricated his arm. 'You haven't by any chance seen him, have you?'

Gwendoline turned from Frank to fix her gaze on Laura. 'A pug; skin fold dermatitis almost inevitable.'

Laura had a vision of the miserable creature they had just encountered. 'He doesn't...'

Gwendoline didn't give her time to finish the sentence.

'I remember meeting you now,' she continued. 'So, the dog is still missing?' She looked at Laura then Frank, then back to Laura again.

'Jealousy.' Her eyes narrowed. She nodded her head in a knowing fashion. 'Yes, that could be the cause of its escape plan. I believe I can see some sort of romance in play between the two of you if I am not mistaken.'

'I hardly think it's any of your business.' Laura was keen to scotch the prying line that seemed to be developing, but Gwendoline carried on nodding with supercilious solemnity.

'Oh yes,' she said. 'I would suggest that this dog of yours has run away. It has run away on account of your duplicitous loyalty. Dogs are most sensitive to the usurper.' She gave Laura an imperious glance. 'It's amazing how naïve some owners can be. Still the dog is presumably quite personable; I would suggest he has adopted a more simpatico domestic arrangement elsewhere.'

'I beg your pardon?' Frank drew himself up in defense of Laura.

'Just like Zaza here, she can be a little tart.' Gwendoline gave a tug on the dog's lead, lifting the white fluff ball's front legs off the ground. 'Still, I'll keep a look out on my travels. Not that there's much chance of my coming across it. I'm off tomorrow and it's hardly likely to be in Holland Park.'

Laura could not find any words of graciousness that the late Queen's Mother might have used, so she let Frank make their farewell, remaining silent until they had returned to the car.

'What an absolute...'

'Don't even think about it,' Frank said. 'He who restrains his words has knowledge. Take deep breaths. Now, how did you get on with Val Farmer?'

Laura took his advice. She began to calm down. 'She thought she saw a man that night. He may have been drunk, and had a hat on, so she had no idea what he looked like. Not much help.'

'I disagree. Who knows, the man might have seen a chance and abducted Parker.'

'Stolen him?'

'Yes. I think we should inform Inspector Sandfield. He should take an interest in strangers wandering around in this vicinity. I left another message for him earlier about the travellers. I feel he's duty bound to respond.'

Laura didn't like to tell him that in her opinion Phil Sandfield was a law unto himself and she was still unconvinced he would see Frank's ecclesiastic duties with regard to his daughter's confirmation as warranting any sort of trade-off. But it made her think. He would have to take an interest if a crime had been committed. In all the upset of the rescue centre she had forgotten Venetia's theory of the possibility of theft. Could Frank be right? Could this suspicious drunk have something to do with Parker's disappearance?

They stopped off at Strudel and Jervis's and decided to discuss it over supper. Laura asked Venetia if she'd like to join them, but she said she too was tired.

'I think I'll stay in, and watch the new series of Love Island,' she said.

As she and Frank gulped a quick gin and tonic, Laura was aware that both Strudel and Venetia were exhausted by a fruitless day searching for her dog.

'Am I wrong involving them?' she asked.

Frank took her hand. 'Don't be ridiculous. We all want Parker back,' he said. 'Now come on, let's go.'

Setting out they took the lift to the ground floor. As the doors opened Laura heard a voice she knew.

'Talk of the devil,' she said.

Ahead of her Phil Sandfield was leaning over the reception desk, a mug of Wellworth Lawns coffee in his hand.

He was busy engaging Mimi with the description of a man.

'… Known to wear a hat…'

Of all the coincidences, Laura thought.

'What kind of hat?' Mimi asked.

'For goodness sake girl. It's part of his disguise. The hat's bound to change.' The inspector took a slurp from the mug. 'Now pay attention. As I was saying, he's medium height – Possibly a little taller. Dark hair. Late middle age, so it's probably dyed.' He removed his own checked cap to scratch his thinning mousy pate. 'Sometimes has a moustache. Could be a beard by now. Weight …' he continued. 'Hmmm, tends to fluctuate …'

'Fluctuate? This sounding nasty,' Mimi said.

'Oh yes, and he's got some sort of foot impediment.'

'Good evening, Inspector,' Frank said, as he and Laura joined them. 'I'm glad we've caught up with you.'

'Ah, Canon. Yes, well, I'm very busy as you can see. The criminal classes don't stop their nefarious activities for a cup of tea and a buttered scone you know.' He turned to Laura. 'I'm sorry to hear about your pug, Lady Boxford. Chipped I presume? Have you spoken with the dog warden?'

'Yes, she has,' Frank said, 'But did you get my message about the vans parked in the wood? It's important because we think Parker might have been stolen.'

'I'm afraid I haven't time for pet theft and harmless campers when I'm tied up with a known gangland member, possibly hiding here in our very midst. I suggest you go down to the station and register the crime.'

'Thank you for the advice, Inspector, but I believe we have information of sightings you might find useful.' Frank told him about the stranger Val Farmer had seen. 'And more importantly Lady Boxford also saw a man matching your description that same night. The night Parker went missing,' he reiterated.

'Matching my description?' Phil Sandfield frowned. 'What are you talking about man?'

'No, not your description, the description of the man in the hat; it's my guess that he wasn't so much drunk as Ms. Farmer surmised but he had a limp.'

'I see,' the inspector said, flipping over a page in his notebook and making a few hasty scribbles. 'Well, I'll bear it in mind. Not that my man would have any truck with a small canine.'

'What do you think the Inspector meant by a gangland member?' Laura asked.

'Here at Wellworth Lawns?' Jervis said. 'Preposterous. Now these Gimlets will go nicely after your G&T's.' He filled their glasses from the cocktail shaker. 'Mind you that new chap who took over poor Frostie Snow's room looks a bit of a rough diamond. He came to our dance class the other afternoon and started swinging Helen Maitland round like a rag doll. I had to tell him we're not in West Side Story now mate.'

'And twice he trod on my toes when I was teaching him a three step.' Strudel raised the remains of the cocktail to her lips before handing the empty glass to Jervis for a top up. 'But let us return to the matter in hand,' she said. 'We have plenty to discuss. Laura must give us her latest thoughts. Tell me, is there anyone you can think of who would wish you or Parker harm? A motive for theft is what I am thinking.'

'Crawford Tuthill,' Laura said without hesitation. She told them of his behaviour the previous evening.

'Filthy drunkard, I wish I'd been there. I'd have given him a piece of my mind.' Frank crossed himself. 'That man can sink to the depths of human depravity.'

'He was in his cups.' The doorbell interrupted Jervis's line of thought.

'There's more to it than that according to Venetia,' Laura said. 'Lulu Vandermoss told Reggie Hawkesmore that Crawford's short of money.'

'Well, it would do no harm to do a little digging into Crawford's financial situation, would it?' Jervis pulled his wallet out of his trouser pocket. 'Half a tick, I'll just get the takeaway.'

Jervis unpacked the contents as they sat round the pine table in the middle of the kitchen. They helped themselves to Chow Mein and the sweet and sour chicken he had ordered, dolloping the food onto the warm plates he took from the oven.

'Let's go back to the evening Parker disappeared.' Frank split a flower shaped carrot between his teeth as Jervis poured a bottle of Riesling. 'Ignoring Inspector Sandfield's mysterious gangster, I believe the man Val Farmer and Laura saw could well be one and the same.'

'That may be true, but we've already covered it,' Strudel said with finality. 'The man was most likely delivering something to Wellworth Lawns, then got lost looking for an address in the village. Laura, you agree with me?'

'It's the most plausible explanation,' Laura said. 'And Phil Sandfield probably only came over for the free coffee.'

'So, there we have it,' Strudel said. 'We must cast the net in a different direction.'

'Oh yes,' Laura said. 'I must tell you about something else that happened today. It was when I was on my way over here earlier.' She told them about the boy with the charity tin. 'It was for retired guide dogs. He was playing with some pebbles. He dropped a few outside the Tuthills. Probably bored, but it got me thinking of all the charity junk mail Venetia receives. I get the feeling a lot of it is fake. There's plenty to do with animals. Ponies and cats, but also dogs. A lot of them are scams, I'm sure.'

'Shocking. I hope she's not falling for them.' Jervis was about to put another helping of Chow Mein on his plate when Strudel put her hand out to stop him.

'Don't eat too much my darling.'

'Why ever not, my love?' Jervis frowned. 'There's masses left.'

'We are short …' Strudel waggled her finger at him.

'Short?'

Strudel coughed. 'Of Ronnies.' She coughed again. 'I mean Rennies.'

Jervis returned the spoon to the bowl.

It was obviously serious.

'Indigestion, don't remind me.' Laura put her chopsticks down. 'But there's another thing Venetia told me. She went to one of those talks in the Recreation Room. It was given by a man called Harry Constantine. He runs a charity, also to do with dogs. It's called "PICS"; stands for, "Pooches In the Care Sector."'

'Whatever next?' Jervis huffed.

Laura explained how it worked. 'Perhaps I should talk to him. He might know about missing pets.'

'Hmmm …' Jervis scraped around his plate with his chopsticks. 'Let's forget about the boy for the moment,' he said. 'Guide dog charities are well known. But this Constantine chap … Pooches In the Care Sector? Sounds like a racket to me.'

'I agree,' Strudel said. 'Perhaps he is stealing dogs from the old folks where he gives these presentations? Then he can rehome them the other side of the country to another lot of old folks when they are giving him nice big donations.'

Frowning, Frank's raven eyebrows began a descent into one another. 'Aren't you letting your imagination run away with you, Strudel?'

'You're too good Frank, that's your trouble,' Jervis said. 'I'd say Strudel's idea makes perfect business sense. But then I come from a background in the insurance industry, not the church.' He put an arm round Strudel. 'Harry Constantine, even his name sounds bogus.'

Strudel smiled up at Jervis. 'You should do some top priority digging into him, would you not say?'

'Of course, my love. We must leave no stone unturned.'

'Thank goodness,' Laura said. 'I thought I might be going mad when I had similar thoughts. So, it's a possibility he could have stolen Parker?'

'And had him shipped out all while he's here innocently promoting his charity.' Jervis held one finger in the air. 'But wait, I have a plan. What about this? Laura arranges a meeting with Constantine. She tells him about Parker. Says she's sure he's dead and she is looking for a replacement.'

'Oh Jervis, you must not say such things.'

'Hear me out, my love. I don't mean it, it's just part of the plan. He may have re-homed Parker for a fat donation to someone else by now, but with his business acumen, he'll offer Laura another dog. After all, he has to show he's running a bona fide charity, or should I say bona fido ...' Jervis disguised his laugh as a cough. 'Bad joke, I apologise. Anyway, to continue, Laura agrees...'

'Won't he know who Laura is if he stole Parker?' Frank asked.

'That's the subterfuge the plan hinges on. Laura's going to be the perfect client. Serenity personified.'

'Your female intuition will tell you when he begins the man-lies,' Strudel said. 'He will be either completely on edge... scrabbling around...'

'Or completely innocent,' Frank said.

'Or a very good actor preying on the emotions of the frail and elderly, but I think Laura's well up to the job of working that one out.' Jervis raised his glass. 'Here's to the set-up.'

Chapter 12

Venetia was far too excited about the idea of a private interview with Harry Constantine to be left out of Laura's potential sting.

He proved, in looks anyway, to be everything she had described. Laura eyed him with cautious attraction. Tall, slim and well dressed in a mud-averse country clothing way, he expressed heartfelt sympathy on the loss of Parker. Strolling around Laura's sitting room with an air of tragedy, he picked up a china Staffordshire pug from the mantelpiece.

'Delightful piece, Lady Boxford,' he said, giving it a swift turn to inspect the base — he had yet to attain scholarship level in the school of charm. 'It must break your heart to see it under the present circumstances.'

Laura almost lost her resolve.

'Lady Boxford is so brave.' Venetia smiled at Laura.

It gave Laura a moment to gather herself. 'Do have a seat.' She indicated to the chair next to the sofa where she and Venetia were sitting. He sat down, legs rather wide apart for Laura's liking, and swept back his mouse brown hair with one hand revealing a tanned and lineless forehead with only the hint of a receding hairline.

'You've got a marvelous set-up here. Perfect for the petite pooch.' His blue eyes twinkled and his smile revealed pre-orthodontic era characterfully imperfect teeth. It was an accomplished act, if act it was.

'I'm sure I will be able to fill the dreadful chasm the loss of your dear Parker has left.' He clasped his hands together for a moment as if in prayer, then rubbed his thighs. 'There's a small amount of paperwork I should go through with you.'

As he explained the workings of the charity, he took out his laptop from the leather satchel at his feet. 'All the dogs at "PICS" are free to approved homes. I'm sure there will be no need for that formality in your case Lady Boxford. Do you like our name by the way?' He gave a little laugh. 'It's meant to sound direct, but with a hint of the feminine. And of course a play on the word pics, in that you chose your pet from a picture. I'll show you what I mean in just a minute. Then when you have your new pet safely installed and all the administration is complete, we give you a special commemorative album in which you can collect your own, "memory pics" of your new best friend. All we ask is a donation. An amount commensurate with the suffering of our canine orphans.'

He gave a look of untold pain, first to Laura then Venetia.

Laura was afraid Venetia might pull out a cheque book along with the paper hankie she had stuffed up the sleeve of her cardigan and she gently held her friend's arm.

Harry Constantine lolled back in his chair, picking up his cup of coffee from the occasional table at his side. He brought it to his full lips, took a sip and flinching from the heat returned it to the table.

'So, Lady Boxford, tell me a little of your circumstances,' he said.

His over emphasis on the use of her name was irksome, but this was her first test. 'I think you know pretty much all there is to know. You are aware of the devastation Parker's loss has caused me.' Steeling herself, she watched for signs that he might be a charlatan, but Harry Constantine was engrossed in something on the laptop that was now resting on his knees.

'Do continue,' he said.

'Well, there's nothing much else to say except that it seems sensible to get an older dog at my age.'

He began typing for a minute. Then he looked up. 'I have to say that you two young ladies are not like most of my clients. I can tell that you, Lady Boxford, have still got much to give and would enjoy a challenge. Now here's my first, "pic". He gave another little laugh, turning the laptop screen to face them. 'He's a very nice springer spaniel; only eight years old, so still plenty of get up and go.'

Laura was reminded by the image of why she had always avoided the breed. Lolling tongue, shaggy brown and white coat – the worst of both worlds when it came to dropping hair. Then the awful floppy ears and a look in the eye of unbounded energy and determination that would only be satisfied after the ten-mile chase involving any living creature prepared to run or fly, preferably including the swimming of a lake.

'Lovely looking dog,' she said. 'But a bit much for me, I fear.'

'Not to worry, he's in Guernsey, so one would want to be sure. Still, I thought I'd run him past you on the off chance.' He scrolled down and had another image at the ready. 'I believe this greyhound might be just the answer. She's past her racing days now. Needs very little exercise.'

Laura liked greyhounds, her hairdresser Dudley had one, but the recumbent bag of bones she was presented with now did not impress her. 'She looks well past anything,' she said.

'This is all constructive information. Building up a picture, or "pic" of the client's needs is what it's all about.' It was as if he'd only just thought of this latest pun on the charity's title and was thrilled by it. He scrolled down some more. 'How about this charming chappie? He's a crossbreed, but I'm sure that's not something, Lady Boxford, that would put you, of all people, off. They're very of the moment, after all. People would kill for a Dalmatian cross corgi these days.'

'I can't imagine anything worse,' Laura said.

'I'd surmise he had some King Charles in him, wouldn't you?'

Laura studied the latest offering. She had to concede that some King Charles spaniels bore similar colouring, but apart from that she could see no resemblance. The dog's monstrous gaping mouth revealed a set of teeth that stretched back beyond a thick wet tongue to the furthest reaches of its throat. The eyes blazed with fervent fury, and around its neck it wore a black and white bandana printed with skulls.

'I don't know much about dogs myself,' Venetia said. 'But it appears to have very short back legs …' Venetia angled her head to get a different view. 'It's difficult to tell what with it half lying down in that sandpit.'

'He lost them in an accident.' Harry Constantine gave Laura and Venetia another of his finest tragic looks. 'But he comes with a set of wheels. Gets himself about without the slightest problem. Remarkable. A true success story, and such a conversation piece.'

'How wonderful,' Venetia said. 'How did he lose his legs, may I ask?'

To Laura's relief Harry Constantine turned the screen back to face him. 'I'm not entirely sure Mrs. Hobbs. I can find out if you're interested.'

It was all getting too much for Laura. She wasn't in any way dog-breedist, well not very, but all she wanted was her dear Parker back. 'I want my pug,' she said, realizing how hysterical she sounded.

With consummate ease Harry Constantine managed to turn the situation round. 'I absolutely agree. In your circumstances I would not be looking just yet. It's too soon. You never know, he may reappear.'

He closed the laptop and put it back in his satchel on the floor. 'I tell you what.' He took a sip of what must have been stone cold coffee. 'I've got all your details. Why don't I call you in a month or so?'

Laura didn't want to upset Venetia by telling her how uncomfortable Harry Constantine had made her with his obsequious banter. It was most suspicious to have shown her such unsuitable dogs, as if he hadn't a clue what he was talking about. She wondered if perhaps he wasn't following his preferred career trajectory.

The paucity of appropriate dogs the charity had on its books may have been to do with its fledgling status, but then Harry Constantine's reasons for starting the charity seemed dubious. Why would a man in early middle age with the demeanour of a city banker, suddenly become so interested in the welfare of dogs and old people? The explanation he gave for the inception of the charity as resulting from a legacy from his grandmother in which she had stipulated that the money be used for the welfare of animals, Laura supposed might have been true. Perhaps it was a final joke at the expense of a wayward grandchild?

Then there was the matter of him saying Parker might "reappear."

'Did he believe in reincarnation?' she asked Venetia.

'You did say you'd "lost your dog." He might have taken you literally was her reply.

On the other hand, the thing that had sparked Laura's interest was the last picture he had shown her of the crossbreed. Like Crawford Tuthill, he had his finger on the pulse regarding their popularity, if not their value. The position of the ubiquitous Cockerpoo, while still widely popular was in danger of being usurped by almost any combination as a must have accessory. Again, she was reminded of Parker's offspring; the three enchanting pughund puppies.

It gave her the germ of an idea and she was more than happy when Venetia said she was missing a vital episode of "Escape to the Country".

After she had gone, Laura rang Strudel and Jervis.

Strudel suggested they meet in the bar as she had laundry drying on her radiators. It was unlike her to be so disorganized, but Laura was too preoccupied to give it further thought as all her attention was focused on the soaring price of what would once have been called mongrel puppies.

Could they be a clue to Parker's disappearance?

The idea was compounded when Laura recalled her conversation with Bryan Bowman in the chip shop on that fateful night.

'Shouldn't really allow dogs in,' Bryan had muttered, his white pork pie hat sitting on top of his cropped coarse brown hair.

Laura knew he could be short sometimes – who wouldn't be working in all that heat? She had only brought Parker with her because she'd had to leave him in the car that afternoon when she went for her pedicure and then he'd looked so angry at the idea of being left again.

'Oh, my goodness, health and safety,' she said. 'I'll take him out.'

'It's alright, he can stay, I know him after all,' Bryan said, and Laura had waited as he got her order ready. As he folded the paper parcel of scampi and handed it to Laura to put in her carrier bag, Sally had come in from the back of the shop. She peered over the counter at Parker who had begun to jump up and down in excitement.

'He's like a little kid desperate for his tea. Mind you I feel just the same. I'm starving, but I've got to wait for my sister.' She turned to her husband. 'Give 'im a crabstick Bry.'

'He does love them,' Laura said.

Bryan opened the fridge and reached for the plastic carton. 'Better for him than fried scampi at his age; he's getting on a bit I should think.' He handed the container to Sally. She tossed one to Parker who caught it midair. Then she handed the container back to Bryan.

'We're missing a marketing trick here,' he said. 'Seafood must be the secret of his eternal youth,'

'Get on with you Bry, you and your marketing tricks.' Sally gave him a gentle nudge with her elbow.

Laura had taken her purse out from her bag. 'He's not that old,' she said. 'But you could be right, not long ago he became a father for the first time.' She had felt as proud as any grandparent.

'Blimey. Potency too,' Bryan said. 'Who'd have thought a crabstick could be as good as Viagra. With puppy prices what they are, you could be on to a winner there.'

They had laughed. Then Laura had suggested she could drop Sally off at her sister's as she was going pretty much straight past the door.

Still mulling over the conversation, Laura went down to the bar.

'Pughunds. Hang on.' Jervis tapped away at his phone as they sat waiting for their drinks. 'The official title of the puppy of a cross bred pug with a Dachshund is a 'Daug.'

'How childish,' Laura said.

'Deputy Dawg.' Jervis said and let out a howl.

Strudel told him to keep his voice down.

'Like it or not, 'he whispered. 'They're fetching upwards of two thousand pounds.'

'Tell me,' Strudel said. 'Is it that you think Parker has been taken for his paternal masterfulness?'

'It may sound improbable...' Jervis was still whispering. '...But good stud dogs don't grow on trees and Parker's got a first-rate track record.'

'You're right,' Laura said. 'I'm going to find out what happened to Parker's offspring.'

'Weren't they taken on by Sir Repton's son Ned Stocking?'

'No need to keep whispering Jervis.' Strudel sighed. 'Ah Ned Stocking, what a lovely young man. Such a good actor himself… and his beautiful wife…'

'That's right, Ned and Pom took them to London.'

Chapter 13

Laura rang Ned's mobile.

'I'm in hair and make-up…' He sounded as if he had a heavy cold. '… At Pinewood Studios working on a film; I'm playing an Antarctic explorer.'

'Shall I try you another time?' Laura said.

'I'm fine to talk. I've got you on loudspeaker and it takes two hours to get my nose to look authentically frost bitten.'

Laura asked about the puppies.

'Pom and I soon realized that having four dogs in a small flat in Clapham was not ideal,' he said. 'We had to keep Sybil Thorndike - no one would take on such an ill-tempered dog as that - but we were loath to sell all the puppies, so we kept the smallest one. Pom called her Whinnie on account of her bossy nature being not dissimilar to that of a certain blonde actress. She rules the roost. Sybil puts up with it – she's much quieter these days.'

Laura heard a conversation going on in the background.

'I'm going to have to go,' Ned said. 'They want me to traverse a crevasse.'

He rang back between takes. The gap was never more than a few minutes as he said his nose started melting under the camera lights.

He told her about the second puppy.

It was another bitch that now lived with Pom's aunt near Lewes in West Sussex.

'She had a similar red coat and body to Sybil Thorndike, but with Parker's smooth grey head. To be honest she's dead ugly and she's got the same nasty temper as Sybil. There was no way we could have sold her. Luckily, the aunt took her off our hands; loves her to bits. She says considering her bum's so far from her brain, it's hardly surprising she's impossible to house train.'

After another break, he started on the story of the third puppy.

'He's a way different kettle of fish,' Ned said. 'He was bought by an actor friend of mine. Much more successful than me, but that's beside the point.

'Would I know him?' Laura asked.

'I don't think so, he's famous for a series partly set in Renaissance Italy.'

'Sound's just my cup of tea.' Laura could imagine Borgia intrigue and heavy ermine cloaks.

'The thing is it's sci-fi. They flip between the Palazzo Farnese and some random planet halfway between Mars and a black hole. It's pretty off the wall, but hugely successful with the kids. He's got hordes of teenage fans all conversant in baroque spaceship art. Honestly, I don't think you'd go for it.'

Laura agreed that she preferred more realistic historical drama.

'I'm going to have to go again,' Ned said. 'The husky team's arrived. Get Pom to finish the story. She's at home, between jobs. She'd love to hear from you.'

Laura rang Pom. In all the commotion of the studios, she hadn't got round to telling Ned the real reason for her call.

'Parker missing? That's terrible,' Pom said. 'I wouldn't have thought of dog napping happening down there in the country.'

'Dog napping?'

'Theft. Here in London, it's different. I hardly dare go out with the dogs for fear of Whinnie being stolen. But what can we do to help?' she asked. 'We're so far away, that's the problem.'

Laura agreed. 'There is one thing I was thinking though. I know it might sound mad,' she said, 'but I wondered if his puppies could have anything to do with his disappearance. Ned told me about the one with your aunt, but he was halfway through telling me what had happened to the third puppy when he had to go.'

'Jensen Darby you mean? He's more famous than Lassie.' Pom laughed. 'After he featured in a commercial selling real estate on an American TV station, he acquired cult status. He's got a massive following on Instagram. Our friend who owns him says he could retire on Jensen's earnings if he wasn't making so much money himself. You should talk to him Lady B. He's met all sorts of weird people because of the dog. I tell you what I'll ask him to call you.'

The actor was at the dog groomers when he rang Laura. In the background she could hear the sound of barking.

'Sorry about the noise,' he said. 'Jensen's very excited. He's having a shampoo and set before we go to Lincolnshire. Don't know why I'm bothering. He'll be covered in mud in seconds.'

The actor explained that they were in the middle of a series of ads for a well-known brand of crisps.

'The company like to promote local potato farmers. We're back up near Louth tomorrow for a couple of days. Been there before, there's a super dog-friendly hotel we stay at, and Jensen's got a bunch of fans nearby. Not like here in London where you have to be on guard the whole time.'

'Pom was saying the same thing,' Laura said. 'She's terrified of Whinnie being taken. Has anyone asked you about Jensen's pedigree?'

'I used to be asked about it all the time,' he said. 'Mostly by Chinese and Japanese tourists; they've been known to pay vast amounts for some breeds of dogs. Obviously during Covid that stopped, but there are still these weirdos who want to know everything about him, not always in a good way. I bumped into a woman the other day just off Kensington High Street. I was about to cross the road out of the park, so I was carrying Jensen. She had a little dog too. She asked about Jensen's breeding. I told her about Sybil Thorndike and you and Parker. She said she was often down that way. It was quite a coincidence, but then she became more forceful. Started going on about how cross breeding should be outlawed and had I got pet insurance because Jensen was bound to get hypothyroidism. Quite unpleasant now I come to think of it.'

'Hypothyroidism?'

'Yeah, I remember that 'cos my mum's just been diagnosed with it. But what annoyed me was that she said that the way I was holding Jensen in my arms was bad for his self-esteem. Tantamount to me giving him mental health problems.'

He might have been reading a script from the Gwendoline Shackleton school of dog psychology. Laura recalled Gwendoline mentioning Holland Park – it was not a million miles from Kensington High Street. She asked him to describe the woman and when he told her what he remembered of the tall manly figure she was even more convinced, but how could Gwendoline Shackleton be involved in Parker's disappearance? She rang Frank.

'I don't quite see how it fits,' he said.

'You saw how odd she was, rude in fact. She almost accused us of driving Parker away.'

'That's not much to go on.'

Laura knew it was thin. 'I had hoped you'd have some divine inspiration,' she found herself saying. It was hurtful and embarrassing. She apologized. But he had nothing to offer and was against her confronting Gwendoline.

'She said she was going back to London,' Laura said. 'You call the parish office. They might know if she's still renting The Rectory.'

'I believe they might.' Frank didn't sound convinced. 'Perhaps we should run your theory by Jervis? I spoke to him earlier. He's busy doing some of his "digging" into Crawford Tuthill.'

'He said we should leave no stone unturned.'

'An archeological metaphor; sifting through layers of earth until you reach the truth, that is our quest, I agree.' Frank sounded more positive. 'I'm going to help Vicar Rachel with her sermon this evening. She said she'd mention Parker at the family service. I'll ask her if she knows about it.'

Laura wondered what the average number of the congregation for the family service was. She hadn't met the new vicar, but she was doubtful that Rachel had managed to fill the pews in such a short space of time.

Laura wasn't piqued by Frank's dedication to assisting the Church's first female incumbent at Woldham, but she hadn't factored in his not being at her beck and call. She looked at her watch. It was the kind of limbo time that happened when the onus of home ownership was removed from daily life. Time that might once have been filled clearing an outside drain or tidying a little used shed. Venetia filled these voids with television and speculation as to what was for the next meal, but Laura already knew this as they'd studied the evening's menu when they arranged to have dinner together. Of course, on any normal day Laura would have taken Parker out, but the idea of walking the grounds again was futile. If he was nearby, he would have turned up by now, she was sure.

Despite this, Laura went to get her coat. She picked up her keys. Thoughts of Gwendoline Shackleton were eating away at her. There she was, right on the doorstep with all her strange ideas. Appearing out of the blue with different, "clients" as she called the dogs. Again, the question arose, what if she was behind Parker's disappearance?

Laura set off down the drive. The days were getting shorter, and she could feel a raw dampness in the air as the gloom of the evening descended. She walked through the village, seeing no one and carried on beyond The Rectory to the junction with the main road. She turned back. Then turned again, so that two or three times she passed Gwendoline's driveway in aimless desperation.

There has to be another way she thought, as she loitered beside the wheelie bins. Some of Jervis's digging was what was needed.

With renewed conviction she carried on to the main road. If she headed left for a few hundred yards she could pick up the footpath that led to the back drive of Wellworth Lawns and on to Mulberry Close.

She would never normally have walked down the side of the road. It was noisy and dangerous. Finding herself having to climb onto the wet tufted grass of the verge as traffic sped past, she was ruing her decision when she heard another car approaching from behind. She listened to the deep thrum of the idling engine, willing it to get on and pass her. She didn't want to draw further attention to herself by turning to see why it didn't, so she carried on in determined annoyance.

Just as she had stumbled for the second time into a drainage grip, the car drew up beside her. She stopped as the passenger window wound down. Stan Kaminski's two dogs stuck their heads out and from behind them he called, 'I thought it was you. Still no sign of your dog?'

Laura shook her head.

'That's too bad. I've seen the posters round the place,' he said. 'I've had an idea about them. Hold on a minute.'

Laura saw the flicker of the Maserati's orange hazard lights. As he came round and joined her on the side of the road, it crossed her mind that something about him was different.

He'd had a haircut, that's what it was. Shorter, glossier; it made a distinguishable difference to his appearance. A small thing, but now the expensive car looked like it actually belonged to him.

'Don't get me wrong,' he said. 'The posters are good, but have you thought of offering a reward?'

It took a second to register.

'You needn't go overboard. Not thousands…'

It was so obvious. Why hadn't she thought of it?

'Five hundred might be enough,' Stan was saying.

Laura marshaled her thoughts. 'That's a very good idea. Thank you,' she said.

'It's nothing. D'you want a lift,' he asked. 'It's crazy you walking along the road on your own.'

'Yes, it was a mistake,' Laura admitted. 'But you're headed in the opposite direction.'

'I'm in no hurry.' He opened the passenger door. Shooing the dogs into the back, he picked up a shotgun in a brown leather slip that was resting on the floor. 'I'll put this away,' he said, "You get in.'

As she waited, she heard the boot slam, then he joined her.

From the back seat Baloo tried to lick his ear.

'Get off,' he said, waving his arm behind him at the dog.

They sped along a mile or so down the road before Stan found a turning space. It was cramped, muddy and smelled strongly of dog, but being a passenger in the Maserati gave Laura an unexpected feeling of exhilaration. She was minded to ask him again about the travellers, but he'd said he would call her and there seemed little point in spoiling her enjoyment. He can't have found out anything, she thought, or he'd have told me.

All too soon he swung into the drive to Wellworth Lawns and drew up outside the entrance to Mulberry Close. She turned to thank him for the ride.

'It's nothing,' he said, polishing the dashboard with the sleeve of his jumper. She found herself studying his features again. Was the colour of his hair natural? If it was dyed, it was expensively subtle. There was also something else she hadn't noticed before. The quality of his nose in profile; neither short nor long, it was distinctive in its straightness.

Strudel and Jervis were preparing for a dance class. Jervis was in the hall tying the laces of his black patent pumps.

'We can't stop now, I'm afraid. We're meant to be in there in ten minutes. Can we catch up tomorrow for a walk?' He turned and shouted up the stairs from where it sounded like Strudel was talking to herself.

He called up again.

Laura knew that punctuality was a priority, but she had not heard such urgency in Jervis's voice before.

Strudel came rushing down, still doing up the zip of her pink taffeta ball gown.

'Laura,' she said. 'I am so sorry; we are quite literally dashing out and you have something on your mind? Why not walk with us and we can discuss it on our way.'

They agreed that a reward was a good idea, but Laura didn't have time to air her concerns that if Parker had been kidnapped, why hadn't there already been a ransom demand?

She left them at the entrance to the Recreation Room from where she could hear the buzz of excited octogenarian ballroom enthusiasts.

She didn't feel that she could bother them again, but Jervis rang later that evening when she and Venetia were about to have supper. He asked her what amount she thought the reward should be.

'One thousand?' she said.

'Excellent call I'd say. You don't want to mess around,' he said.

'Will you revise the posters?'

'I'll get on it right away, have it done by supper,' he said. 'I mustn't upset Strudel. She's cooking her "speciality."'

'Not…'

'Fraid so.'

Jervis was manful in his pretence at liking Strudel's Bavarian take on the great French classic, Tripe a la mode de Caen and Laura felt guilty as she and Venetia sat in front of the TV having finished Alfredo's veal escallops. They were watching a programme about offshore banking in Jersey that Venetia said she wanted to see. Laura couldn't understand why, but it was only as she was getting ready to take Venetia back to her room that she asked her.

'It got me thinking when we were listening to Harry Constantine - I quite went off him you know. There was something very fishy about that dog being in the Channel Islands and I'd noticed a couple of those charity letters I got were registered there. I think you should treat him with the utmost suspicion.'

Laura went to bed thinking about the way Venetia's mind worked; the random connections she made. She agreed with her intuition regarding Harry Constantine's character, but was it relevant to Parker's disappearance? And what about Gwendoline; was she involved? Or Crawford Tuthill?

And then most recently there was Stan Kaminski. That profile... His distinctive Roman nose that reminded her of the traveller man.

Chapter 14

Laura joined Strudel and Jervis the next morning. Strudel had corralled a team from the dance class, plus four singles who had recently signed up to Ancient Eros suggesting to them that the Sunday walk would be an ideal opportunity for a first date. They concentrated on local footpaths and well-known dog-walking areas. Jervis had borrowed the office laminator and printed a smaller version of the original poster that could be strung up easily on gates and fences.

Frank met them after helping Vicar Rachel with the family service.

'She's going to let me know if she finds out anything about Gwendoline Shackleton's tenancy,' he said.

Before Laura had time to ask if he was joining them for lunch in the pub, he told her he couldn't stay long, as he had letters to write. Then he was helping Vicar Rachel with evensong.

'Twice in one day?' It popped out ... Did she sound very needy?

'She's finding her feet.' Frank said. 'But if you'd prefer not to be alone?'

'Look at all these people.' Laura waved her arm in the direction of Strudel and Jervis, who were giving the helpers more directions. 'I've more than enough to keep me company.'

'I thought as much. Why don't I meet you in town after your hair appointment tomorrow?'

As Laura parked outside Dudley's Hair Designs the next day, she saw that he already had a copy of the new poster in his window.

She heard the familiar tinkle of the bell as she opened the salon door. Tall and gangling with short platinum blond hair and heavy dark-rimmed spectacles, Dudley came out from behind the desk to greet her.

'Lady B,' he said, taking her hand. 'I haven't seen you since the truly awful news about Parker.' He ushered her to her usual seat. 'But you mustn't give up hope.'

Laura was glad of the sound of the dryers in the busy salon. She felt as if she might start crying as she saw Dudley's elderly, and unlike the picture Harry Constantine had shown her, well-covered greyhound. The dog was lying deep in contented slumber in its bed. Laura remembered how Parker used to barge his way in with it. He'd try to snuggle up, turning round and round and scuffing the bed with his toenails while the greyhound looked on with dispassion. Then just as Parker had got comfortable, the greyhound would invariably get up, stretch and vacate the bed.

Laura saw Dudley eyeing her in the mirror. She pulled herself together.

'I'm sure he'll turn up,' he said, wrapping a black towel round her shoulders. 'The new poster will attract attention. Money's a great incentive to get people's grey matter on the boil and I'm glad you haven't held back on the reward. Too little and you get a load of time wasters. But I'm not going to bang on about it, you must be sick of people telling you what to do.' He ran his fingers through her hair. 'So, what about this? The usual?'

Dudley always liked to add plenty of body to her generally untidy short, blonde hair. 'Hold back on the curls if you don't mind. I do so hope you're right about him turning up.'

Dudley picked up on the tremor in her voice. 'Let's get you to the basin,' he said. 'I'll do your shampoo myself. I've got a lovely new range for you to try. Black pepper, tamarind and fennel. I know it sounds like the ingredients of a curry, but it smells gorgeous. Everyone says they feel invigorated afterwards.

Massaging her head, he asked if she had any clues about Parker's disappearance. She told him she had a few tenuous leads, but that despite all their efforts to date it remained a complete mystery.

'No local sightings?' he asked.

'All misguided, some well-intentioned, I'm sure.'

'Have you been to the poodle parlour in the old market?' She knows a lot of what goes on round here.'

Poodles? It triggered a couple of thoughts in Laura's head. Firstly, that Poodles were clipped and Stan's little dog Kuko with its funny tail had almost certainly been clipped that way.

The second thought was about hair in general. There was only one men's barber in Woldham. What she would describe as of the sawdust era. Frank used him and while he was a perfectly good barber, he was not the sort who would have anything other than a bottle of Grecian 2000 on his menu.

'Have you ever come across a man called Stan Kaminski?' she asked.

'Nice enough guy,' Dudley said. 'Not that I approve of guns, but then he only deals in top dollar kit.' Dudley rubbed his fingers and thumb together. 'Showed me a couple of Purdey's the other day when I was doing his hair. Obviously, I'd no idea what they were.'

'You mean he brought a pair of Purdey's into the salon?'

'Heavens forbid, you know we don't cater for men in here. What would the ladies think?' Dudley picked up his scissors. 'No, I go to his place. I've a few male clients who I make an exception for.'

'So where does he live?'

'Very nice house in the old part of town, Bull Street. A bit near the pub, but you can't have everything. Interesting furniture. That's how he made his money originally.'

'Antique?' Laura asked.

Dudley held the scissors in midair. 'Old, but not antique. I think you'd call it rustic chic. I'd have shown you some pictures, but I chucked all the magazines when we were in lockdown. He used to give me his old copies of Interiors for the salon.'

'So, it was expensive?'

'Some of it, for sure. He had a dealer in London. Stuff sold like hot cakes. If only they'd known it was his brother making it all out of ripped up pre-communist kitchens back home.'

'His brother?'

'Yes, he showed me a photo of them both together. Stan's shorter, otherwise they look very alike, but Stan has all the dosh, and it's amazing what a difference that, and a good haircut, can make. Then of course I add a bit of magic with a few hints of colour woven in.' Dudley could always be relied upon for indiscretion.

'I should know,' Laura said.

'Don't get me wrong,' Dudley continued. 'I'm not saying the brother's a peasant. Oh dear that sounds terrible…' He caught Laura's eye in the mirror.

'I know what you mean,' Laura didn't want to put him off revealing more indiscretions.

'Simple sort I'd say. Oh dear that sounds worse…What I mean is, heaven knows what he'd have thought of his stuff turning up in those shops on Pimlico Green. Good thing he's stuck in Lithuania.' Dudley gave a knowing nod.

'So how come Stan now deals in firearms?' Laura asked.

Dudley turned on the hair dryer. 'Sporting weapons, Lady B, get with the lingo. Stan's made a bob or two, enough for the Mazzer, so he can afford to expand into something that ticks his boxes big time. Mind you everything's an investment for a bloke like that. And why not, I say.'

When Laura left Dudley's, Frank was waiting for her by her car. She took his arm.

'You'll never guess what,' she said.

'Tell me in the car. I've had some new ideas for the posters.'

As they reached the edge of town, Frank asked what Stan Kaminski's latest career in firearms had to do with Parker.

'It's the brother. Don't you see, Stan's lied to me about him,' Laura said. 'He knows his brother and family are here, because I told him. So, what are they doing here?'

'Trying to make a living I suppose,' Frank said.

'But that's hard, since Stan no longer needs their furniture. So, what I think is, they've come over to try a bit of diversification.'

'What do you mean?'

'Selling dogs. You saw the one that had recently had a litter. They won't be registered or vaccinated I bet.'

'Well, it's a good thing I've told Inspector Sandfield about them.' Frank twisted the roll posters in his hands. 'He rang me about the man with the limp. I think it was an excuse to say he was sorry to have been so short with me the other evening.'

Laura turned to him. 'You what?'

'He was most interested in the vans. Said he'd make it a priority to check on them. Could be a hideout for his gangland leader. He's going to owe us one big time now.'

The lights changed. Laura stamped on the accelerator.

'Steady,' Frank clung to his seatbelt. 'What's the mad rush?'

'Phil Sandfield is the mad rush, that's what. If he's got there first, we'll never find out.'

'Find out what?'

'If it's just the brother importing dogs, or if it's Stan too, and if one or both of them are, what's to stop them adding any other lost dog they chance upon to the list. Particularly if it's a pedigree pug.'

'I'm sorry Laura but I don't quite follow your logic.'

'It's what Alfredo said. I didn't think anything of it at the time, but now it makes sense. He saw the Lithuanian woman hanging round outside the kitchens at Wellworth Lawns. Why bring dogs all the way from Lithuania when you can steal them on the doorstep.'

'Let no one deceive you, it says in John, Chapter 3, but just how do you intend to prove it?'

'This time I am going to buy a dog from them. The man virtually offered me one, don't you remember he even said he could get me a pug.'

They could see tyre marks in the grass and the remains of a campfire, but the vans were gone.

'We're too late,' Laura wailed. 'What if they did have Parker with them and now they've moved on so they can sell him elsewhere.'

'But if Stan is the man's brother, why would he have given you the idea of the reward.' Frank said.

'Perhaps that's all part of it. Stan's tipped them off. Blood runs thicker and all that. That's why they've moved on. Maybe now they're planning how to get the money.' Laura bent down and picked up a charred piece of wood. She could see it was partly painted. 'We've missed our chance. Now there's nothing we can do but wait.' She tossed the piece of wood away. 'And with them gone, Stan can deny everything.'

Frank was fiddling with one eyebrow pondering this when they heard a vehicle approaching. Turning, Laura saw a police car making its way slowly along the poplar-lined track. It came round the corner and drew up beside them.

Phil Sandfield got out. 'What the hell are you doing here?' he shouted.

'I'm afraid we're all too late,' Frank said.

'Well, that's just brilliant.' The inspector slammed the car door. 'I've a good mind to book the pair of you for obstructing a crime scene.'

'What crime?' Laura asked. 'Anything to do with the theft of my dog?'

'Of course not. Why would I be wasting my time on canine pilferage when I'm closing in on a wanted criminal and potentially a load of his accomplices.'

'Maybe they are connected,' Laura said.

'Money laundering? Firearms offences? Pugs? I think not. Now please Lady Boxford, try and follow the correct channels. I've said it before, stop your meddling and go through the dog warden. That's what he's there for.'

'Steady on Inspector.' Frank raised his index finger in a meek attempt at reconciliation. 'The dog warden's doing all he can I'm sure, but we must be allowed to follow our own course of action if we see fit.'

Inspector Sandfield sighed and pulled open the car door. 'Canon Frank,' he said, getting in and starting the engine. 'To be blunt, stick to what you're good at, tending to the sick and needy.'

'His impudence is astounding,' Frank said, as they stood alone in the bare campsite.

Frank's dealings with the Inspector were limited compared with Laura's and she felt sorry that he had been the recipient of his charmless tongue on her account.

'Let's not get side-tracked by him,' she said. 'There's still a chance we can flush out Stan. We must find him as soon as possible.' Laura ran to the car. She got her mobile from her bag, but there was no signal.

They rattled back down the track onto the main road. It was only two miles before they reached a new development on the outskirts of a village. Laura stopped the car. She tried the number again. This time it went to answerphone. She left a message asking Stan to call her.

She put the phone down on her lap. 'This is unbearable.'

Chapter 15

Stan remained elusive. Days passed. Whenever Laura tried calling it continued to go to answerphone. She left messages for him. She even drove past his house one evening, but there were no lights on and no sign of his car. She felt powerless under the interminable weight of loss.

The amount of the reward had made no difference either. Jervis fended off a lot of what he described as chancers. One man even offered his own mother's pug as a replacement. He said it was nice enough but was in the habit of eating the carpets.

Frank remained vigilant. He and Laura took a few rides out to put up posters on the gates of a footpath or bridleway they had previously missed. They stopped at a local business park. They thought about going into the recycling plant as they passed, but the idea was too grim. Both knew what the other was thinking.

Laura took her meals downstairs accompanied by Venetia who always had some gem she had gleaned from her latest TV fad to keep the conversation going. The staff and other residents acted as if nothing had happened. New arrivals were more interesting. Parker's disappearance was yesterday's news.

Laura felt friends were avoiding the issue, in order to save her from discomfort and that she was being subtly urged to move on. To accept what they saw as inevitable. Whatever had happened to him, Parker wasn't coming back.

She tried to come to terms with it, but every time the telephone rang she tensed for news. Jervis reported in regularly. There was still a steady stream of on-line activity, but in general it had moved away from the specifics of Parker to the joining of related groups. Even Jervis said he was overwhelmed by the amount of sites that were devoted to missing dogs and cats.

Desultory and disconnected, Laura battled through the days. Victoria rang to ask if there was anything she and Vince could do, but this was one occasion when all her husband's wealth amounted to nothing. Laura felt as if a part of her was missing. She was constantly aware of small gaps in her existence. The tension in her arm she once felt when Parker was pulling on his lead; the action of patting him or brushing his teeth. This in turn brought on a series of memories; the way he would shake his head and yap when she had finished, as if to say, 'right, I've let you get away with that, so now let's get on and have one of those dental chews that are absolutely useless, but taste quite good and fill in the time until my supper.'

There was only silence now where his wide range of vocality had been. The jealous yap he would make when she picked up the phone to make a call. The greedy growl when she entered the kitchen. The hysterical yelp when he saw the pink wrapping of a packet of prawn cocktail crisps. The endless endearing snorts and snores...

She knew she couldn't continue like this. She'd had countless dogs over the years; the pet cemetery was testament to that. OK, none had ever gone missing; none had ever had to be 'presumed dead,' but that was something she would have to grin and bear. She had to move on.

With this in mind, she asked Venetia if she'd like to accompany her to the library in Woldham. Venetia never read a book, there was far too much on TV to entertain her, but she liked an outing and had made friends with a man she fancied who scanned the library cards.

'He probably won't be there,' she said, tipping the stack of audio books she'd borrowed and never listened to into the footwell of Laura's car.

The usual parking spaces they frequented were full. Laura had to do a circuit round the one-way system. She wished she'd brought Venetia's disabled parking badge, as they'd come without her Zimmer, but eventually they found a spot which wasn't far if they went through the bicycle shop. Laura wasn't keen. It made the shopkeeper apoplectic as everyone did it all the time. But more than that, the short cut meant they ended up in Tileman's Road, a short way from The Blue Dolphin. There seemed no escape from the memories it conjured up.

They set off with the audio books in a brightly striped beach towel carrier that Laura kept in the boot to use as a shopping bag.

As luck would have it, the cycle shop owner was busy with customers. They passed through the shop and out the back unnoticed into Tileman's Road where they heard the warning bleeps of a reversing lorry. Laura turned. She briefly saw the dark blue cab, then taking Venetia's arm she walked on to the junction with Sheep Street and waited for the traffic before they crossed the road to the library.

Venetia's friend happened to be behind the counter, which meant that what with the returns procedure, then making a new selection on his advice, they were there for nearly an hour. Laura was getting hungry and irritable as she lugged the beach bag back down the street carrying not one, but three Dickens' audio books - the librarian's favourite author, all with at least twelve discs.

They were about to go back through the cycle shop when two men came out pushing mountain bikes. It meant Laura and Venetia had to wait on the pavement while the men put on their helmets and mounted. Laura watched them cycle off down the street. They passed The Blue Dolphin and on through the bollards at the end. Her hunger acute, Laura's gaze reverted to the chip shop. She was torn between her craving and the guilt of being without Parker. She saw the shop door open. It wasn't that far.

A man came out and started walking towards them, his head down, a brown hat obscuring his face. The checked deerstalker was an incongruous piece of headwear. For some reason it reminded Laura of someone. She couldn't think who, but anyway she was more interested in the contents of the white plastic bag he was carrying. Her imagining of its tantalizing contents was cut short by a vision of Parker barking at her, a cross staccato bark of annoyance at being left out. How could she have even thought about it?

The man was getting closer. He gave a sideways glance in their direction. Laura saw a hint of his face. She was sure she didn't know him, but still there was something about him that was familiar.

He took a step down off the pavement; head bent low again and carried on in the middle of the road until he had passed them. Laura waited a few seconds then turned to see where he was going. At that same moment he also turned. Their eyes met. Laura sensed a hint of recognition before he lowered his head again and resumed his journey. What was it about him ... and his irregular gait?

Laura realized she knew.

Her heart pumped. She swung back round to Venetia.

'It's the man with the limp,' she said. 'I must follow him. Quickly now, before he gets to Sheep Street.'

'I'll never keep up,' Venetia said. 'Give me the bag. I'll go back to the library and wait for you there.'

Laura pulled the bag off her shoulder and handed it to her. 'I don't know how long I'll be. If you can't wait, call a taxi.' She took a brief look down the street. The man was about to turn the corner. 'I must hurry.' She started running as the man turned left at the end of the road.

She knew if he got wind of her he might simply leg it, so when she reached the junction, she peered round the corner. He was only a few yards away. Pedestrians were hampering his progress. He had to wait as the parked cars meant he couldn't walk out into the road. Laura followed, keeping a discrete distance between them. She stopped as he paused at the next junction before crossing the road.

He carried on, crossing two more streets before he took another left. They were nearing the end of Sheep Street now. The turning was not a road Laura knew well. It didn't have any shops, but she knew the Baptist Chapel was on the right and the public conveniences further down on the left. There were less people now and he had picked up his pace, the plastic bag swinging at his side. Laura's head was thumping. Her legs were beginning to ache. As she passed the chapel, she wondered how much longer she could continue. He must stop soon to eat his food, or it would be cold. She paused to catch her breath. In a moment he had disappeared around the corner. She followed again. Stopped at the corner. Peered round. The sound of traffic had subsided. She looked from left to right. The street was empty.

He was nowhere to be seen.

Laura leant against the wall, gathering her thoughts. There was nothing to be done. It was probably a wild goose chase anyway, but still it proved one thing, the man was local. He knew his way around. Slowly she retraced her steps. As she neared Sheep Street the sounds of traffic increased. She heard a siren as she waited at the traffic lights to cross the road, then dodged her way back through the shoppers until she reached the library.

There was no sign of Venetia when she got there, so she set off back to her car. She reached the cycle shop to find that it had closed for lunch. The detour made her wish that, like Venetia, she had taken a taxi home and by the time she reached the car, her feet felt like someone had stuck lumps of dough to the soles of her shoes. She slumped into the driver's seat, yearning to get home to Wellworth Lawns.

The traffic was bad. There was a queue out of Woldham that she sat in before turning off the main road for the last few miles, only to find herself stuck behind a bus. She thought of overtaking, but the road was too narrow. An opportunity arose as it stopped on the edge of a village, but the effort of concentration was too great. Hot, exhausted and hungry, she resigned herself to the wait. Thinking she would be free of it at the turning to Chipping Wellworth, Laura flicked the indicator, but then just yards from the turning, the bus came to a halt in front of her. She knew the village had a request stop, but it was rarely used.

As the door slid open, she wondered who could be getting off.

She saw a white plastic bag swinging as a man stepped down.

It was him.

She bowed her head. Waited. Took a peek. He was turning down the road to the village. She realized she would lose sight of him. Wishing her car was electric, she followed at a distance, keeping in a low gear.

She rounded the corner past The Rectory and saw him again as he walked through the village to the gates of Wellworth Lawns.

She knew now that there was only one way he could be going. She drew up beside the gates, got out and peered over the hedge.

But there was no sign of him. The drive was empty.

The only other way he could have gone was through the shrubbery. How stupid of me, Laura thought, he must be a new employee. She supposed he didn't want to be seen by the other staff or residents. Cross with herself, she drove round the other side of the house to the parking area by the old stables. She leant across to pick up her bag from the passenger seat well. As she sat back up, out of the side window she saw the man again. He must have come out of the undergrowth to get to the kitchens.

Except that he was now heading in the opposite direction...

Towards Mulberry Close.

She started up the engine again. Waited until he had got to the entrance to the close, then followed. He was heading for one of the houses. He checked to left and right. Took something from his pocket.

It must have been a key, because he let himself in to Strudel and Jervis's.

This is none of my business, Laura thought, making her way back to find Venetia. But then again it was. She was sure he was the same man she had seen the night Parker went missing. She had discussed it with Strudel and Jervis. She could even recall the conversations. Then it dawned on her that when she had mentioned the man and Frank had tried to get her to elucidate further, it had been Strudel and Jervis who had diverted the conversation and had even suggested the man was irrelevant.

Laura's hunger had vanished. As she strode into the hall, she saw Mimi filing her nails absently at the reception desk.

'Lady B,' Mimi gasped on seeing her. 'You been to see Mrs. Hobb?'

'Mrs. Hobbs, Venetia, you mean? I'm just going upstairs to find her now.'

'But she not up there now time. She is in the hospital. Mrs. Harcourt is having phone call. Mrs. Hobb she is running over a car. Right outside library.'

Laura sat with Frank beside Venetia's bed. The bruising on her face was bad, but she said it didn't hurt and her wrist was quite comfortable now that the morphine was taking effect. There was a covered plate resting on her lap. She asked if Laura would move it for her, as she wasn't hungry.

Lifting the lid Laura saw a moist-looking cheese sandwich. She asked if Venetia would mind if she ate it.

'Go ahead dear,' Venetia said, waving her plaster cast wanly.

Laura took half the sandwich, offering the other half to Frank.

'As it happens, I had something earlier with Vicar Rachel,' he said.

'Really?' Laura wiped the corner of her mouth with one finger.

'She wanted assistance with a small matter that I was pleased to help with. We'd just finished when I got your call.'

'You've got him very well trained up with his mobile, Laura.' Venetia's speech was becoming slurred.

'I'll have to get you one,' Laura said. 'Not that it would have helped.'

'The ambulance was very quick getting to me and the nice young woman whose car I hit was holding my good hand all the time we waited.'

Laura noticed Venetia's eyelids begin to flutter. 'You should rest now. I'll come and see you tomorrow,' she said.

'Just one thing,' Venetia said. Her eyes were only just open. 'I have a feeling I was pushed.'

Chapter 16

Laura and Frank walked back down the seemingly endless corridors to the hospital exit.

'Venetia's so fragile. She was probably jostled off the pavement. Not helped by the fact that she was carrying all that.' Laura gestured to the beach bag full of audiotapes that Frank had slung on his shoulder. 'The slightest thing could have unbalanced her. It's all my fault for chasing that man.'

'What man?' Frank pushed open the swing doors that led outside to the car park.

'The man with the limp.' It was a relief to be in the fresh air. Laura could feel the afternoon sun warming the back of her neck, easing the ache in her shoulders. 'We saw him coming out of The Blue Dolphin carrying a bag of fish and chips. I followed him. That's the reason I had to leave Venetia.'

'You followed him? Where?'

Laura squinted up at him. She held one hand to her forehead to shield herself from the glare. 'To …' She was about to tell him when she heard her name being called from across the car park.

They both turned to see Strudel and Jervis jogging double time in their direction.

'You ask them where he went,' Laura said.

The passers-by who were privy to the tears and wailing from Strudel in the hospital car park must have assumed that there had been a bereavement. The situation could have escalated as Laura accused Strudel and Jervis of lying, had it not been for Frank's swift intervention. He suggested they retire to the privacy of his house a short distance away.

They parted company in opposite directions to their respective cars. Laura took Frank with her, as he had walked from Vicar Rachel's.

'There must be some rational explanation,' he said, as he opened the front door to his cottage.

It was in a row of Victorian Alms houses in a street near the church. A benefactor with a sizeable purse had donated them to the parish; hence the cottages were of generous proportions considering their age. Laura was fond of Frank's tastefully ramshackle sitting room. She went over to the French windows that opened onto a charming garden filled with late blooming rambling roses. He had once suggested that there was space enough in the house for the two of them. Laura had conferred with Parker and shaken her head. They were too set in their ways to cohabit at this stage of their lives was her excuse. Frank had offered to empty his shelves of ecclesiastic literature in order that she have a place for her collection of Staffordshire pugs, but it would still have been much too cramped, and he hadn't mentioned the copious volumes on Ancient Greece and Rome. She did though covet his Georgian silver teapot that now appeared on the tray he carried in from the kitchen.

He was pouring her a cup of Lapsang when they heard Jervis's car draw up outside.

'We can explain,' Jervis said, bursting through the front door into the sitting room where Laura had arranged herself on a battered leather chair away from the sofa.

'The man …' Arms outstretched, Strudel collapsed onto the sofa. 'He is my Ronnie come over from Spain.' She began to cry.

'Can we start from the beginning?' Frank handed Laura her cup. 'I'm afraid I'm not up to speed on all of this.'

'He's Strudel's husband …' Jervis flopped down beside Strudel. 'Ronnie Black.'

Laura had heard a few tales of Ronnie Black. The whirlwind romance when they had met in Strudel's hometown in Bavaria. Their somewhat haphazard married life in London, then his departure and subsequent dubious antics at a bar he owned somewhere near Marbella. But Strudel had not divulged the fact that she was still married to him.

'His arrival is most unfortunate as you can imagine.' Jervis coughed. 'Not to put too fine a point on it, he's on the run. Well, perhaps not so much on the run, more needing to keep a low profile.'

'He has nowhere else to go,' Strudel wailed.

Frank frowned, eyebrows closing in on one another.

'But he will be leaving very soon. He has promised. Please believe me,' Strudel implored. 'We never meant to deceive you.'

'I don't know how you can say that,' Laura said. 'I thought you were one hundred per cent behind my search for Parker.'

'We are, of course we are.' Strudel said. 'I beg of you believe me.'

'I do think we deserve some sort of explanation as to why you are harbouring a wanted man,' Frank said.

'Steady Frank; it's complicated. He says he has business to conclude. I can't say I understand the whole story myself,' Jervis said. 'He was returning from negotiations in London when Laura saw him.'

'Negotiations?' Frank's frown returned.

'As I said, it will all be wrapped up most shortly.' All of a sudden, Strudel had regained her composure. She leant forward. 'But importantly for now, my Ronnie could be useful.'

'I can't possibly see how,' Laura said.

'He told us an interesting story.' Jervis tapped the side of his nose with an air of hush-hush nonchalance. 'While he was on the train to Woldham, he bumped into Lulu Vandermoss. They got into a conversation. According to Ronnie, Lulu had quite a lot to say about our friend Crawford Tuthill and none of it was complimentary.' Jervis hesitated. 'Look,' he said. 'It would be much better if he told you what transpired. I wonder, would you agree to a meeting with him?'

Unsure of the relevance but intrigued by Jervis's revelation, Laura agreed.

'I feel that now is rather late in the day,' Frank said.

'Tomorrow then?' Jervis suggested. 'I know Ronnie has one or two things to attend to during the day. How about we meet early evening – break the ice with a cocktail?'

It was a long time to wait … 'We may need several,' Laura said.

Chapter 17

'He's a tad nervy,' Jervis said, holding the door open.

Laura and Frank followed him to the kitchen and waited to one side of the pine table.

Ronnie Black was pacing unevenly up and down on the other side, his face hidden under the brown deerstalker. Aside from the limp, Laura now remembered what had struck her as familiar about him. The hat belonged to Jervis. She had seen him wearing it at a point-to-point they had attended.

Ronnie stopped in front of the sink and drew down the blind on the window. Beside him, Strudel flicked the hat from his head, grasped him by the wrist and pulled him round to face them.

Jervis made formal and somewhat unnecessary introductions, then suggested they all take a seat.

Ronnie wrenched himself free of Strudel, turning back to the sink.

'Sit down, in the presence of Lady Boxford, how can I? I'm brought low with mortification. What's the time, I could use a drink.'

Strudel looked up at the cuckoo clock.

'Get him one Jervis, it's nearly six.'

'I was going to make Mojitos…'

'I'm sure a glass of Sherry would suffice,' Frank said.

'Should hit the spot.' Ronnie stuck one arm out and gave a thumbs up.

While Jervis went to find the bottle from the drinks trolley in the sitting room, Laura and Frank sat down. With Strudel the other side of the table, they eyed one another nervously.

Jervis returned with a bottle in one hand and five schooners in the other.

At the sound of the glugging bottle, Ronnie turned from the sink. He reached for the nearest glass, downed it in one, then slid the glass across the table in Jervis's direction. After a slight hesitation Jervis refilled it. He pulled out the spare chair between himself and Strudel and beckoned to Ronnie. With a screech of chair legs on the kitchen floor, Ronnie pulled himself in so that his stomach was pressed against the table.

He was out of condition, that was for sure, but a good-looking man all the same. He reminded Laura of a fat Humphrey Bogart in his later years. Grey stubble on his rounded jaw mirrored his short cut receding hair and deep lines scored his forehead. She wondered how old he was – definitely not as old as Strudel who Laura knew had recently celebrated her eighty-second birthday.

It didn't take long for the alcohol to take effect. Ronnie's confidence grew.

'Bit like an inquisition, this,' he said.

Laura glanced at Frank. There was no way he was going to take the role of a sixteenth century Spanish Cardinal. She would have to take the lead and hope that Strudel was right in thinking Ronnie was going to be useful.

'We're not here to pass judgment on your present circumstances Mr. Black,' she said.

'Please call him Ronnie,' Strudel said.

'I'm presuming that you know why we're here. The fact that I saw you on the night my dog went missing and that in colluding with your secrecy, Strudel and Jervis may have hindered my hope of finding him.'

'Hang on Laura,' Jervis said. 'In Ronnie's defence, he's been out at all hours delivering leaflets. He did all the pubs and off licenses. And he helped with the wording. Granted his knowledge of wanted posters may have helped.' Jervis laughed.

'That's a bit below the belt Jarvie,' Ronnie said.

'But it's still hardly a quid pro quo for my having to chase you all around the streets of Woldham, or the fact that that particular wild goose chase ended with my friend in hospital with a broken wrist.'

'What can I say, Lady Boxford …' Ronnie's confidence ebbed. 'I am humbly filled with remorse.' He rested his elbows on the table, hands clasping the sides of his lowered head.

'Nibbles?' Strudel suggested, breaking the ensuing silence. She got out a tin of cheese footballs from a cupboard.

'There's another thing,' Jervis said. 'Ronnie's had an idea as to why the boy you saw outside the Tuthill's was dropping pebbles.'

'I can't see how that's going to help find Parker?' Laura said.

Ronnie looked up. 'I've a hunch the kid was using the charity as a cover. He was leaving the pebbles as a sign for someone else. Could even be something to do with the chap who's been touting the other dog charity…'

'Harry Constantine?' Laura popped a cheese football in her mouth.

'Maybe to show him where there's a potential dog to be nicked,' Ronnie continued.

'Mmm…' Laura had forgotten the texture as the biscuit wafer melted and her tongue met the soft salty cheese interior. She pulled her thoughts together. Could Ronnie be onto something?

'Might all be a coincidence?' Ronnie pushed against the table with his knees, so the chair was balancing on its two back legs. 'But if Jarvie and I can find a connection between the charity the kid was touting and the other one run by the Constantine bloke.' He ran his hands over his stubble. 'Who knows, it could turn out the lad's a key player.'

'In Parker's disappearance?' What with everything else that had been going on, including with Ronnie himself, Laura had to admit that they hadn't resolved the issue of Harry Constantine.

Ronnie leant forward so the front two legs of the chair landed back on the floor.

'Please, you will break it,' Strudel said.

'Sorry Strue.' Ronnie held up his hands. 'Blimey this sherry's reminding me of home. Top up Jerv?' He held out his glass. 'On the other hand, there's what Lulu Vandermoss told me.'

'I was wondering when we'd get to that,' Laura said, as Jervis filled first Ronnie's glass and then others while he was at it.

Laura watched Frank take a handful of cheese footballs. He was about to put them in his mouth when the cuckoo in Strudel's clock on the wall shot out and began tweeting.

Frank dropped the footballs on the table. Ronnie leapt up, looking furtively from left to right. 'Darn thing,' he said. 'Gets me every time.'

'Calm down Ronnie.' Jervis scooped up Frank's wayward nibbles and handed them back to him. 'But it's seven now. What say I knock up some scrambled eggs, if anyone fancies it?'

'I will do the scrambling,' Strudel said. 'Some gherkins on the side will add refinement.'

'Gherkins?' Ronnie asked.

From his apprehensive tone, Laura felt they had something in common.

Jervis opened a bottle of Chilean Sauvignon Blanc to accompany the food. Ronnie sniffed the glass and took a sip. He said it wasn't half bad but suggested another vineyard for future reference.

The meal complete and a few glasses later Laura noticed the timbre of Frank's normally sonorous voice was raised an octave as he suggested they return to the subject of Lulu Vandermoss.

'How did you happen to get into a conversation with her?' he warbled.

Laura knew he wasn't very good at holding his drink.

'I'd met her before,' Ronnie said. 'She came into my bar in Puerto Banus a couple of years back. She was in a bad way, drowning her sorrows. She'd come over to bury a friend of hers who'd recently passed.' He raised his glass with a downcast expression, downed the wine then turned to Jervis. 'I think Lady Boxford could do with a top up.'

'Please call me Laura.'

Jervis filled the glasses.

'Puerto Banus used to be such a charming little fishing village,' Laura said. She remembered her horror when the yacht she and her late husband were guests on had sailed into the modern marina. 'Now it's full of...' She looked at Ronnie and checked herself.

'Undesirable ruffians.'

Ronnie took the words from her mouth.

'Russian oligarchs and their women filled with Botox,' he continued, undeterred. 'All good for my business, though it saddens me to say it.'

'A friend of mine had botox. When you kissed her on the cheek it was like bumping into a block of alabaster.' Laura smiled hazily, as Jervis opened another bottle.

'Let's get back to Lulu,' he said, refilling their glasses.

'So, when I saw her on the train it took a minute or two to place her,' Ronnie continued. 'But once I had - I never forget a face - I decided to reacquaint myself; engage her in a spot of banter. I was surprised she didn't remember me, or the bottle of Bolly I'd bought her before I realised the friend who'd passed was her actual partner, but there you go.'

'Her partner?' Laura asked.

'They were in a civil partnership. She called her, her wife,' Ronnie explained, carrying on without drawing breath. 'So, then we got on to Wellworth Lawns. She must have thought I worked there.' He turned to Laura. 'What I didn't say was that I'd seen her out the night you lost Parker.'

Laura gathered her senses. 'What were you doing out that evening?'

'Strudel and I had had words. I'd gone outside to cool off. Took a little amble. Thought the coast would be clear at that time of night. Got a bit near the big house. That's when you clocked me.'

'So, where was Lulu?' Laura asked.

'That's the funny thing; she was near the entrance to Mulberry Close. Don't forget, I was on the scarper from you, so I'd lain low in some bushes for a while. When I thought the coast was clear I was making my way back here when I almost ran into Crawford Tuthill. Then, blow me if I didn't narrowly miss bumping into her.'

'Lulu, you mean?' Laura said.

'Yes. I'm pretty sure she'd been waiting outside Crawford's place. Then she followed him. He was going in the direction of the big house.'

'I saw Crawford having a drink in the bar,' Laura said. 'That's when he said he couldn't come out to help look for Parker because of a bad knee.'

'So, this was sometime after Parker went missing?' Frank said.

Ronnie's lower lip jutted forward. 'I guess so.'

'You didn't hear the search party?' Laura asked.

'I went back indoors. Strudel and Jervis had the music playing, practicing a samba I think, quite a racket either way. I left them to it and snuck off upstairs.'

There was a moment's silence as they all tried to make sense of the information.

'Go back to meeting Lulu on the train from London,' Jervis said.

'As I said, she must have thought I knew the place because we started chatting about this and that and I said wasn't it a shame about the dog that had gone missing.' Ronnie directed himself to Laura. 'Knowing how important it is to Strue and yourself.'

'He is our man in the background wings.' Strudel smiled wistfully at Ronnie.

'So, Lulu says she knows what happened to Parker,' Ronnie continued.

'What?' Laura took a gulp of wine.

'She says she's sure Tuthill's done the dog in. Said she saw him with a spade the night the dog went missing.'

'Why did she think he would do something so dreadful?' Frank asked, his face ashen.

'Something about Lady Boxford ruining his prospects; I didn't quite get it. Then the train was coming into Woldham, and she asked me if I ever had time off. She was thinking of joining ballroom dancing classes.' Ronnie winked at Strudel. 'Said I could be her partner.'

'The cheek of it,' Strudel said. 'We are the ones making this sort of decision.'

Ronnie laughed. He got up and stretched. 'Can I interest anyone in a glass of Pedro Ximinez?' he asked. 'I've got one bottle left. Been keeping it under the bed. A very fine vintage if I say it myself.'

'But I have vacuumed in there,' Strudel said.

'She'll be wanting a new hoover next.' Ronnie winked at Jervis. 'Fancy a drop?'

Jervis jumped up from his chair. 'I'll get some clean glasses,' he said, and headed out to the sitting room. Ronnie limped after him and they heard him clump up the stairs.

'Wait,' Strudel said, following him out. 'I am coming to see this hiding place.'

Laura and Frank were left alone.

'One has to wonder at the reliability of either Lulu or Ronnie,' Frank whispered. 'I mean would Crawford Tuthill go that far?'

'And does he honestly think Parker is to blame for Elodie's inability to have puppies?' Laura kept her voice low. 'And detest me so much he would kill him because he believes, wrongly, that I made money out of Parker's puppies?'

Their conversation was halted by the return of the others. Ronnie opened his prized bottle. He poured the thick dark liquid into liqueur glasses.

Laura took a sip. It was comforting, but definitely a step too far. As she savoured it, Ronnie pulled a chair round to the end of the table next to her.

'Top ranking bevvie, wouldn't you say, Lady Boxford? I sell a lot of it to the ex-pats.' He raised his glass and grinned at her. A wide beguiling smile.

'Returning to the subject of Lulu again,' Frank said,' Do you think we should ask Inspector Sandfield to interview her?'

Ronnie's smile crumpled. 'Please don't do that. I'm that near sorting things...

'What things?' Laura asked.

'Least said the better.' Ronnie turned to Strudel. 'Then I'll be off, I swear.'

'We must keep him safe. He will help us.' Strudel clasped her hands together. 'I will have a small flirt with Crawford to see if Lulu is speaking any truth.'

'And Ronnie and I will get on with the Harry Constantine angle,' Jervis said. 'Scam charities and pet abduction. Safe houses; fences and what have you...You must have some connections who know about that sort of thing don't you Ronnie?'

Ronnie turned to Laura, staring deep into her eyes. 'Believe me, I'll do whatever I can to help you Lady Boxford.'

Laura woke with a headache. She stretched her legs down the bed in the forlorn hope that Parker would be there, curled up waiting to push his way up the bedclothes and give her a wet lick on the face. Of course he wasn't.

The hangover was a terrible way to start a Sunday, but on the other hand the evening before had not been in vain. Whatever his motivations were, Strudel's husband might turn out to be a bonus in the search for Parker. Thinking about him as she picked up the phone that was ringing beside her, she found herself in the strange position of rather liking what she had seen of Ronnie Black.

'Laura, are you paying attention?' Strudel asked, as if reading her mind. 'I have seen Crawford taking Elodie out and engaged myself with him at the bottom of the path. I made a great fuss of Elodie. Then I asked him if he would like to join us at our ballroom dancing. I know Melissa won't, so I said we have a spare lady who is new to the art form.'

With her free hand, Laura gulped the contents of the water glass on her bedside table. 'How did that go down?'

'He made no mention of a bad knee, but asked how much it will cost. When I say it is the most minimal subscription, he starts humming and hawing. Then he asked me who the lady might be. I told him it was you.'

'Me? Strudel, how could you?'

'Don't worry; it is only part of my plan to reveal his true colours. "Of course, it is no problem for Laura

Boxford who probably does not have to pay at all as she owns the place." These were his words. He is not fond of you as we know, but I do not think this would lead him to acts of criminal violence against our dear Parker.'

It was only Strudel's opinion, but Laura had to agree that it was unlikely Crawford was involved. For whatever reason, Lulu must have her own agenda for maligning him.

She wanted to ask Frank his opinion, but he had a long-standing arrangement to stay with an old friend in Salisbury and wouldn't be back until the next day when they had agreed to have supper together.

How was she to fill in the time without the daily punctuation marks of having a dog? It wouldn't have been so bad if Venetia had been there, but she had been kept in hospital with an irregular heartbeat and when they had spoken the day before, Venetia had told her not to bother with visiting as Gladys was coming. Suddenly she hated the weekend. It was like being back at boarding school when one longed for an exeat.

She went to the kitchen to make a cup of tea. Beside the kettle stood Parker's tin of treats. 'Where are you?' she implored, twisting the Navajo bracelet around her wrist. Perhaps Ronnie's suspicion about Harry Constantine would bear fruit when he and Jervis looked into the affairs of his so-called charity?

Chapter 18

Monday morning couldn't come soon enough. Laura was wondering if it was too early to call Strudel when Strudel called her.

'Are you awake?' she asked.

'Of course I am, I'm about to get dressed.'

'Well, you will never guess what happened last night…' Strudel paused as if waiting for Laura to have some form of psychic transmission.

'What?' Laura had to ask.

'Elodie went missing.'

'What?'

'When Crawford let her out, she didn't return. We heard him and Melissa calling and calling. We went out to help. Half of Mulberry Close joined in, but there was no sign of her.'

'I'll be straight over,' Laura said.

As she rounded the corner into Mulberry Close, Laura saw Melissa standing outside their open front door.

'Any news?' Laura asked.

'I'm staying here in case she turns up,' Melissa said. 'Crawford has gone to see Jayne Harcourt. I couldn't stop him. He's adamant he saw a man acting suspiciously and he's blaming Jayne for not taking dog theft seriously after Parker's disappearance. Oh Laura, I don't know what to do, Crawford can be so... hot headed.'

Laura silently commiserated with Melissa for having to live with such an ogre. 'I'm sure Jayne will do everything she can,' she said. 'But what happened?'

'Crawford said that when Strudel waylaid him yesterday morning, she told him she knew he always took the same route with Elodie, so last night he went a different way. When he returned, he left Elodie outside the front door because he needed to put the poo bag in the bin round the side of the house. Normally, because of her lameness she would just wait for him, but when he came back, she wasn't there. That's when he saw the man running out of the close.'

'What did he look like?' Laura asked.

'Crawford said he was more of a boy, but then everyone looks young when you get to our age.'

Laura's thoughts raced. As delicately as she could she took her leave and hurried on to Strudel and Jervis's. She knocked and let herself in.

Standing in the hall, she heard the scrape of a chair. Ronnie came to the kitchen door. 'Excuse my appearance,' he said, rubbing his still unshaven chin. 'But to be quite honest I'm that shagged. D'you want a coffee?'

Strudel ran downstairs. 'Let me make it.'

'Morning Laura,' Jervis said, coming in from the sitting room. 'I saw you talking to Melissa. Still no sign of Elodie? I'll go out again in a while.'

'There's no point,' Laura said. 'If you want my opinion, the boy Crawford saw last night stole her. I think Ronnie's right; the pebbles were a sign.'

Ronnie gave an exaggerated bow.

'We need a description of the boy from Crawford,' Laura continued. 'Could you ask him Jervis?'

'Steady Laura, we must think this through,' Jervis said. 'Ronnie spent most of last night on the phone to one of his connections in Spain. He's come up with some interesting facts. Did you know Crawford Tuthill used to be a plastic surgeon?'

'I had this hunch about him that I couldn't pin down,' Ronnie said. 'It was Lady Boxford's mentioning Botox and all those Russians that kicked it off. They used to hang around in my bar; the women with their frightening trout pouts and eyelids starting somewhere up above their ears. I remembered the name of Tuthill. Some Russian man had given me a card to put on the notice board in the bar. Tuthill and Kempinski; the combination of names had struck me a bit odd at the time. They were advertising reconstructive surgery. There's quite a call for it in the south of Spain and I don't just mean the Ruskies.' Ronnie winked. 'I Googled the practise, but nothing doing. So, then I asked a mate of mine if he knew where Tuthill and Kempinski was.' Ronnie crossed his arms. 'You tell her Jarvie.'

'Puerto Romano; it's a couple of miles down the road from Ronnie's bar in Puerto Banus.'

'And another mate of mine who lives in Puerto Romano told me they shut up shop in something of a hurry a couple of years back. He also said he didn't think there was ever a Kempinski.'

'It sounds like old history,' Laura said. 'We have to concentrate on what's going on now.'

'You may be right, Lady Boxford, but it occurs to me that there might be more to this than meets the eye. Him doing a fast one smacks of trouble. Probably financial.' Ronnie pursed his lips, nodding his head as if agreeing with himself. 'Looking to the present day, how about this as an idea; Tuthill, short of dosh as a result of the closure, engineers his own dog's theft in order to get an insurance payout.'

'That's not going to keep him in hot dinners at Wellworth Lawns for long,' Jervis said.

'Short-term fix? Or, how about this – he's going to sue Wellworth Lawns for the loss of the dog.'

'Melissa's mental health…' Jervis hummed. 'Could be mileage there.'

Laura was beginning to wonder if Jervis and Ronnie weren't suffering from mental health problems themselves. 'What would be helpful is a link between Elodie and Parker,' she said, but Jervis wasn't paying attention.

'I wonder if Crawford's got a history of litigation?' he said. 'A spot more digging could be in order.'

'Good plan Jervie,' Ronnie said.

They were transfixed by their own agenda. Laura left them to it.

Pacing around her apartment as if measuring up for new carpets, she tried calling Frank. He must get the description of the boy from Crawford. If there was even a hint that Parker was one in a series of dog thefts, there was room for hope.

Frank didn't pick up. He had said he'd be leaving Salisbury mid-morning. Lunchtime came and went.

She left a message for him, then tried to calm herself by watching an old episode of Morse. It wasn't the same with Venetia still in hospital and she kept looking at her watch at crucial moments so she hadn't a clue what was going on.

As she was about to reach for the gin bottle in a meltdown of exasperation, Frank appeared.

'You won't believe what happened,' he said, making himself comfortable on the sofa. 'I got your message about Crawford, so I dropped in at the bar on the off chance and there he was. I was about to engage in conversation with him as you wished, when Jayne Harcourt came in saying his wife had called to say that Elodie had been returned. Melissa heard the doorbell and when she went to open it, there was the dog, sitting outside.'

Yet again Laura's hopes were dashed.

Frank took her hand. 'It's a setback I know, but let's go down and talk about it over dinner. At least the Tuthill's won't be there.'

But they were.

'You wanting sitting room in middle somewhere?' Mimi pointed to a table only two away from Crawford and Melissa.

Laura hesitated. She wanted nothing to do with them…But on the other hand…It was mystifying that they should be there at all when Elodie had only just been returned. If Laura and Frank took a table nearby, they might be able to listen in.

Mimi took them over. Between their table and the Tuthills a couple Laura vaguely knew from her occasional forays to the book club were finishing their main course. Laura smiled in recognition. She was about to exchange some pleasantry or other when to her astonishment Crawford called out.

'Frank, you've told Laura about Elodie, I presume?'

'Wonderful news,' Laura said.

'Amazing how many kind people there are around,' Crawford continued. 'Returning our lovely dog to us.' He gave a jovial snort and returned his attention to Melissa.

'He really is ghastly,' Laura whispered across the table to Frank.

'I thought sitting here might be a mistake,' he said.

'The thieves must have found out how lame Elodie is,' Laura said. 'That's why she's been brought back. I'd have thrown her in a ditch.'

Frank's disapproval was evident.

Laura gulped. 'You know I don't mean it.'

She was saved from further embarrassment by Mimi's arrival with the wine. After she had taken their order, Laura kept the conversation on a level of inconsequential small talk, while keeping half an eye on the Tuthills who were starting their main course.

By the time that Laura and Frank's starters arrived, the couple on the next table had finished their meal. They got up to leave. It left no barrier between Laura and Frank and the Tuthills, but the dining room was full and there was a general clattering of plates and glasses that made it hard for Laura to hear what they were saying. She did though notice, after a surreptitious sideways glance, that Melissa was looking flustered. Her pink complexion gave Laura encouragement that something was brewing.

She was cutting into a slice of smoked salmon when there was a temporary lull, and she heard Melissa's words.

'Not now, please Crawford,' she said.

Crawford batted loudly back with no regard to who could hear him. 'Why can't I? I've just as much right to be here as the next man.'

'Please Crawford.' Melissa got up, squeezing her napkin like a dishcloth in her hands. 'We shouldn't leave Elodie alone this long.' She was directing herself more at the room in general than her husband. 'Not after all she's been through.' She dropped the napkin on the table and left.

Crawford muttered something under his breath and downed the remains of his glass before following her out.

'Well, that was something,' Laura said.

'But what?' Frank said.

He was right. Laura felt deflated. She had reveled in the Tuthill's spat, but when it came to it, she had simply overheard a matrimonial disagreement like hundreds of others. The only difference was that Crawford Tuthill was so odious that he didn't care if he hung out his dirty washing in public.

Her hopes of Elodie's theft being somehow related to Parker's disappearance had come to nothing. Suddenly she didn't want to be in the dining room a moment longer. Frank was so annoyingly right sometimes. She sighed, thinking about how to remain calm.

'You not having heartburn?' Mimi asked, putting the empty plates on a tray.

They had not got far into their main course when Laura felt a tap on the shoulder. She looked up and found herself staring into the doleful eyes of Lulu Vandermoss.

'I don't mean to disturb you, but I saw that too,' she said. 'Melissa knows something that Crawford's trying to hide.'

'What do you mean?' Could one believe anything Lulu said?

'My lips are sealed, but on another matter, I was in Woldham the other day when our friend Venetia had her accident. I witnessed the whole thing.'

'Really?' Venetia, "our friend"? And why were Lulu's lips sealed?

Sickly as sherry trifle Lulu continued sotto voce. 'I believe she was pushed. I didn't see who it was, but I thought I'd let you know.'

Laura watched the emaciated figure glide out of the dining room.

'What do you suppose she meant by that?' Frank asked.

'She must have rung Venetia in hospital. I didn't know they were that close. I hate to say it about my dearest friend, but Venetia's becoming a bit of a liability. I think she probably made it up about being pushed and now it suits Lulu to make it look as if I'm the one who doesn't care. She seems intent on stirring for no apparent reason.'

'All the same, we shouldn't entirely disregard her,' Frank said.

Chapter 19

Laura was wincing at the acidity of the grapefruit juice when, for the second morning running, the telephone rang, and Strudel and Jervis's number came up.

'I tried you last night, but you were out,' Strudel said. 'I have important news. Ronnie saw the man returning Elodie in a small silver vehicle. He got the registration number and has spent much time identifying the owner. We know who it is. Jervis has sent an email with a photo to your mobile. Call us back when you have looked at it.'

Laura was unprepared for Strudel's decisive tone of voice. She plucked her mobile from the bedside table and looked at Jervis's attachment.

Smiling broadly at her was an image of Harry Constantine, one arm placed nonchalantly round the shoulders of a young man.

She rang back.

Jervis answered.

'It's the boy I saw dropping the pebbles,' she said. 'But who is he?'

'He's Harry Constantine's eighteen-year-old son, Ludo. The car that delivered Elodie back is registered in his name. Ronnie was up half the night finding that out, don't ask me how.'

'Harry Constantine's son?' Laura's tray slid off the silk eiderdown. She tried to catch it with one hand, but it crashed to the floor.

'I thought you'd be interested,' Jervis was saying.' We found the picture on Harry's Facebook page. I'd say they could have some questions to answer regarding Parker's disappearance. It's looking like a hopeful lead.'

Laura stared at the contents of the tray on the floor. 'You mean they could be in it together? Using the charities as some sort of cover?'

'Good question. The Guide Dog Rehab Ludo said he was working for is well known. I'll call them; find out if he's on their list of volunteers. Alternatively, it could simply be something innocent, like the father training up the son to follow him into the charity sector.'

'But that's beside the fact that Ronnie saw the boy returning Elodie after she'd been stolen.'

'That's where it's a bit tenuous. He could have found the dog roaming around and returned it, as he'd seen where it came from.'

'I need to speak to him.'

'We know where Harry Constantine lives. Not far away, a village called Drayton Copestake.'

'Brilliant Jervis. I'll get Frank to come with me and have a sniff round.'

On her way to visit Venetia who had been kept in hospital having developed a chest infection, Laura stopped at the hairdresser's.

'I'm sure we weren't expecting you this week Lady Boxford.' The receptionist said, scrolling down the tablet. 'Here we are, I've got you down for your colour in two weeks' time.'

'I just wanted a word with Dudley. Is he around?'

'He's out the back having a break. Hang on, I'll go and get him.'

As Laura waited, she watched a woman sitting staring straight ahead of herself in the mirror, her sculpted head encased in little foil packages like an art installation. Then, beyond her, the staff room door opened, and the receptionist came out with Dudley. As he made his way over, Dudley stopped at the silver head, unwrapped a single packet and gave it a scratch. The woman looked up in expectant adoration as he wrapped it up again.

He reached Laura, stepping over the basket containing his sleeping greyhound.

'How can I help?' he asked. 'Is it Parker?'

Laura nodded.

'We'll go into the staffroom. My lady in the foils has a little more cooking time to do.'

She followed him to the inner sanctum where he offered her a seat, pulling out a metal chair tucked under a table piled high with boxes. Then he lifted a mound of towels covered in clear plastic wrappers to reveal a small wooden stool.

'No luck with Stan Kaminski?' He squatted on the stool, his lanky legs bent double as he tried to fit his feet into the cramped space. 'I must say I wasn't sure you were on the right track there, Lady B.'

'You may be right, but one thing I know is he doesn't always tell the truth: about his own brother, for example. He's got some questions to answer for sure, but right now he's proving elusive,' Laura said. 'In the meantime, I'm following a new line of enquiry and as the fount of all local knowledge, I was wondering if you'd ever come across someone called Harry Constantine?'

'Sure,' Dudley said. 'His ex-wife, Milly's a regular.' He stood up and moved a stack of boxes off the table onto the floor. 'Blonde highlights.' He pushed the stool against the wall, sitting back down with a sigh. 'That's better,' he said and put his legs up on the table.

'Is she from round here?' Laura asked.

'They started off as weekenders. Like a lot of the women who come here now, they know the colour chart from their hairdresser in London, then come here and get it done for a fraction of the price. Half a head mostly – they're not fools. Don't get me wrong, I'm not knocking it; it's my bread and butter after all. Well, you're my bread and butter Lady B, they're more the caviar on top.'

Laura might have taken this the wrong way were it not for Dudley's idiotic high-pitched laugh at his own joke.

He took his feet off the table, stretching his arms above his head. 'But seriously, Milly Constantine's all right. I don't know anything much about him.'

'They've got a teenage son…'

'Ludo? He's a wild child from what she's told me. Been expelled from his school. Parent's divorce was acrimonious; probably what sent him a bit off the rails. He was driving Milly mad living with her, so she's palmed him off on Harry. It's a shame to be honest. She kept the family house and he's living in a rented cottage somewhere on the old Copestake estate.'

'Have you any idea where?'

'No, but she did mention something about him taking the Range Rover. Might give you a clue? She was pretty miffed about that.'

'Thank you, Dudley. I'm so sorry to ask so many questions.'

'It's nothing. You know I've got no secrets from you.' Dudley adjusted the turquoise rimmed glasses he was sporting that day, then crossed his arms and leant forward. 'But what's the angle?'

'I think the boy may be involved in dog theft.'

'Parker?'

'I haven't got much to go on at the moment.'

'If I can help with any information that might lead to finding him, you know I'd do anything.'

'Do you know why the boy was expelled?'

'Drugs probably, but listen Lady B, I better go,' he said. 'There's nothing these ladies hate more than a feeling of abandonment.'

As Laura left the salon, Dudley's greyhound rose from its basket, stretched with lethargic elegance and lay back down. Her mouth went dry with yearning.

Laura rang Frank from Venetia's hospital bedside. He was waiting in the car park when she came out and as they headed out of town, she told him what she had learned from Dudley.

'The thing is, Range Rovers are two a penny round there,' Frank said. 'Do we know what colour it is?'

'Venetia says it's black, or very dark blue. She saw him getting into it after the talk he gave.'

'How is she?' Frank asked.

'Her breathing's better and they've stopped monitoring her heart. She's got a mass of new pills.

They're aiming to discharge her tomorrow. I said I'd collect her. She wants to drop in at The Blue Dolphin.'

'Is the hospital food that bad?'

'To thank Bryan Bowman. Apparently, he was there when she fell. He called the ambulance. She wants me to buy him something as a token of her appreciation. What on earth can I get?' Laura pulled up at a set of traffic lights. She looked out of the side window at a row of houses. In one of the gardens a crab apple tree was laden with a late autumnal crop.

'I know, I'll get him a basket of fruit.'

They were discussing the suitability of such a gift as they neared the village of Lower Copestake. From almost a mile out the verges were neatly mown.

'I thought Dudley told you Harry Constantine had come out of the divorce badly?' Frank said. 'This all looks very expensive.'

'He's in Drayton Copestake. Quite different to Lower Copestake that the Henderson family sold off in the sixties to pay for the roof of Copestake Hall. They've regretted it ever since. Wall to wall weekenders.' Laura pointed to the small village green, newly planted with a eucalyptus tree below which brick red geraniums were still flowering in the brown soil.

'Quite wrong.' Laura shook her head, as they headed up the hill towards Drayton Copestake.

The road steepened. The verges grew wild with nettles and dying rose bay willowherb. It flattened out onto a ridge and then dipped down again from where they could see the start of the estate cottages bunched here and there along the side of the road that led directly to the drive of Copestake Hall. The mansion itself was partially obscured by ancient woodland. As she drove on Laura could just about make out the Victorian towers that had been added to the original building.

She remembered the house from years gone by. Dinner parties held in the sepulchral cold of the mock-Tudor hall. Tough venison stew eaten off cold plates. Randolph Henderson trying to touch her thigh under the table. Then after dinner the ladies were ushered into a lifeless drawing room with a fireplace that smoked and let out precious little heat. It was a monster of a place. The present generation had done nothing to improve it, or the rest of the estate by all accounts. Dudley had told her that rents in Drayton Copestake village were cheap because none of the houses were modernized. Harry Constantine had obviously had to tighten his belt.

'I don't think there are that many properties,' Laura said. 'It shouldn't take us long.'

'I'd say we need look no further.' Frank pointed down the hill to a pair of semi-detached cottages. The nearest one was covered in ivy. Parked outside on the muddy lane was a dark-coloured Range Rover with a battered silver hatchback in front of it.

Laura drew up a few yards behind the two cars. As they got out, they could hear raised voices. The side door of the cottage was open.

'You're not going there again,' a man shouted from within. 'I told you, the basement's off limits.'

'Try stopping me.'

The same young man Laura had seen with the charity tin and in the photo Jervis had found, came out of the house, slamming the door behind him. It immediately opened again, and Harry Constantine stormed out.

'Ludo, come here,' he shouted.

Both men saw Laura and Frank simultaneously. Laura wished she'd made a better plan. It was all happening too fast. She had no clear idea of what she was going to say or do.

Before she had time to think further Harry Constantine said, 'You've missed the footpath, it's back on your left.'

He used the same tone as he had used on his son. Meanwhile the boy was slinking off towards the silver hatchback.

'Hello,' Laura said. 'Do you remember me. We met at Wellworth Lawns. Laura Boxford.'

Harry Constantine put one hand up to his forehead and tilted his head against the pale almost non-existent midday sun.

'Oh my goodness, I do beg your pardon Lady Boxford,' he said, coming towards them. I didn't recognize you in this light. We get so many ramblers round here. They're always losing their way. I assumed…'

'Not to worry.' Laura stepped forward. 'This is Canon Frank Holliday,' she said. 'We really wanted a word with your son.'

'I might have known,' Harry Constantine muttered. He walked briskly back towards Ludo who was opening the door of the car.

'Come here a minute,' he said, pulling the boy by the sleeve of his hoodie.

Ludo tried to shake himself free. 'What d'you want?'

'It's about a neighbour of mine whose dog went missing yesterday.' Laura felt Frank's steadying hand on her arm as the boy gave an impertinent huff. He pulled his sleeve from his father's grasp, proceeding to get in the car.

Aware that she might be running ahead of herself, Laura tried to assemble her thoughts. She didn't want to lose him now. 'Canon Frank here believes he saw you returning it.' It was bad enough that it was a lie, but worse, Laura knew her haste was a mistake.

'Oh that.' The boy seemed relieved. 'Yes, I found the dog wandering around.' His face was pale and sweaty. 'I've met you before, haven't I?' he said. 'I remember now, it was outside their house. That's how I knew where it came from. They should look after their pets better.'

It was just as Jervis had predicted. Laura could have kicked herself.

Ludo slammed the car door and put his key in the ignition. 'If that's all, I've got to get to Woldham.' He turned to his father. 'See you, mate,' he said and drove off.

They watched as he went down the road to the main gates of Drayton Copestake, circled round driving back towards them. As he passed, he wound down the window and waved.

'Kids,' Harry Constantine laughed with jovial irony. 'He's not a bad lad. I shouldn't complain, but what's all this about a missing dog?'

'Small misunderstanding,' Frank said.

Returning to Woldham, Laura and Frank agreed they couldn't be sure whether Harry Constantine was playing the innocent father covering for his son or even if there was anything that connected either of them to Parker's disappearance.

'There was a certain desperation in the boy's appearance,' Frank said. 'Tormented almost. I'd like to have offered him spiritual guidance.'

'That's not much help if it's drugs he's after.'

'How stupid of me.' Frank cleared his throat. 'I must keep up with these things.'

'Dudley told me. That's the only reason I knew. He said Ludo was most likely kicked out of school for drugs.' Laura patted Frank's knee. 'What do you think, "the basement" is?' she continued. 'It sounded like a nightclub to me.'

'I'm rather out of touch with the youth of today and what they get up to. Vicar Rachel tried incorporating rap music into the family service, but I'm afraid it didn't go down well. The oldies hated it, and the kids started talking about some sub-genre called drill and I don't think it had anything to do with National Service.'

'What are you talking about?' Laura could feel her exasperation level rise and she took a corner faster than was sensible. Vicar Rachel was getting everywhere. She yanked the wheel to avoid the ditch. They ended up skidding into the middle of the road. An oncoming car honked its horn as it took to the verge to pass them.

Frank delved into his jacket pocket. He pulled out a handkerchief to mop his brow. 'We won't be meeting anyone young or old if you carry on like that.'

'Sorry,' Laura slowed down. 'I was trying to think. Mimi's often telling me how she goes out clubbing with her boyfriend, Tom the handyman.'

Chapter 20

By the time they got back to Wellworth Lawns the lunchtime shift had finished and there was no one on at the reception desk.

'I'll see if there's anyone still in the kitchen,' Laura said. 'Wait for me in the lounge; there'll be tea and biscuits.'

Laura found Alfredo clutching a large bowl in one hand, a whisk in the other. He said it was his evening off, but he didn't trust the team with making Hollandaise for the salmon later.

'Is Mimi around?' Laura asked.

'She should be back soon. Anything I can do?'

Laura knew he was avoiding mentioning Parker and she didn't want to take up his time. She had a feeling that he, like most of the staff, while concerned for her, was quietly resigned to the fact that Parker was not coming back.

But she was wrong.

Alfredo put the whisk down. 'I got an idea you're onto something Lady B,' he said. 'Holy Uova, you gotta keep at it whatever it is. There's plenty of bad people out there I'm telling you.' He put the whisk back in the bowl and began to beat the contents with vigour. 'I seen that Roma woman by the bins again. I told Jayne Harcourt, but she just laughed and told me to make the citizen's arrest next time.'

By the time Mimi came back on duty Frank had polished off most of the complimentary biscuits in the lounge. Laura watched him stuff another bourbon in his mouth as they waited for Mimi to put the tea things away. Then they joined her at the bar while she re-stocked for the evening.

'I no understand, you want go clubbing?' she said, as she wiped down a bottle of Fernet Branca.

'My word, no,' Frank said.

'Oh, I thinking maybe fun you two dancing. Maybe not in Woldham club. How 'bout you give the ballroom dancing a go Ladyship? I know you not so fond of this, but maybe Canon Frank throwing some nice moves?' She put her arms into waltz position. 'I got the snowstorm toy from my hometown Burgas; is a ballerina; she dancing with her man just like you two.'

Frank leant heavily on the bar and wiped one eyebrow with his index finger. 'You're getting the wrong end of the stick.'

'She's not...' Laura felt confused by Mimi's romantic notion. 'Well maybe she is.' She turned to Mimi. 'We just want to know where young people might go to have fun. Not necessarily dancing. Maybe a bar that's in fashion now. You see we're looking for a boy we've seen who might know something about Parker.'

'Parker, Oh my.' Mimi tightened her ponytail, both elbows sticking up in the air as she pulled on the long dark tresses. 'Now I thinking, my Tom and me we going sometimes One Oh One club. Very nice cocktails.'

'Is it below ground?' Laura asked.

Mimi gave her a vacant smile.

Laura pretended she was going down some steps.

'The Basement?' Mimi's eyes widened. 'You not serious? My Tom never taking me there no more. Is full of scum.' She put her hand on Frank's arm. 'This is very bad place. Beer and crisps all mashed into the floor. Feet sticking like in Russian state vodka bar.' She lifted her feet like an astronaut, her hand over her mouth as if she were about to vomit.

Laura laughed. She promised she had no intention of visiting such a place.

Jervis pointed at the map on the computer screen. 'Here it is. Sack Lane; not an area of Woldham one would normally frequent, although we did put a poster in the 24-hour shop on the corner. Are you sure you want to be going there?'

Clouds gusted over a waning moon as they parked a few yards up the street from the 24-hour shop. They walked round the corner into Sack Lane. It must have been about the only remaining street in Woldham to retain the original Victorian cobbles. With no street lighting, Frank insisted Laura take his arm as they made their way over the bumpy surface past a row of workmen's cottages. Through their torn and shabby half drawn curtains flickering lights from TV screens gave out some illumination. Laura could hear the sounds of laughter, adverts and soundtrack music of the different channels, all of which she knew Venetia would have been able to identify.

The houses ended abruptly and with them what little light there was. Frank fumbled in his jacket pocket. He took out a small torch. They could see a gap in the street, then some industrial units followed. They were a mish mash of architecture, some Victorian, some from the 1950's, now mostly derelict, the windows smashed or boarded up. They could hear a background throbbing hum, but it was hard to figure out where it was coming from. The cobbles broke up into a cinder track. They followed it for a short distance, an area of wasteland to one side of them, before being faced with padlocked metal gates barring the way. Ahead in the gloom lay the old coal merchant's depot.

'I suppose the railway track must be the other side of those buildings.' Frank shone the torch onto a conglomeration of sheds. Their rusty corrugated roofs creaked, casting eerie shadows in the limpid dirty light.

'It must be ripe for development,' Laura said.

'Possibly the whole street,' Frank agreed.

Laura shivered. 'We must have missed The Basement. Let's go back to where we heard that noise.'

Turning, they were startled as a pair of car headlights turned into the top of the street. They stumbled out of the beams into the rough grass to one side. Laura could feel wet penetrating the soles of her shoes and an acrid stench as she lifted one sodden foot out of the mud.

'Stay still.' Frank gripped her arm. The lights were moving. The beams were almost upon them.

'Duck down,' he said.

Laura heard his knees crack. She squatted. Bent her head low. How was she ever going to get up? She waited. Took a peek. 'It's turning round,' she whispered.

White reversing lights went out. The car disappeared round the corner leaving them in almost total darkness. Frank stood up. He held his hand out to her, pulling her up.

They were about to step back onto the track when they heard voices coming up the street.

'Duck,' Frank whispered.

As Laura lowered herself to the ground once more, she tipped forward. Her hands went out to save herself. With knees and palms covered in wet gritty dirt, she regained her balance and looked at Frank beside her. His back was arched; head tucked in like an enormous turtle. As she wiped her hands down the sides of her jeans, a door in one of the factory units opened and a shaft of light lit up the cobbles ahead. She saw three figures as a blast of music emanating from the opening. Then the door banged shut and all that was left was the throb of bass.

'That's got to be it,' she said, as Frank pulled her up again.

They retraced their steps until they reached the old red brick building. It had three sets of double doors set at intervals along the exterior wall. A chink of yellow light seeped out of a crack where the middle doors had not quite shut. It was obvious from this and the thud of bass that it was the entrance to The Basement.

'We can't go in there,' Laura said.

'Wait.' Frank edged up to the door. He got hold of the heavy iron latch and opened it an inch. They could see a set of steep stone steps leading down.

'You're right.' He pulled the door too. 'We'll have to find another way.'

They edged round the side of the building and found a wooden gate set into a prefabricated concrete wall. Frank tried the handle. He shook his head.

'Give it a shove,' Laura said. 'No one's going to hear anything above that racket.' She watched as he turned the handle in one hand. Then let the full force of his body thump into the door.

To her astonishment it gave way. Frank was thrown forward by his own momentum. He stopped himself from falling by a miracle of backward propulsion of his arms that flailed like a pair of out of sync propellers.

With the gate swinging open, they found themselves in an empty paved back yard. Uneven concrete slabs underfoot met the side of the factory walls. Stunted silvery Buddleia shivered as their branches squeezed out of the cracks.

The noise of the music was much louder now. Why could she see so clearly? Laura looked up at the sky. There was no sign of the moon. They walked a few paces further into the yard. In front of them was a tall stack of abandoned wooden pallets through which the light was filtering.

'Stay here,' Frank said.

Laura crossed her arms and waited as Frank skirted the pallets. Minutes passed. It was getting cold. She tried to read the dial on her watch. Then she thought she heard a thud. She crossed her arms again, wishing she'd put on an extra layer.

A few moments later he reappeared.

'There's a cellar window open.' Puffing with excitement, he pointed to beyond the pallets. 'I had to lie on the floor, but I could see him; Ludo's in there.'

Laura lay on the cold ground peering through the diamond shaped windowpanes held in place by a metal frame coated in peeling white gloss paint. The glass was covered in misted dirt and cobwebs, but the three figures sitting at a table in the club below were dauntingly close. Ludo Constantine was with his back to the wall. Laura felt she could almost reach out and touch his blond hair. On the white plastic table in front of him was a half-filled tumbler of colourless liquid. Of the two others with him, one was a boy of about the same age as Ludo; more heavily built and with a mass of unruly brown hair. The third boy looked younger; perhaps only about thirteen? Laura didn't really have a clue. He was thin and pale with mousy hair and a long jutting nose. Around them other tables were filled with groups of people. All three of them were texting on their phones, occasionally looking at one another to make some comment. Their conversation was impossible to hear above the sound of the music.

After a while Laura began to question the validity of this nocturnal escapade. Her chin, resting in her hands, had gone numb. The nerve endings in her elbows felt like ever increasing electric currents were passing through them as they dug into the paving slabs. Beside her Frank appeared to be in the same amount of soundless agony. Small puffs of vapour were emanating from his nose with the rapidity of an athlete under pressure.

She was about to suggest they call it off when she saw all three boys get up. Ludo's head was so close to the bottom of the window that a rush of fear passed through her. He lifted his arms up and stretched. She held her breath, her eyes transfixed on a small tattoo of an eye at the base of one thumb, so close to her that she was sure it must have ocular powers. Her heart pounded.

Then the boys began walking slowly away through the maze of crowded tables. She turned to Frank. He was already on his knees. He let out a pent-up cry of pain as he straightened up. Then held out a hand to help her.

They returned to the corner of the street. Laura stood pinned against the wall behind Frank as he peered round the side of the building.

His head swayed back and forth for a few minutes. 'I think we've missed them,' he said. But at that moment they heard the bang of the door. He poked his head round the corner again.

Laura waited for it to retract, but then he beckoned to her with a swift hand movement.

They edged along the front of the building. Took cover in a doorway beyond the club entrance. Both peered out.

The boys were twenty yards in front of them, deep in conversation. One of them laughed, but now they were losing definition in the darkness.

Laura and Frank edged forward to the next building and another doorway. Frank made a further recce. 'There's a gap then a phone box with no door on it,' he said.

They crept up to the dilapidated stinking relic from the 1970's. Squashed inside it, they couldn't see anything ahead. Then they heard a knocking. Some seconds later a door opened, letting light out onto the street; in front of one of the workman's cottage stood the three boys. They heard the sound of barking. Holding her breath behind the graffitied BT logo Laura watched as a small white dog ran out.

One of the boys bent down. He caught it in his arms. Then all three of them went in and the door shut.

Laura and Frank waited. Half an hour passed. People started coming out of the club.

'We should go,' Frank breathed in her ear. 'It's nearly midnight. They could be staying there all night.'

They hurried back to the car and as Laura drove him home, she reiterated the whispered argument they'd had in the phone booth.

'I know you don't believe me, but I've seen that dog before,' she said.

'How can you be so sure? They all look identical to me.'

'That's the difference between us. Anyway, dogs like that just don't turn up in places like that.'

'Are they rare?' Frank asked.

'Not particularly but they're for old people,' Laura said. 'Kids are far more likely to have a French Bulldog or a Staffie these days.'

'Perhaps it was their granny's or they're training it for the circus?'

She pulled up outside his house. 'I don't care what you say, I'm going back tomorrow.'

He sighed. 'Well, you can't go alone.'

'So, you'll come? Good,' Laura said. 'Because I'm telling you, it was the same miniature poodle I saw with Gwendoline Shackleton.'

Chapter 21

Before collecting Venetia from hospital, Laura rang Strudel.

'Is Ronnie there?' she asked.

'He returned very late last night and now is sleeping,' Strudel said.

Laura told her about the night before. 'I wonder if he would agree to go to with us to Sack Lane?'

Strudel hesitated. 'For why?'

Laura explained what they had seen. 'It could be part of the whole Harry and Ludo Constantine dog theft set up and maybe Gwendoline Shackleton's part of it. A fence or something... Or she makes sure the dogs are house trained and won't bite before they get sold on. Maybe she even writes them some kind of fake certification.'

'I see.' Strudel sounded as unconvinced as Frank.

'Jervis did say Ronnie might have connections who know about pet abduction. He'd know if it looked like that the kind of set up.'

Strudel said she'd ask him.

As Laura waited at the greengrocers to pick up the fruit basket she had ordered for Venetia's gift, she felt she was making real progress. Parker had probably been re-homed by now, but that was not a problem. He was easily identifiable, if nothing else by his microchip. She'd be cross if his new, "owner" had got rid of his leather collar with the Masai beadwork and his beautiful silver charm, but it was a small price to pay for his return.

She carried on to the hospital wondering if it would be better to call Inspector Sandfield now, but no, she thought, that man doesn't deserve the accolade of breaking a ring of dog thieves. She and Frank, with the help of Ronnie, would bring the criminal activities of the Constantine's and whoever else was involved tumbling down around their heads.

Frank was waiting for her in the hospital foyer. She sent him to find a wheelchair, while she went to gather up Venetia and her belongings.

It took Frank some time to find one, but there was no rush as Laura and Venetia waited for the nurse to collect Venetia's new prescription. When he arrived, they waited further as Venetia said goodbye to her new friends on the ward. They went to the hospital pharmacy, and all waited again while the prescription was dispensed. Then she and Venetia waited in the car as Frank returned the chair to the hospital entrance.

Laura felt that she was learning the art of patience when finally they set off to The Blue Dolphin.

Venetia sat in the front. She seemed to have diminished further in size since the accident. It looked like she could benefit from a booster seat to see over the dashboard. On the other hand, from her mirror Laura could see Frank compressed in the back, the top of his head squashed sideways by the roof.

'I do hope Bryan likes fruit,' Venetia mused. 'Aftershave would have been much too forward.'

'Remind me, what exactly did he do to help?' Laura asked.

'He was so kind. He knew who I was; because of coming into the chip shop with you and Parker I suppose.'

'Yes, but what did he do?' Frank said.

'He was walking down the road with his sister-in-law, Val Farmer and another man I hadn't seen before.'

'How do you know Val Farmer is Bryan's sister-in-law?' Laura asked.

'Because she works at Wellworth Lawns. She sometimes checks up on me when she's on night duty and we have a chat. She's been trying to lose weight but Sally and Bryan... well Sally mainly is always giving her fish and chips. Val says Sally doesn't want her to go on a diet because then she'll have to. Anyway, I stopped to say hello. We talked about you and Parker, then I walked on and then it happened.'

'So, they were all there when you had the accident?'

'I think so. He asked someone to call the ambulance when I was lying in the street. He must have seen the whole silly thing.'

'What silly thing?'

'Me tripping. I know I said I thought I'd been pushed, but I may have got it wrong. It was all such a crush... but as I said I felt most comforted to know he was there.'

'Well, here we are.' Laura drew up on the kerb outside The Blue Dolphin. 'You can thank him yourself.'

Frank held Venetia's arm while Laura carried the basket as they all went into the chip shop. There was no one to be seen, so Laura rang the bell on the counter.

'Keep an eye out of the window for traffic wardens could you Frank?' she said. She supposed Bryan and Sally were taking a quick break before the lunchtime rush.

They heard Bryan's voice from out the back. He came into the shop carrying a stainless-steel container filled with freshly cut chips.

'Hello.' Venetia waved gaily at him.

'Well look who it isn't,' he said, a broad smile on his face as he put the potatoes down beside the fryers. 'And don't you look the picture of health.'

Venetia beamed at him. 'I've brought you this,' she gestured to the basket. 'As a token of my thanks for the help you gave me.'

Laura pulled away the wrapper and lifted the basket onto the counter. There were quite a lot of lemons in the selection, but the blue satin bow was impressive.

Bryan gaped at it with a blank expression. 'Now hold on a minute, what's this? I don't need charity.'

Frank swung round from the window. 'Mrs. Hobbs was eager to show her appreciation for your assistance. You were there when she had her accident, weren't you?'

Bryan gave him a look of bemused irritability. 'Yes, I was there. I was on my way to the bank, but I didn't actually do anything.'

'On your own were you?' Frank asked.

'Yes, on my own.'

'What about the person you asked to call the ambulance?' It was unlike Frank to ask such exacting questions.

Bryan pulled his white hat back from his forehead. His short brown hair popped out at the front like an escaping hedgehog. 'What is this? I've no idea who called the ambulance. The woman looking after Mrs. Hobbs must've done it. To be honest there were plenty of people by that time. I left them to it.'

'But…' Venetia gave a plaintive cry.

Bryan turned to her. 'Look I'm not wanting to appear ungrateful, but I really don't deserve this. And to be honest both Sally and I have a fructose intolerance.'

'I'm so sorry, this is all my mistake.' Venetia pulled a tissue out of her pocket.

Laura took the basket off the counter. 'Mrs. Hobbs must have been concussed,' she said. 'Give my regards to Sally. I'm sure we'll be in again soon.' She handed the basket to Frank, took Venetia by the arm and guided her back to the car.

When she had strapped her in, Laura turned to Frank who was hunched over the basket, his nose inches from a small bunch of grapes.

'What made you behave like that?' she asked.

'I don't know, there was something disingenuous about him.'

She turned back to Venetia and was about to admonish her, but there was little point. It wasn't her fault she had become so confused. Who wouldn't under the circumstances? She must have recognised Bryan as a friendly face amongst the crowd and latched onto that. 'It's as much my fault as anyone's,' she said.

'He was bound to have something like a fructose intolerance surrounded by fried food all the time.'

Laura dropped Frank off and took Venetia back to Wellworth Lawns. She left her lying on her bed with the TV on, eating the grapes from the basket of fruit. It was a blessing that she seemed to have forgotten that the fruit had been for Bryan and was now convinced that Laura had bought it for her.

'So kind of you,' she said, delving further into the basket. 'We can make lemon and ginger tea later.'

Laura went to ring Strudel and Jervis.

'Ronnie's just gone,' Jervis told her.

'Not for good?' Laura asked.

'I'm hoping so. Things could be getting a bit hot round here for him. We think our old friend Phil Sandfield's on the prowl. I saw him coming up the drive this morning when I went to collect the paper. But don't worry, Ronnie had a word with Frank about Sack Lane before he left. He was a bit worried about you two going back.'

'We will be fine.'

'Just friendly advice.' Jervis hesitated. 'OK the Constantine boy's got the dog for some reason, but he could be in with a bad crowd. We know he's been kicked out of school. Maybe he's involved with drugs. In that area of Woldham it's highly likely. Those kids could be mixed up with traffickers. Ronnie says they use children to move drugs around. It could be a drop off point.'

'Even if it is to do with drugs,' Laura said. 'That doesn't preclude the dog theft aspect.'

Chapter 22

It was Frank's idea that he curl up in the boot of Laura's car. He said it looked less suspicious if she was alone. They had removed the parcel shelf and put the back seats down. Now, as she turned off the engine, she could see his dark silhouette occasionally in her rear-view mirror as he elevated himself to peer out of the back window.

'This area is definitely ripe for drug dens,' he said.

'What do you know about such things? Anyway, you're meant to be keeping your head down. So much for the craft of stealth.' Laura said.

'I've been getting up to speed with Ronnie, if you'll excuse the pun. He's been telling me all about substance abuse. You wouldn't think it would happen in a small town like Woldham; crack cocaine and heroin, county lines and such like.'

Laura was about to ask him what his understanding of county lines was – she'd had a short lecture on the proliferation of regional drug gangs from Venetia who had been watching a programme about it – when he changed the subject.

'You don't think we're a bit too obvious?' he said.

Laura was parked tight into the side of the pavement a few yards up the road from the 24-hour shop but far enough from the next street to remain in the dark.

'I'll pretend to look in my bag for my purse. Anyone will think I've stopped for a pint of milk. I won't take the key out.'

Laura looked at her watch but couldn't see the dial. She guessed it must be about eleven o'clock. From her mirror she watched as a few people came and went from the shop, mostly buying a bottle and hurrying off into the night. Studying what she could of her fingernails, she hoped Frank would forgive her for what he almost certainly thought was another of her ill-conceived ideas. She was about to ask him if they shouldn't call it off, when coming towards her, she saw a figure.

'It's him,' she called out in a pressing whisper as she ducked her head. 'Ludo Constantine. He's coming our way.'

'I'm taking a look,' Frank whispered.

She could hear his rasping breath coming from the boot. It sounded as if it was being magnified through a stethoscope.

'He's gone round the corner into Sack Lane,' Frank said. 'No dog with him.'

Laura began to fret. What if it was just a drug den he'd gone to?

Then Frank whispered, 'keep down, they're coming.'

With her forehead pressed into the steering wheel she waited. Then, thinking they must have passed, she was about to sit up when she heard noises from the back of the car. It started to rock. Were they being attacked? Abruptly she was shunted sideways, squashed into the car door. Frank, in a surprising move, tipped headfirst forward into the passenger seat beside her.

'Sorry,' he said, levering one foot off the roof. His leg swung round narrowly avoiding Laura's head and landed in her footwell. He held onto the steering wheel, pushed himself into an upright position and pointed to the road ahead. 'Look.'

Ahead, three boys were walking down the pavement. Even from the back, Laura recognized them under the light of a streetlamp. Ludo was in the middle; the smaller boy walking beside him on his left. On his other side, the older one with the curly hair was holding the little white poodle on a lead. What was it called? Laura wished she could remember.

'OK. Turn on the engine but make sure the lights are off,' Frank said, putting on his seatbelt.

She fiddled with the automatic dial then switched on the ignition. The sound seemed deafening; akin to the rumble of the old Wellworth Lawns heating boiler as it cranked into action.

They watched the three boys walk to the end of the road and turn left. They gave it a minute before following. At the junction Laura edged round the corner. Immediately she put her foot on the brake. Twenty yards in front of them the boys had crossed the street and were standing on the pavement opposite.

'It's a bus stop,' Frank said.

'What shall we do?'

'Don't move, we're in luck.' Frank pointed down the road. A night bus came towards them and slowed to a halt at the stop, obscuring the boys.

'It'll take them a minute to pay,' Frank said. 'Get ready to make a U turn.'

Laura put the car in gear, but as she did so they saw Ludo. He hadn't got on the bus. He was walking back towards them.

Frank lowered his head. She followed suit.

'OK. He's passed us,' Frank said, a few moments later. She looked up. She could see the bus was indicating to move off.

'Drive on and turn as soon as you can,' Frank urged. 'I hope you're up for a trip to Cheltenham; that's its destination. The drug capital of the Cotswolds according to Ronnie.'

'What about Ludo? It's him we want.'

'But the poodle's on the bus, that's what we have to follow. D'you want Parker back?'

'Of course.' He was flustering her.

'Why chase the sprat when you've got the mackerel in your sights and they're leading you straight into the jaws of the shark.'

Laura didn't have time to mull over Frank's unexpected analogy as she made an untidy three-point turn.

They followed the bus at a discrete distance out of Woldham into the open countryside. She was glad there were few other vehicles on the road as they passed through the villages en route. Only once did the bus indicate and slow into a stop where a young couple got out.

Laura glanced at the dashboard clock. It was nearly midnight. Not for the first time she began to rue her rash behaviour, but the adrenalin was pumping and beside her she knew Frank had no intention of quitting now.

As they drove on the sky took on an orange hue. They had reached the outskirts of Cheltenham.

'We're going to end up in the middle of the town,' Laura said. But then the bus indicated. It pulled in. They waited a distance away.

The doors opened and the boys jumped down the step. The older one, who was carrying the poodle, deposited it on the pavement as the bus drew away. Then they set off down the road a short distance before turning off.

Laura and Frank followed them through the suburbs. Once, they thought they'd lost them as they entered yet another of the many streets of identical rows of houses.

'Damn it,' Frank swore, but before Laura had time to properly register the expletive, the boys came back in view. The older one had picked up the dog again and they had quickened their pace. They appeared to be heading for the town centre, but then changed direction. The houses became more sparsely separated with larger gaps between the parked cars on either side.

'Keep your distance,' Frank said.

It was harder to remain undetected, but the two boys didn't appear to have any suspicions as they walked on together.

Laura was starting to think tailing was easy with Frank beside her telling her what to do. She saw a crossroads ahead and was waiting for him to say something when the lights of a car coming in the opposite direction dazzled her.

'Which way?' There was a hint of panic in her voice as she realized she had lost sight of the boys.

'Keep left,' Frank said.

She drove on. The houses stopped. The road narrowed.

'Draw up,' Frank said. 'You'll have to park on the pavement.'

She bumped up onto the kerb and came to a halt on the gnarly roots of a tree that had broken through the paving.

'We'll have to walk.' Frank pointed to an overgrown hedge. 'They've gone up that lane.'

Laura could see there was a gap in the hedge with an inconspicuous stony track leading away.

As they got out Frank put his finger to his lips. They closed their respective doors with a gentle push and click.

Turning down between the thick greenery, it felt as if they were back in open countryside. The street lighting no longer illuminated the scene and the sky was dark.

'I can hardly see,' Laura whispered.

'Grab hold of the back of my coat,' Frank said.

She grasped the vent of his tweed jacket with one hand. This time at least she was wearing her old pair of trainers, but still she kept slipping on the grassy tufts that lined the middle of the track. She followed him as the track narrowed. At one point a low branch to one side whipped her face. She turned to wipe her eyes and saw the glow of the lights of Cheltenham behind them.

Just as she was feeling they were heading somewhere too remote for her liking, a light came on in front of them. Frank stopped short. Laura bumped into the back of him. She saw a gateway and then the side of a small farmhouse from where the light was casting shadows on a yard surrounded on two sides by outbuildings.

They heard a door slam. The light went out.

'We'll go round the side,' Frank said.

Laura followed him blindly a few yards further up the track before he turned off to one side into a field. The terrain became even rougher. She kept stumbling forward, having to put her other hand on his shoulder to stop herself from falling.

At last, he came to a stop.

'Listen,' he said.

Laura heard a sort of short high-pitched cough. As soon as it began it stopped abruptly

'Hear that?' Frank whispered.

They stood stock-still.

It happened again. It was as if something was trying to clear its throat but couldn't.

'What is it?' Laura asked.

'A digital bark controller. My neighbour had one fitted to quieten her neighbour's three Alsatians.'

Laura heard the sound again. Now she knew what it was, it made sense. She listened as another nascent bark fell away into pitiful silence.

'Ultrasonic. Does their heads in, according to my neighbour.' Frank said.

Does their heads in? Laura had always assumed Frank's street was a quiet genteel area.

'Now,' he said. 'I suggest you stay here while I see what's in those sheds.'

'But…'

'Better this way, Ronnie would agree,' he said and disappeared through an open gateway.

Cold and tired, Laura sat down on the damp ground, resting her head against the gatepost. Her heart was beating fast. Why hadn't she gone with him? For a time she stared into the darkness, straining for noises to indicate his whereabouts, but the cold was making her drowsy. She rubbed her hands together, blew on them. Her eyelids felt so heavy, as if an invisible spider was weaving strands of web in her eyelashes.

I'm not letting him go without me again, she thought.

Laura heard him call her name.

'Come on,' Frank said. 'We must go.'
Something in his tone brought her out in a cold sweat. As she pulled herself up and grabbed his jacket, she thought she heard voices. He set off at a brisk pace, almost too fast for her to keep up.

'Are we being followed?' she managed to ask between breaths.

'I'm not sure, but I've seen enough,' he said.

It began to rain. Her feet were slipping as she stumbled onto the track behind him. Her ankles hurt. She was getting out of breath. The track seemed to go on forever.

Finally, they came to the opening in the hedge. They rounded the corner and Laura felt the safety of tarmac beneath her feet.

As she let go of his jacket, Frank turned to her and held out his hand. 'Car keys,' he ordered.

Under any other circumstances his terse command would have been unacceptable, and she would have refused, but now she felt too tired to protest.

Frank held the door open for her. She slumped into the passenger seat and was still putting on her seatbelt when he started up the engine. He yanked at the steering wheel, lurching off the pavement. For the next few minutes Laura gripped the sides of the seat in silence. The car swung at speed round street corners as Frank negotiated his way out of the suburbs.

By the time they reached the main road she was feeling queasy and was thankful for the route he now took. The Roman road was empty and straight.

'Are you going to tell me what happened?' she asked, as he slowed to seventy up a steep hill.

'Stables and sheds full of 'em. No idea how many. Absolute disgrace,' he said. 'Fancy treating God's creatures like that? I can only be thankful you didn't come with me.'

He was right. She would have demanded to let them out.

'Then someone came out of the house; maybe they were checking on them, I can't be sure, but they could've been after me so I legged it.

'I don't suppose…'

'No way of telling if Parker was amongst them, I'm afraid.' Frank's jaw was set firm as he concentrated on the road.

Of course he couldn't possibly know. Why hadn't she gone with him? Laura saw the clock on the dashboard. It was half past three. They could hardly go back now.

'What kept you so long?' she asked.

'I had to get round the side of the house to avoid the lights coming on. Then I saw them through a window.'

'The boys, you mean?'

'Them and another man; it was definitely to do with drugs.'

'How do you know?' she asked.

'Ronnie's crash course; I think the boys must be supplying the man with stolen dogs to get their drugs.

We'll go to the police station first thing in the morning. Explain to Inspector Sandfield. He'll have to act.'

'We don't need him. Can't we go now?'

'It's not open until nine. I'll collect you at a quarter to. But I shouldn't worry, I'm sure they were getting stuck in for what Ronnie termed, 'a session'. If the police move fast enough the boys might still be there. They'll be able to arrest the lot of them.'

There was no alternative. If Parker was there the police would find him, but the wait was almost too painful to bear.

Chapter 23

It was with some relief that when Laura and Frank arrived at Woldham Police station shortly after it opened the next morning, they found Phil Sandfield was out. The memory of their last encounter with him at the travellers' camp still rankled.

After a short wait they were ushered in to the office of his second in command, Lizzie Bishop. She got up from her desk and greeted Laura warmly.

'I haven't seen you for ages… not since…' She smiled at Laura. It had been on the occasion of the WPC escorting Laura to Woldham hospital's psychiatric unit when Laura was erroneously sectioned for a short period.

'Phil can be overly cautious at times,' Lizzie said. 'Still all in the past now.' She smiled, clapped her hands together and took on a more serious tone. 'So, I gather you have information on some stolen dogs? I heard about your loss Lady Boxford; d'you think he could be among them?'

'Parker? That's what I'm praying for.'

'Of course, Parker, bless him.'

Laura couldn't believe she was hearing such a positive response. 'But this is much bigger than just him,' she said. 'There are a lot of dogs involved.' She wondered why she hadn't come to Lizzie in the first place. 'My friend Canon Frank Holliday and I...' she gestured in his direction '...Late last night, we were following our own enquiries when we happened by chance to come across the place where they are being kept,' she continued.

'I took the opportunity of drawing a map.' Frank handed a rough drawing he had made to Lizzie.

'Excellent recall if I may say so,' she said, studying it. 'I'm very grateful to you. It confirms some suspicions my friends over at Cheltenham have had for a few weeks now. If you don't mind, I'll get on to them right away.' She picked up the phone on the desk. 'I'll get word to you at Wellworth, as soon as I have something to report.'

It was mid-afternoon the next day when Jayne Harcourt got hold of Laura to tell her that Inspector Sandfield had requested to see her in Jayne's office in an hour and a half.

Laura rang Frank and asked if he could join her.

'It's pushing it,' he said. 'But of course, I'll meet you in the bar.'

She was waiting at a seat by the window that looked out onto the driveway, wondering what it was that kept Frank so busy, when she saw Phil Sandfield arrive. Not wanting to be seen, she hid out of view beside the curtains. When she checked that he was gone, she saw Frank running towards the house.

She met him in the hall. 'He's just arrived,' she said.

They waited while Frank caught his breath then headed for Jayne Harcourt's office.

'Thank you,' she whispered outside the door. 'I just couldn't face him on my own.'

She knocked and heard Jayne call out, 'Come in.'

Jayne was seated at her desk as Phil Sandfield paced around cap in hand, he slapped it against the side of his chunky thigh. 'Ah, there you are Lady Boxford,' he said, giving a curt nod to Frank. He deposited the cap on top of a filing cabinet. 'If you'd like to take a seat.'

Laura looked around. Apart from the one Jayne was sitting on there was only one chair at the desk and that was opposite Jayne's.

'If you wouldn't mind Ms. Harcourt?' The Inspector was making his way round to her side of the desk. Jayne got up.

'There's another,' she said.

'Let me help.' Frank took the spare chair that was positioned against the wall and placed it beside the desk. Then he and Jayne played a sort of game of music-less chairs that ended with them both saying they would stand.

Laura wondered how the Inspector had this effect on people as he took out a small notepad.

They waited in silence for him to make his mind up what he wanted to say.

'Right.' He stuffed the notebook into his breast pocket. 'So, the good news is the Cheltenham team have raided the farm. They've caught the perpetrator and there are at least thirty canines now in custody with the RSPCA awaiting identification. We're almost certain they're all stolen.'

'That's marvelous news,' Frank said.

'Wonderful.' Jayne clapped her hands together.

Laura was on the edge of her seat. 'Can we go over there?'

The Inspector swung his gaze over the three of them. 'Hold on a minute I haven't finished. Here at Woldham we generally take a welcoming approach to any information the public may be able to provide. We are after all, here to serve. But in this instance…' He narrowed his gaze to Laura and then Frank. 'I have to warn you that your interference has very nearly caused a major incident between us here in Woldham and the Cheltenham branch.'

Laura looked at him in disbelief.

'Hang on,' Frank said.

Phil Sandfield raised a finger motioning him to be quiet. 'This particular man was already on their radar, and they were planning imminent intervention.'

'But that's good,' Laura said. 'We've only hastened the process. Hopefully preventing further thefts.' She was longing to find out more. Was Parker one of the dogs now with the RSPCA?

The Inspector put his glasses down on the desk. He rubbed the bridge of his nose between his forefinger and thumb before putting the glasses back on. 'I'm not sure if Ms. Harcourt here is aware of your past, Lady Boxford.' He looked up at Jayne then back to Laura. 'And I don't see any reason why she should be. But let me make this clear. If I find out that you and the Canon here have been interfering with legitimate police matters one more time. Believe me, I won't hesitate to take matters further.'

He got up from behind the desk and headed for the door, stopping briefly in front of Jayne. 'Ms. Harcourt, I'd like your assurance that Lady Boxford will be dissuaded from making any further public nuisance of herself.'

The manageress, her mouth slightly open looked baffled, but agreed.

Before Laura had time to question him, the Inspector continued.

'So now that we all understand one another. I'm afraid to say there were no pugs amongst the dogs that were apprehended. I'll see myself out.'

Laura's face fell. Her hands felt like lead resting in her lap. She stared at a Wellworth Lawns prospectus lying on Jayne's desk, tears dripping down onto its glossy surface.

Frank ran out after the Inspector as Jayne attempted to console Laura. He reappeared some minutes later and they returned to Laura's apartment where he made her some tea. The cup and saucer were from a pretty Coalport set she had. She was in the habit of filling the saucer half full and putting it on the floor for Parker to lap – he loved milky Earl Grey. Her eyes blurred. Why out of all those stolen dogs was Parker not amongst them? It was all so meaningless and unfair.

'I think I managed to wrong foot young Sandfield if that makes you feel any better,' Frank said.

'What do you mean?'

'I asked him if a white poodle was amongst the dogs they'd found. Obviously, he said it was none of my business, but he admitted he didn't know and asked me why. I told him we'd seen two boys arriving with a white poodle and I recognized them as known drug users from Woldham. He asked me how I knew. I spun him a story that it was through my community work with Vicar Rachel, and we had reason to believe they were selling dogs for drugs.'

At last, Vicar Rachel was proving useful. 'What did he say to that?' Laura asked.

'He didn't. I did. I told him I could identify the boys and that I'd be making a statement to the police in Cheltenham if he wasn't prepared to take it further.'

'So, he's got to keep you in the picture?'

'He'll prevaricate I guarantee, but I pointed out the urgency as I said there was a possibility Parker may have gone through their hands already and could still be traced.'

'This is brilliant.'

Buoyed by his success Frank continued. 'We'll have to give him a day or two. We don't want to interfere unnecessarily, especially as he's determined we're trouble-makers, but that's no reason why we can't continue with our own investigations. The link could still be Ludo and Harry Constantine along with Gwendoline Shackleton. We should try and find out independently about the white poodle. I'm not entirely sure how…'

With a lightness of heart, Laura said, 'So you believe me?'

'Why not? One thing I'm beginning to understand is that there are plenty of people out there prepared to steal a dog for any amount of reasons. We'll see if Jervis can get hold of Ronnie; between them they might have some ideas. You see this is far from over, there are still plenty of paths open to us.'

Laura smiled at him as he stirred his tea methodically, not allowing the spoon to touch the sides of the cup.

'Then there's your friend Stan and the Lithuanian travellers. Have you tried his number recently?'

'Oh my goodness, what with all this I forgot to tell you, Alfredo saw the Lithuanian woman outside the kitchens again. Laura said.

'Recently you mean?'

'Yes.' Laura remembered Stan's lie about his brother and the reward being Stan's idea... 'But if they had Parker, why haven't they demanded the ransom money?' she said.

'Perhaps they'd already sold him, but I doubt it was for more than the reward.' Frank looked at her, one eyebrow raised. 'Or maybe they're trying to get him back?'

'Stan must know something.' Laura tried his number, but still there was no reply. Where was he?

Chapter 24

Nearing the end of a weekend spent fruitlessly searching for the travellers, Frank suggested on Sunday afternoon that Laura call her grand-daughter Victoria and ask to use the drone again.

Now on Monday morning, as Laura paced back and forth outside the main entrance, she heard Mimi call her name.

'Is pilot. Not Mr. Robin. Friend of him in same drone club. He coming kitchen way. He waiting now at reception desk,' she said.

Laura described the vans to the new pilot. She suggested accompanying him, but he said it wasn't necessary and he'd be back in a couple of hours.

Laura whiled away some of the time having coffee with Venetia in the lounge before returning upstairs to try Stan's number again.

When, yet again, he didn't answer, she decided to call the kennels thinking they might know where he was. It was the same huntsman that she had talked to previously who answered.

'We've been trying to find him ourselves,' he said. 'Problem with an urban fox in Woldham; seems it's run out of baby nappies and turned to eating a flock of domestic chickens that are being kept in a back garden due to avian flu. It's good PR for the hunt if we're seen to get rid of vermin for the public. I mean in a humane way of course. Re-homing; re-wilding all that wokery pokery. I'm afraid the late Sir Tony would have turned in his grave. But then where's Stan when we need him? Only shooting doves in Argentina, as you do.'

'How did you find that out?'

'My young whipper-in said texting him was the answer. Don't know why I didn't think of it myself, but there you go, thick as a plank when it comes to technology I am. Anyway, he's on his way back now. Said he'd see me tomorrow. So, I'm afraid I'm first on his list.'

That was Stan's story, was it? Laura wondered whether to believe it. She resolved to get Jervis to teach her how to text. She was about to ring him when Mimi called.

'Pilot is back,' she said. 'He here in reception for you.'

The lift was on the floor above so Laura took the stairs. She found him waiting by the front door.

'That was easy,' he said. 'Well, quite easy. They've hidden the vans in a barn, but the little girl gave them away; must have heard the drone. Lucky you told me about her. You should get over there as soon as you can if you think they're likely to be on the move.'

From his description Laura knew exactly where they were. It was as quick to walk, so she wasted no time in setting off for the deserted farmyard. She remembered the low swoop of the barn owl they had disturbed as the helicopter flew overhead and then the search she and Frank had made on the ground. The ultimate sadness of the place. The feeling of desperation she had felt. All the same it was strange that a place like that could still exist in an area of such wealth. Jervis had found out who owned it and was told the land was contract farmed. It was only a matter of time before the owner put in for planning permission.

Now Laura took the most direct approach. She headed into the open country at the back of Wellworth Lawns, the wind blowing her hair. Her route involved some trespassing, but as long as she kept to the hedgerows, she was confident of not getting into trouble.

She walked up a gentle incline, passed round a ploughed field, then crossed through a wood. It was warm and quiet amongst the trees, but she was pleased at the feel of the breeze gusting on her face as she came out the other side. How Parker would have loved gallivanting about with her.

Stopping to look down across a field of empty pasture, she could see a narrow plume of smoke wafting thinly in the air from the barns below. Was this the answer to her prayers? Could she finally be getting nearer to finding him?

She climbed a gate, tramped through the tussocky grass and met the track that led to the farmyard. Ahead was the half open door of the main barn. Then, as she rounded the corner into the courtyard, she saw the bonnet of one of the vans.

The man was sawing wood next to a small fire. He didn't see her until the dog barked.

'Truda,' he shouted, as the dog bounded up to Laura and began licking her outstretched hand. Laura noticed Truda's coat was matted and scurfy. She could see the bones of the dog's spine.

'Hello,' she called out.

The man put down his saw. 'I remember you. You're the lady with the missing pug dog,' he said.

'That's right. My name's Laura by the way. I don't live far from here.'

'Tomas.' He held out his hand. 'So, you haven't found it?'

'I'm offering a reward now.' She watched him. His face was gaunter than she remembered. 'A thousand pounds.'

His expression gave nothing away, although he conceded it was a lot of money.

'How's your business going?' Laura wondered if it was even legal for him to work.

'My wife Eva and my daughter are out in the other van trying to sell from the side of the road.'

Eva. So that was her name. The woman Alfredo had seen.

'It is very difficult since we are no longer having the main outlet,' he continued. 'Eva, her driving is very bad, but her English is worse. It's a big worry for me.' He laughed. 'Then Camilla sold a chair for three pounds because the man gave her a guinea pig.'

'She must have loved that,' Laura said.

'Truda ate it.'

'Oh dear.' Laura looked at the dog lying asleep in front of the fire. 'So where was your main outlet?' she asked.

'My brother. Never trust your family.'

'He's let you down?'

Tomas turned his head and spat.

'That's bad.' Laura crossed her arms and took a step nearer the fire. 'What will you do?'

'We can't stay here much longer. I'm hoping we can sell the stuff we've got then maybe take something back to Lithuania.'

'Like what?'

'Maybe Miele washing machine; Dyson hoover? I could sell those things… but…' He raised his shoulders and let them fall, kicking at the fire ash with the toe of his leather boot. 'I don't know.'

'I remember you said you could get me a pug if I wanted. I'd pay well, as much as the reward.' Laura watched out of the corner of her eye as he weighed up the offer. His thin lips remained motionless, but she could see a tic below his cheekbone as he clenched his jaw and stared into the middle distance. After what seemed an age he said, 'I will try and get one for you.'

'You made it sound as if it was easy last time I saw you.'

He gave her a sharp look. 'Nothing is easy right now, but maybe I know someone.'

Laura set off back to Wellworth Lawns with a spring in her stride. She would meet Tomas again in two days. Perhaps he hadn't known there was a reward. Why should he if he wasn't speaking to his brother Stan? So, did he know where Parker was? Was he going to actually get him? Laura found she hardly dare think what might be possible. It was selfish she knew, but whatever circumstances Tomas and his family found themselves need not concern her even if their misfortunes were a way for her to be reunited with Parker.

But what if he found her another pug? Would she take it? A feeling of treacherous joy at the idea of having a dog, any dog, almost overcame her before she dismissed it. Replace Parker? It was out of the question.

Back in her apartment she hunted in the kitchen cupboard for something to eat. There was nothing but a sachet of tomato soup.

She was stirring the mug when she heard her mobile ringtone. Rummaging in her bag, she found it just before it went to answerphone.

'Sorry it's taken me so long to get back to you,' Stan Kaminski said.

Was she prepared for this? Keeping it light, she asked him if he'd had a good trip.

'Fantastic,' he said. 'But it was mainly business. A cousin of mine introduced me to a new client.'

'A cousin?'

'Yes.'

'Who knows about guns?' It was hard to hold her nerve.

'How did you know? The Argentines are crazy for English shot guns. But what about you; did you find your dog?'

'I'm afraid not. I did as you suggested and put out a reward, but as yet there's been nothing.'

'There could still be time, you never know.'

'But talking of this cousin of yours, I've just met another of your relatives.'

'What do you mean?'

'Your brother, Tomas.'

'Oh God, they're back.'

Laura wished she could see his expression. 'Why did you lie to me about him?'

At the end of the line Stan paused. 'How can I say this without sounding like I have no heart.' He paused again. 'When my brother said he was coming to England I told him there was no work for him. I'd finished with the furniture business. Then he rings me and says he's nearby. He doesn't know my actual address, but I have told him, there's nothing I can do for him; he must go home.'

'He's desperate. They've got no money.' Laura thought of the little girl in her thin cotton dress. 'Do you think he would do anything criminal?' She wondered if she had gone too far.

'No of course not; he's a carpenter.' Where did you see them?' There was urgency in his voice.

'I was out walking.' She realized she was risking her plan if she told him.

'Where?'

'I'd taken the car. I expect they've moved on by now. They were packing up when I left.'

'But where?'

Laura gave him the name of a wood the other side of Woldham.

She felt guilty when he thanked her. He'd said his brother wasn't dishonest, but she hadn't told him about Tomas's wife Eva being seen at the back of the kitchens at Wellworth Lawns by Alfredo. He had no idea how precarious their situation was or what it could lead to, but he mustn't know where they were, not while there was hope that they knew something about Parker's whereabouts.

Chapter 25

'Where have you been?' Frank said. 'I've been trying to get hold of you. Have you listened to your messages?'

'I'm sorry. It took longer than expected.'

'With the drone?'

'Yes,' she said, happy that he was on the end of the line, unable to see her face as she lied. 'When I got in, I had some disgusting soup I found in the cupboard. Then I fell asleep and when I woke up it was too late to call you.'

'I was up…'

She cut him short. 'But now I'm feeling right as rain. Shall we go for a walk later? I can tell you all about it.'

Laura didn't want to tell Frank all about it. He might question her rationale, and he would certainly not agree to her going alone. It was easier to keep him in the dark; it was only for two days after all. If Tomas did have Parker when she met him as arranged then it would all be different, but if he didn't, nobody need ever know what she'd been up to.

'That sounds a good idea,' Frank said. 'Let's go through the village. We might call by at The Rectory. See how Ms. Shackleton's getting on.'

'We could drop in on Strudel and Jervis on our way,' Laura suggested. She was aware that she had not contacted them either. 'I wonder if they've been in touch with Ronnie recently?'

Frank said he'd already talked to them. There had been no word. 'But Inspector Sandfield left me a message,' he continued. 'No poodle was found during the Cheltenham raid.'

'Oh.'

'You don't seem very interested,' Frank said.

'Yes, I am. No really. Let's go.'

It was a dank overcast afternoon and by the time they had reached the bottom of the drive Laura could feel her feet getting cold.

'Shall we take a short cut up the lane?' She wished she'd taken out her winter boots from the back of the cupboard.

'If you'd like,' Frank said. 'But I think before we go any further you might as well tell me what happened with the drone. I met Mimi at reception. She said you were being most mysterious about it.'

Laura pretended to get something from her pocket. The only thing she could feel was a tissue, so she took it out. Frank waited as she blew her nose, his arms folded across the front of his tweed jacket.

'Well, are you going to tell me what happened?'

She put the tissue back in her pocket. 'It wasn't Robin, it was a different pilot,' she said. 'He was very nice, but it didn't come to anything.'

'No?'

'He told me to have a look at those barns, that's all. You know, the ones we went to before.'

'I knew it. You didn't go on your own, did you?'

'Don't worry. There was nothing there anyway.'

'No sign of the travellers?' Frank sighed. 'Disappointing.'

She knew he was thinking her foolhardy, so to change the subject she told him something of her conversation with Stan.

'He made contact. Why didn't you tell me?'

'I am now. He's been abroad.' She was thinking about her deception as they crossed the road. 'It was all above board: a business trip. He's going to try and find them. He said he'd let me know.'

'But do we trust him?' Frank said.' Has something changed?'

'No, but we know where he is now.'

They were about to turn down the narrow lane that led behind The Old Rectory when they heard a voice.

'Come, Prendy!'

Of course, that was its name. Why hadn't Laura remembered earlier? She pulled Frank behind a privet bush on the pathway leading to the nearest cottage. They heard the snap of a branch and from out of the lane Gwendoline Shackleton appeared pulling the white poodle behind her. She marched round the corner in the direction of her own house.

'I'm going to confront her,' Laura whispered.

'Wait.' Frank took her arm. 'Be careful. What are you going to say?'

'I'm going to ask her who Prendy's owner is.' Laura strode out of their hiding place and down the village street. She had almost caught up when she called out, 'excuse me.'

Gwendoline let out a screech as if she'd been bitten on the rump by a piranha.

'I'm sorry,' Laura said. 'I didn't mean to frighten you.'

'Well, you made a pretty good fist of it.' Gwendoline frowned at her. 'You should know better than to approach people from behind like that. What do you want anyway?'

'You remember me…'

'I'm sure I have no idea who you are.'

Frank came up beside her. 'It's Lady Boxford; she had only friendly intentions and a curiosity for your charming companion. Ms. Shackleton, isn't it?' he said.

'Why, yes.' Gwendoline fluttered her lash-less vapid grey eyes at him. 'I do recall we've met before, haven't we?'

There was something almost improper about such coquettishness coming from someone well past the normal age for flirtation and it was making Laura cross.

'D'you mind my asking how long you've had that dog?' she said, pointing at the poodle.

Gwendoline turned to her with a hostile glare. 'I beg your pardon?'

'It's just that I've seen it with someone else. I think it might be…'

'Lady Boxford was most concerned that you might have lost the dog and now by good fortune, it has been restored to you.'

'What are you talking about?'

'I don't suppose you remember, but Lady Boxford has tragically lost her own dear pet pug, and she is most concerned that others should not suffer the same fate. She is alert to any small inconsistencies in…' He was running low on hyperbole. '…the welfare of our canine fidus achates.'

'The faithful friend; now it's coming back to me. A pity I don't know the Latin for proprietorial pug. Still no sign of the poor suicidal creature?'

Laura clenched her fist and wondered what would happen if she threw a punch.

Again Frank came to her rescue. 'Lady Boxford, as you can well imagine, has been distraught.'

'No surprises there.' Gwendoline had begun the eye fluttering again. 'I've said it to countless potential owners, if you can't provide a secure setting, there is no point going into the expensive business of dog ownership. That's why I've got this wretched poodle Prendy back and just when I thought he was emotionally stable.'

'So where has he been?' Laura felt as if she was on the verge of something. Why when one avenue looked like it was leading somewhere, did it take this chance encounter for another route to suddenly look wide open? 'You see I think I've seen Prendy in Woldham,' she said. 'And personally, I would not be happy if I knew my dog was keeping that kind of company.'

'A peculiar observation considering you have no idea of the whereabouts of your own dog. Anyway, I can't be held responsible for what Prendy gets up to when he is not under my professional aegis. He may have been having tea at the Ritz for all I care.' Gwendoline twirled one manly hand in the air like the late Duke of Edinburgh. 'All I know is that I get paid for picking up the pieces.'

'You mean he's come back to you for re-training?' Frank said.

'He didn't fulfill the required level of toileting. So now I am left with the onerous task of getting the little wretch to remember only to piss on tarmac. You'd have thought these people would have thought about it earlier, living in a mansion block flat with only a small balcony and the added confusion of Astroturf.'

'So, who are these owners?' Laura knew she shouldn't have asked.

Gwendoline let forth a barrage of disdainful waffle about client confidentiality.

Frank followed it with a stream of placatory verbiage that Laura listened to with mounting indignation. Then he made excuses for the two of them. As they walked back up the drive, Frank tried to make her see the funny side of it, but for Laura it was too late, and they parted where Frank had left his car.

'It was too humiliating,' Laura said, as she and Venetia sat down at a table in the dining room for dinner.

'Just one course, don't you think?' Venetia took the napkin from the plate in front of her and spread it on her lap. 'So Frank annoyed you because he was getting you out of a spot of bother with the dog psychologist.'

Laura's napkin gave a starched crack as she flapped it open.

'Generally, I'm all for them,' Venetia continued. 'Graeme Hall on Dogs Behaving Badly can work miracles.'

'I coming just one minute,' Mimi said, as she passed them carrying a basket of bread.

'Frank did not get me out of a spot of bother,' Laura said. 'I was perfectly capable of doing that myself. No, it's that he didn't back me up. She's got this dog I was telling you about and I was on the verge of finding out about it when he butted in. It could have been a vital clue to finding Parker.'

'I know how hard this is for you.'

'He acquiesced to her the whole time.'

Venetia picked up the menu. 'I'm sure he meant well. Smoked salmon and scrambled eggs will do me fine.'

'I don't like being treated like a child.' And yet she was behaving like one. Petulant.

Venetia seemed to have lost concentration again.

'Well, it's not exactly that,' Laura continued. 'It's just that sometimes Frank always being right is a bore.'

Venetia was gazing over Laura's left shoulder. 'Hello,' she said.

Laura felt a presence behind her. She turned.

Hovering like as spectre in a shapeless grey linen frock was Lulu Vandermoss.

'I couldn't help overhearing you,' she said, brushing a wisp of hair from her face with one knobbly, white finger. 'In my opinion men are driven by a desire to please but if something gets in their way, they have no qualms about hiding the evidence.'

'Quite right Lulu,' Venetia said. 'What a pretty dress you're wearing.'

Laura turned back to Venetia and frowned at her.

'Oh, and by the way…' Lulu continued.

Laura had to turn back round.

'… I overheard your Frank Holliday talking to Vicar Rachel in church.'

'My goodness,' Laura said. 'What a lot of things you overhear.'

'It must be on account of my quiet demeanour, but as I was saying they were talking about the grieving process. He was asking her if she thought it was an illness or a mental disorder. Very deep thinkers both of them.'

'That's very interesting,' Venetia said.

'It's not, it's preposterous. Grieving; a mental disorder? I've never heard anything so ridiculous.' Laura hated the idea of Frank discussing her situation behind her back.

'Are you staying for supper?' Venetia asked. 'Would you like to join us? Laura and I are often having philosophical discussions, aren't we? I do love watching Sherlock.'

'I'm afraid I'm not feeling up to it,' Lulu said. 'I was in two minds as to whether I was well enough to eat. And now I'm sure I feel far too sick. In fact, I must go and lie down.'

'Well, goodnight.' Venetia shook her head as Lulu wafted out of the room. 'Poor dear, I fear she's mentally disordered.'

'What are you talking about?' The evening was in danger of becoming tiresome.

'Grief,' Venetia said. 'She's grieving on account of her best friend being murdered. Well, it was her wife as a matter of fact. I don't think I told you that bit.'

Laura didn't like to say that she already knew, but a needle of guilt pricked her as she remembered how dismissive she had been of Venetia previously. She was about to ask her what else she knew of Lulu's story when Mimi returned to take their order and after that Venetia became waylaid by tales of cookery shows she had been watching.

Laura was only half attending to her account of the finals of 'Masterchef' as they finished their scrambled eggs when Mimi ran over to their table.

'Ladyship,' she gasped. 'Alfredo, he want you… right now I thinking?'

It was unlike Mimi to be so insistent.

'You go,' Venetia said. 'Come up and find me later, won't you?'

Laura followed Mimi through the swing doors at the other end of the dining room. They rushed down the corridor passing a waiter carrying a tray of food.

In the kitchen there was a general air of steaming chaos. People shouted as they prepared the orders. Standing over a gas ring Alfredo stood shaking a pan of flaming sauce.

Mimi called to him.

'Kids,' he shouted. 'Finish this off for me, one of you, I must speak with Lady Boxford.'

A young man ran over and took the pan.

'Come with me,' Alfredo called to Laura, throwing his hat onto a counter as he passed.

She followed him out to a small shelf-lined pantry filled with neatly stacked jars and cans. He took something out of his pocket and held it out to her.

There, nestling in the palm of his calloused hand was the silver charm from Parker's collar.

Chapter 26

Laura lay awake with the pug shaped amulet clasped to her chest. She felt the rough edge of the open link that would have attached to the D ring on Parker's collar. It must have caught on something and pulled open. Then fallen and that's where Alfredo had found it.

He had gone out to dispose of some food waste from dinner and had seen the glint of something in the corner by the drain. He said the area was cleaned each week after the bins were wheeled out ready for collection. It could so easily have been swept away by the pressure washer. Instead had come to rest in a cranny.

What did this mean for Parker? Laura opened her hand. Surely the silver should have tarnished by now, but it was as if someone had only recently polished it. Just like she would do after Parker's weekly shampoo.

The glint of shiny metal.

It had to be Tomas's wife Eva. How else could it have ended up at the dustbins? Alfredo had described the woman again. But what was her reason to be near the bins?

Laura held the charm tight. She remembered the Lithuanian hound. It had appeared to be in such poor condition.

Could it be that they were looking for food for their dog… or even for themselves? She remembered that Tomas had said how difficult things were as he had tightened his leather belt. She had thought then how thin his waist seemed by comparison to his broad shoulders. It made sense. They were starving and the Wellworth Lawns bins were a ready supply of food. For a moment Laura felt disgust at the idea of all that waste.

Gradually her vague theories fell into place. They knew about the bins when they had stolen Parker. Frank was right, they had sold him, but they had no idea about the reward until Laura told Tomas. But Tomas knew where Parker was. He had to buy him back.

Laura began to relax. They had sold him, but Eva had kept the charm for a trinket to add to her necklaces. Somehow it had fallen off when she was scavenging.

Laura was so close. She was meeting Tomas at six – All she had to do was get through the next day and then she would see Parker again. She sighed and closed her eyes.

When she awoke it was seven forty-five in the morning. She felt for the charm, sat up in a panic. Where was it? She scrabbled around amongst the bedclothes and found it under her pillow. Getting out of bed, she went to the kitchen where she found a pair of scissors. Holding the open link on the charm between the blades she pressed it closed before returning to the dressing table in her bedroom. In the drawer where she kept her jewellery, she opened the leather box and rummaged round until she found the gold chain with her St Christopher on it. She added the silver pug. She was putting it round her neck when she heard a knock on the door and Mimi brought her tray in.

'Look,' Laura said, showing her the necklace.

'Oh Ladyship, I hoping this is good news and we are finding Parker soon. Some people downstairs saying nasty things but I not believing them.' She began pouring the coffee.

'What are they saying?'

Mimi put the pot down and started playing with her ponytail.

'Tell me.'

'Well, they saying this is showing…'

'Showing what?'

'They saying Parker he must be dead and someone putting him in the bin.' Mimi sat down in a heap and began to cry.

'That's nonsense,' Laura said. 'I've no doubt that Parker is alive. In fact, I've a good idea I'm going to be seeing him later today.'

The maid looked at her in amazement.

'But you must keep it quiet. Can you promise?'

Mimi nodded with enthusiasm as she wiped her eyes with her sleeve. She ran back to the tray. 'I putting milk in now?'

'I'll do it,' Laura said. 'You must get on. I wouldn't want you to be running late on my account.'

What gossips people were; it was out of the question that Parker could be dead. Dead? She felt a moment of unease. It couldn't be…No, the real question was how she was going to keep her rendezvous that evening a secret from Frank, Strudel and Jervis.

As it turned out, the little lies she had concocted in her head were unnecessary. Strudel rang to say they had heard about Alfredo's discovery. She was delighted of course but seemed uninterested in the significance of its whereabouts.

'Ronnie has returned,' she said. 'You must come over immediately; he has an announcement of an important nature. Jervis is calling Frank.'

As Laura made her way to Mulberry Close, she wondered what this revelation could be, but even when they had all gathered round the kitchen table, she was more concerned with biding her time until her meeting with Tomas.

'Ronnie has been preoccupied with his own business,' Strudel said. 'But has found time to visit us once more and brings news of further research.'

'Into the affairs of our friend Crawford Tuthill, ex-plastic surgeon.' Jervis waved his tea mug in mock salutation in Ronnie's direction.

Ronnie reciprocated with his own mug. 'Good to be back.' He put the mug down and leant forward at the table. 'So, I happened to have some contacts in the Spanish press. I took the opportunity of getting in touch with them while I was awaiting… err… further developments of my own.'

'I don't think we need go into that,' Jervis said.

'Would I?' Ronnie held his hands up. 'So, to continue, we know Crawford ran a practice in Porto Romano. And that Miss Vandermoss was, when I met her, living a couple of kilometres down the road mourning her wife's death. I'd remembered the wife's name, so I decided to call my mate at The Marbella Herald on the off chance. And there it was. Bingo.'

'What was Bingo?' Frank asked.

'I'm getting to it. It turns out there'd been an investigation by the Spanish police into Crawford Tuthill for malpractice. A woman he was treating had died after…'Ronnie hesitated. 'I don't like to say this in front of the ladies…'

'We're all grown ups here.' Jervis urged him to get a move on.

'If you're sure,' Ronnie said. 'She was having her rear raised. It was after a Brazilian butt lift.'

Venetia had told Laura about BBLs, but she noticed Frank wince.

'What was the result of the investigation?' he asked.

'The police dropped the case due to lack of evidence. But it's shortly after this that the practice closes and Crawford Tuthill retires, not as you might think staying put on the Costa del Sol but legging it back to grey old Blighty.'

'Get to the point Ronnie,' Jervis said. 'Tell them who the woman was.'

Ronnie rubbed his hands together. 'It was Lulu Vandermoss's wife.'

Laura sat up. 'Having the BBL?'

'You got it.' Ronnie sat back and folded his arms.

'That is certainly strange,' Frank said.

'Many women are wanting to improve the contours of their bodies,' Strudel huffed.

'I mean strange it's Lulu's wife and Lulu happens to be here now,' Frank said. 'Tuthill can't possibly know this can he?'

'Now you're getting it.' Ronnie took a slug of coffee.

'Curious don't you think,' Jervis said. 'But what makes it crucial to the present is that Ronnie has discovered that due to new evidence the Spanish police have reopened the murder investigation into Crawford Tuthill. If it comes to trial and Crawford is found guilty, you know what that means?' He looked at Laura.

'He'd have died of old age before they managed to extradite him,' she said.

'That's as maybe, but on the other hand he could be found guilty in absentia and you can't stay at Wellworth Lawns with a criminal record. It might account for what he said to Strudel about you, Laura.'

'You mean he sees me as having some sort of control here? I know he doesn't like me, but he must realise I don't have anything to do with the running of Wellworth Lawns. No one could possibly think that.'

'Ah but they see you with Victoria and Vince.' Jervis waved his arm in the direction of the window through which the roofs of Wellworth Lawns could be seen. 'I'm not saying that's got anything to do with the terms and conditions of the place, but I'm afraid it does smack of influence.'

'Jealousy,' Strudel said. 'His envy drove him to a terrible act… and now the tag from Parker's collar. Oh Laura, I am most afraid for you.'

'There's really no need. This whole Lulu business is starting to make sense. It's a misguided vendetta. Mimi told me Lulu pretty much said to her that Crawford killed Parker and threw his body in the bin. She's saying that's how the charm from his collar ended up there.'

'But that is horrible,' Strudel said.

'It's a lot of rubbish. Lulu's plainly trying to darken Crawford's name in any way she can.' Laura couldn't admit to the vision she had had of Parker's limp body being tossed in with the rubbish. It was too awful to contemplate. 'Crawford's a bully,' she continued. 'And he may be in financial trouble, fearful of this prosecution, aggrieved at my comfortable position, but that's never a good enough reason to kill an innocent dog.'

'Proof would be almost impossible to come by,' Frank said.

'I suppose you're right. We may never know.' Jervis got up from the table and headed for the sink. He gazed out of the window in the direction of the Tuthill's bungalow.

'He's not dead,' Laura almost shouted the words.

'And on that note,' Ronnie said. 'I suppose we can put Tuthill on a back burner until we find further evidence, however in the meantime there's something else.'

'What else?' Time was ticking by, and Laura was impatient to get on.

'I had another encounter at Woldham station,' Ronnie said. 'Well, I didn't meet them in the flesh as such. It was more from a distance. I'd seen Harry Constantine's picture on his website, so I knew what he looked like and from Laura's description it was definitely the Shackleton woman.'

'They were together?' Frank took Laura's hand.

Ronnie nodded. 'Much as I hate to say it, you should go to the police. She was handing over a dog to him. A white poodle.'

Chapter 27

After all the distraction of Crawford Tuthill and Lulu Vandermoss, Laura had listened to Ronnie make the case for involving the police in the matter of Harry Constantine with a certain amount of impatience. Jervis said it was now their best chance of finding Parker and Frank had wanted to go with her then and there.

'Alright,' she said. 'But I think it would be best if I went alone.'

In all probability it was only what she had suspected. Gwendoline Shackleton and Harry Constantine were running some kind of business selling pets to unsuspecting and possibly vulnerable elderly clients. She had been misguided in thinking Ludo and his druggy friends had something to do with it; he had simply been carting the dog round with him for his father as it was shunted between prospective owners. It was despicable but bore no tangible relation to her own situation with Parker, because by far the most likely explanation for his disappearance was that he had been taken by Tomas and that was why Eva had the charm.

She made an excuse and left them sitting round the table as she hurried back to Wellworth Lawns. There was still the afternoon to get through, but she wasn't going to spend it at the police station. Of course, she would go at some point, but she hadn't specified when. Perhaps tomorrow? She'd come clean with Frank later on.

She sat down at her desk and did some paperwork. She wrote a letter to an old friend suffering from arachnophobia in a thatched cottage in Somerset recommending conkers or a specialist bug vacuum, but all the time she was thinking about her meeting with Tomas.

As the time drew nearer, Laura hardly dare think that soon she might have Parker with her. It was hard to contemplate his dear, funny face close to hers after so many days. She pondered walking to the farmyard. It would take up more time and she'd have liked the fresh air, but the light was already fading.

She started to get ready. As she located her handbag, a panicked thought occurred to her. How could she have allowed this oversight? How was she going to pay? Tomas would want money either way. If, heaven forbid, it wasn't Parker, she was going to take the pug he brought. That was the time to go to the police. And if it was Parker as she hoped and prayed, then Tomas would get the reward. But he wouldn't want a cheque. Cursing herself for being so stupid, she rummaged in her purse and found sixty pounds.

She checked the time. She should get going. What could she possibly use as some sort of promissory note?

Instinctively, she turned the Navajo bracelet, rubbing the warm smooth metal in her fingers. She went to the wall safe in her bedroom, opened it and took out the sparkling diamond and platinum ring her first husband Tony had given her on the occasion of their engagement. It had recently been valued. She remembered being a little underwhelmed by the figure the insurance broker had suggested, but they'd been so young, and Tony was always strapped for cash. It was worth marginally more than the reward. She added the ring to the chain around her neck and stuffed it down the neck of her jumper.

Driving through the gloaming she was filled with hope. The moon was coming up and filled the sky with a bluish grey light that lit up the rolling hills. She wound down the window and took in deep breaths, filling her nostrils with the early evening air.

So elated was she that she missed the turning and had to back up before heading down the track. She parked; looked around. Barns, sheds and outbuildings in remote locations; never again would she have to visit these places.

She opened the door and got out. There was no smell or sight of wood smoke. Turning on her torch, she skirted the buildings, but as she rounded the corner into the yard there was still no sign of either van. She called out wondering if Tomas had changed their place of concealment and come on foot. There was no answer, so she went into the main barn and sat down on the side of an old metal cattle feeder.

She waited. What else could she do? Tomas was now half an hour late. How stupid of her to think that he would respect punctuality. She wondered how long he would be.

More time passed. When she looked at her watch again it was five past seven.

She needed to make a decision. Perhaps something had happened to them? If only she had brought a pen and paper, she could have left a note. She was so sure he would be there, but now she began to doubt her reasons for believing in his integrity.

It was soul destroying, but there was nothing for it but to leave. She returned to her car, her whole body leaden with the wasted effort. She thought about the silver charm. Tomas couldn't know where Alfredo had found it. No, there was some other reason why he hadn't shown up.

A dog fox howled, echoing her thoughts. She started the engine. The only answer was to find Stan. She would have to tell him. It was her only option. He sounded like he wanted to find his brother and family as much as she did. They didn't appear to go far when they moved and with his knowledge of the locality, he was bound to find them sooner or later.

It was nearly eight by the time she got back upstairs and for one of the few times in her life Laura felt like having a drink with the sole intention of getting drunk. As she took the ring off the chain and put it back in the safe, she wondered what was best for drowning one's sorrows, a massive gin and tonic or a triple brandy?

In the end she knew it wouldn't change anything. It was too late to go down to supper and anyway she couldn't have faced the dining room even though she knew Venetia would be there. She couldn't even face having something sent up, so she decided on a bowl of cereal, milk being about the only fresh commodity she kept in her fridge.

Sitting with the bowl on a tray on her lap, she flicked through the TV channels. An old black and white western was far enough removed from reality for her to have a small chance of being able to concentrate on the storyline.

It wasn't the case and in a short space of time she realized she hadn't a clue what was going on. As she flicked through the TV guide, she heard her mobile ringing in her bag. She thought of ignoring it, not because she might catch up with the plot, but because she couldn't think of a single person, she could face speaking to. I suppose I should, she thought. It might be Victoria. She turned down the volume and picked it up.

'They're with me,' Stan said.

Someone told him they had seen a woman and a young girl trying to sell furniture outside Woldham on the London Road and he'd gone out searching for them.

'I found Eva and Camilla parked in a layby. I made them take me back to the farm where they've been camping,' Stan said. 'The place you were meant to meet Tomas.'

'That was a wasted journey.' Laura was glad she hadn't resorted to alcohol and was in command of her faculties.

'I'm sorry,' Stan said. 'Tomas only just told me. I thought it was best to get them out as soon as possible. They're in a bad way. I'm going to have to sort the whole mess out. Eva's in no fit state to drive a van back to Lithuania. I'll have to sell one of the vans and lend them the money in the meantime.'

'But what about the dog he promised me? He said he could get me a pug. That's why I was meeting him.'

'He's told me about that,' Stan said. 'I don't know what he was thinking. He could no more find you a pug than he could make a Chippendale chair.'

'So, what about Parker's dog tag?'

Stan said he didn't know what she was talking about.

They were lying, Laura was sure.

'Just let me talk to them before they go. I'll come over first thing tomorrow,' she said. 'I'm sure Eva knows something she's not telling you.'

Chapter 28

Even after filling up with petrol on her way into Woldham, Laura was still early. She parked in the garage and watched the numbers come up on her mobile as first Strudel then Frank, and then Venetia tried to call her. She knew they'd have already tried her landline, but she ignored them and set off again.

Stan had given her his address in spite of the fact that she already knew where he lived. She turned into the street expecting to see the travellers' vans, but there was no sign of them. In a panic that she was already too late, and they had already gone, she squeezed her car in at an angle behind Stan's Maserati. At least that was here. She leapt out and ran up the path. As she pressed the doorbell she could hear barking.

To her relief, the little girl, Camilla, let her in. The Lithuanian hound tried to barge past her through the open door.

'Truda,' Stan shouted, running up behind it. He grabbed the collar, pulling the dog to one side.

Laura followed him through the hallway. He opened a door to one side and pushed the dog in before continuing down the passage.

It was one of those town houses that are deceptively large inside. The polished floors were of reclaimed oak. Laura wondered if the planks had come from Lithuania as she walked on into the living room. Nearest to the door the sitting area consisted of an L shaped grey velvet settee on which Stan's two dogs were stretched out. Camilla skipped in and sat down beside them, putting her arms round Baloo who raised his head to check that Truda wasn't present before relaxing back, his interest in Laura minimal. A large chrome standard lamp arced over them, illuminating the glass coffee table on which lay countless piles of books and magazines, that Laura could see were of an artistic nature. The walls were bare apart from a set of four large prints of hunting scenes by Snaffles. Laura wondered if they were originals.

At the far end was a modern kitchen. The back wall was almost entirely glass, with doors leading outside onto a paved area with garden furniture. Tomas and Eva were sitting on two of a set of four chrome bar stools that stood around an island unit on which a vase of lilies stood. They were eating hunks of baguette, the crumbs spilling onto the polished cement surface.

Seeing Laura, Tomas dropped the bread. He slid off the chair, putting his hands together as in prayer. He appeared out of place in the urban setting, pale and lank despite his outdoor life. Eva, still perched on the bar stool, also seemed older than Laura remembered, smaller too and altogether uncomfortable.

Tomas took a few steps forward. 'I am so sorry,' he said. 'I have let you down. Please forgive me. I have tried to find your dog, believe me.'

'So, you knew where Parker was?'

'Well, a dog like him I had seen; I was hoping this I could do for you, but I had no luck.' Tomas held out a hand in his brother's direction. 'And then Stan came, and we went with him.' He hung his head.

'And now we've had proper food,' Camilla chipped in from where she was now sprawled out next to Baloo.

'What can I say?' Stan threw up his arms. 'My brother is ashamed, believe me.'

'More to the point what can you do?' Laura said. It was hard to know how to conduct the conversation standing in the middle of the room. She decided to sit on one of the bar stools. It was Eva she really wanted to speak to.

Ignoring the one Tomas had vacated, she pulled out another on the opposite side of the island. She realized she was going to have to hitch up her skirt to climb onto it. She had deliberated on her outfit for some time before choosing her Cameron Hunting Tartan shift dress. It was elegant and normally gave her confidence when she was wearing it. Now it was hampering her. 'I'm never much good with these things,' she said, smiling at Eva as she balanced herself on the stool.

Eva smiled back; her cheeks full of bread. She put her hand over her mouth and nodded her head from side to side.

Straightening her skirt, Laura gave an encouraging laugh. 'So, Eva.' She put her hand down her shirt and pulled out the chain round her neck. 'I think you probably recognize this.'

It was like watching a smoker being asked by the doctor how many a day they smoked. The thought of the lie was overtaken as a million tiny blood vessels dilated on Eva's face giving the game away, but before she had time to reply Camilla came bouncing up.

'Let me see,' she said.

Laura took off the chain and showed her the silver pug.

'Oh Mama, the lady has found it!'

In a nervous reaction, Eva's hand reached for the gold chains round her own neck.

Laura turned to Stan. 'She knows where Parker is. This was on his collar, and it was found behind the kitchen rubbish bins at Wellworth Lawns two days ago. Alfredo the chef has seen Eva there on more than one occasion. Ask her how she can explain that.'

Stan walked over to the island. He leant across it, his face close to Eva's. 'What does this mean?'

'I don't understand.' Tears were forming in the corner of her eyes.

Laura recalled Alfredo telling her about the conversation he'd had with the woman when she was pretending to be from the council. 'I think you understand more than you're letting on,' she said.

Eva shook her head from side to side.

'Stop this,' Stan shouted.

Laura was aware of the little girl between them. She could see Camilla was sensing something wasn't right.

'Stan,' she said. 'You need to make them understand that I will go to any lengths to find my dog. I'm sure Camilla would feel the same if Truda were to go missing.'

'Oh please,' Camilla begged.

'We don't know anything about your dog, I swear,' Tomas said.

Ignoring him, Laura thrust the charm in front of Eva. ''But you've seen this before. Camilla said as much, and you also know where it came from, my dog Parker's collar. I beg you, tell me where he is.'

Eva sat in silence, her bottom lip quivering.

'Well, the only thing I can do now is call the police,' Laura said. 'Alfredo will testify that it was you he saw outside by the bins.'

Eva didn't move, but Tomas stepped forward. 'Don't do that please.'

'What is this about,' Stan said. 'Was Eva there?'

'Papa?' Camilla's plea drew all of their attention. They stared at her in silence.

After a few moments Eva said, 'We had no food.'

Laura sighed. She had been right all along.

'You mean you've been getting food from the bins at Wellworth Lawns?' Stan seemed genuinely shocked. 'Tomas, is this true?'

Tomas mumbled something and Stan began to speak quickly to his brother in their native language. Tomas hung his head again. Camilla looked from her uncle to her father. She too was starting to cry.

'But wait.' She held her hands in the air. 'Mama never found it there. She never saw the dog. She found it in the town. It was just lying there so she picked it up. She had it round her neck, but then she lost it.' Camilla slumped onto the kitchen surface, her head in her arms. 'We thought it would bring us good luck.'

'Thank you Camilla.' Laura gave her a gentle pat on the shoulder.

The girl lifted her head to one side and blinked at Laura.

'So where in the town did your Mama find it?' Laura asked.

'At the back of the chip shop,' Tomas said.

Stan frowned at his brother. 'The chip shop? So, you were buying fish and chips when I thought you said you hadn't eaten in weeks.'

Tomas gave him a mournful look. 'We didn't buy anything.'

'Which chip shop?' Laura asked.

'I don't know. We tried many.'

'It was the one with the big blue fish on the outside,' Camilla said. 'On the road we couldn't get through in the van.'

'The Blue Dolphin.' Laura said.

They had discovered the chip shop when they had got lost driving in Woldham. They were trying to find their way out when the van got stuck in Tileman's Road. It was too narrow to turn, so Tomas put the van in reverse, but then he had seen a lorry coming up behind him. They waited while the lorry backed up into a small yard at the rear of the chip shop. They saw the sign on the side of the lorry; it was delivering potatoes. They watched as the driver got out and went to the back of the truck.

Tomas saw a chance. Keeping out of sight, he followed him. The man opened the back of the truck. He lowered the tailgate and climbed in. The tailgate raised and a few minutes later lowered again revealing half a dozen sacks of potatoes on a trolley. The driver wheeled the load to the rear of the chip shop and left them there as he went in. Tomas took a chance that he'd be gone a few minutes. Luck was on his side. He ran over and slit a hole in a sack with the knife he had on him, stealing a handful of potatoes before anyone appeared. Then he ran for it back to the van, still undetected.

'We thought we'd see if the delivery came again the next week,' Tomas said. 'It did. The driver was regular as clockwork. This time Eva came to help. We took a carrier bag.'

Eva sat up. 'That's when I saw the charm,' she said. 'It was on the ground near the back of the truck. Shiny. I put it in my pocket before Tomas handed me the potatoes.'

Laura let the words sink in. Eva had found the charm from Parker's collar in the chip shop yard... What did it mean?

Tomas was talking now.

'I didn't know she had it,' he said. 'Not 'til we got back and then when we looked at it, we thought it must be from a bracelet or something. With that and the potatoes we were thinking it was fortune calling on us.'

'Did you go back again?' Laura asked.

'We tried,' Tomas said. 'But they must have sniffed a mouse, after all it had happened twice that a bag had been broken into. Always on a Thursday. The next time the man took the sacks straight into the back of the shop. We waited, but then Eva got scared.'

'I heard a dog. It was making a noise.' Eva made the sound of whining. 'I thought it might come out and bite me.'

Laura remembered the day she and Frank had returned to The Blue Dolphin after Parker had gone missing. It seemed an eternity ago. She had thought she heard whining then. What had Sally said? It was Bailey, her brother's dog.

The brother who delivered the potatoes to them.

'And did you ever see a dog?' she asked.

Eva shook her head. 'No, we never saw it.'

'But we saw a crate,' Tomas said. 'A metal one; it was on the seat in the cab.'

'What kind of crate?' Laura asked.

'A dog crate, not so big; only for small dog.'

She asked them if they had seen a dog, but neither had.

Laura wished she knew what kind of dog Bailey was and if he could have fitted in the crate. Her mind raced back to that day. Hadn't Sally's behaviour been strangely defensive? The way she'd shouted to Bryan, 'Lady Boxford's here.'

Laura's heart began to thump. Could the crate in the lorry's cab have been for another dog?

Parker?

Could it have been him whining? Had he been in The Blue Dolphin all the time? Was he there, waiting until Sally's brother arrived and only then taken away. The realization was too awful. She must confront Sally… No, she must find the brother.

'You said it was always on a Thursday…' She looked from Tomas to Eva. '… But that's today… What time of day was the lorry there?'

Tomas thought. 'Maybe two-thirty?'

Laura looked at her watch. She had about two hours to wait.

Chapter 29

By the time Laura had gone back to the garage to buy a sandwich and a bottle of water, then driven into town, it was half past one. She got to Tileman's Road and looked for a parking space but could find nothing. She turned the car round and reversed the short distance to the end of the street and parked up against the bollards, blocking in the car beside her. She ate half the sandwich, hoping someone would move. Time ticked by. She could drive round to the next street to try and find a space, then walk back through the bike shop, but then she would have to pass the front of The Blue Dolphin. It would leave her too exposed.

In a state of agitated indecision, she switched on the engine trying to think of another plan. Her hands were clammy on the steering wheel. She found the napkin that had come with the sandwich and wiped them. Still wondering what to do, she saw a man come out of a house. He walked over to a car parked about three doors up from the chip shop's yard. The lights flashed as he zapped the lock. He got in. His indicator light flashed. Yes.

Laura put her car in gear, but then a car was coming in the opposite direction. Eager not to lose the space, she drove right up behind the exiting car so that the road was blocked. For a moment she thought it was going to reverse back into the space, but then the oncoming vehicle flashed its lights and backed up. The parked car slid out, and Laura edged into the vacant space.

She turned off the engine, hoping her blood pressure would decrease. From her rear-view mirror, she could see the chip shop yard. Anxiety mounted as she sat waiting, but the sandwich was making her soporific. She turned on the radio and listened to the news. The Archers came on and then a play – she knew she was losing concentration. Her eyelids lowered as the voices droned. She changed channels. Radio 2; the songs were easy, some she knew and liked.

Then an oldie came on, Dancing in the Moonlight. It held a particular memory for her. Why had she eaten all that bread? She hummed the tune, her thoughts blurring. She was staying with Victoria and Vince in a castle on a Scottish Island that Vince had taken to celebrate their wedding anniversary.

There was dancing after dinner. Laura had taken Parker in her arms and twirled him round the baronial hall. Everyone was laughing as Parker howled in delight, a green velvet ribbon that matched her dress tied in a bow round his neck.

In an instant the reverie was broken as Laura heard beeping. She was alert. A dark blue lorry was reversing down the road in front of her. She flicked off the radio. It was drawing closer, the beeping getting louder. It passed her and then reversed slowly into the yard of The Blue Dolphin. As it turned, she could see emblazoned down the side was a red sign that said, "Glover's", and below, "Lincolnshire's Finest Potatoes." On the cab door was a potato with a yellow crown.

Laura got out. The engine stopped and she heard the slam of a door. She walked to the corner; looked round but couldn't see anyone. She took a few quick paces to the passenger door of the cab and climbed the steps. Gripping the door handle, she peered in. Stuck to the dashboard was a circular advertising sticker. On it was the photo of a snub-nosed dog. Its face was predominantly black with a long chestnut coloured body, and curious curly tail. It was sniffing the air, and in front of it was a packet of crisps. Underneath a strapline read, "Jensen says they're the best."

On the passenger seat, lying beside a pale blue cotton cap was a pile of paperwork and a packet of the same crisps. Laura looked up and saw dangling from the mirror a flat plastic effigy of the same dog. There was a familiarity about the smiling cartoon creature with its pink tongue sticking out one side, that Laura recognized.

It had to be Parker's offspring.

She had seen what she needed and was about to climb down when she heard voices. In a panic, she slipped catching her shin on the metal step. Blood oozed through a hole in her stockings. Twice now the Cameron tartan dress had let her down. Why hadn't she worn jeans? She hurried back round the corner and pressed herself against the wall.

A woman's voice called out, 'D'you want a pie, Brandon?'

It was Sally, Laura was sure.

'Go on then,' a man with a low rasping voice replied. 'I can't stop long, I've got to be in Leicester by five.'

'That's not your normal run,' Sally said.

'It's not for spuds. I'm meeting a man on other business.'

'Honest Brandon, haven't you enough?' Sally asked, her voice getting closer.

Laura stumbled back to her car and drove to Mulberry Close.

Jervis let her in.

'Frank's here,' he said. 'We've been worried about you. Have you been to the police?'

'No.'

'But what the hell have you done to your leg?'

'It's nothing. I don't suppose Strudel's got a plaster?' Laura said. 'But what I really need is for you to find me an address.'

'Hang on a minute, let's sit you down.' Jervis took her arm and guided her into the sitting room.

Strudel held her hands to her face. 'Oh my darling, let me get my first aid kit.' She ran from the room, her pink ballroom dress fluttering out behind her.

'Where have you been?' Frank asked, coming to sit next to her on the sofa.

'I know where Parker is,' Laura said, as Strudel returned holding a large metal box.

She knelt down on the floor in front of Laura and opened it, revealing a mass of medical equipment.

'It's just a graze,' Laura said, but Strudel insisted on using the full panoply of antiseptic and wound dressings at her disposal.

When she had finished bandaging her up, Laura told them about Eva finding Parker's silver charm in the chip shop yard. 'Parker's disappearance has got nothing to do with the travellers. It's Sally Bowman's brother Brandon who I'm sure is at the bottom of it. He supplies the potatoes. The business is called, "Glover's" and its somewhere in Lincolnshire. Can you find it Jervis?'

Jervis dashed to his computer and started typing. 'There's only one with that name. This must be it,' he said. 'Merrifield Farm, Near Louth.'

'I'm going there tomorrow,' Laura said.

All three of them looked at her in consternation.

She told them about the lorry and the pictures of Jensen Darby. They said she was being irrational. There was only the slimmest of evidence and it could lead to more trouble.

'We've been discussing it, and we think you've been doing rather too much sailing close to the wind. I mean look at how you've hurt yourself now,' Frank said. 'Wouldn't it be more sensible to go and see that nice WPC?'

Laura rebuffed the hand he was about to put on her arm. 'Lizzie Bishop? It would be a waste of time,' she said, returning to her theory on the potato farmer. 'I'm convinced he knows something. The dog cage in his truck. The fact that there's never been any sign of his supposed dog Bailey. Then his comment about his "other business." But more important is the connection between him and Jensen Darby. I'm going to ring the actor who owns him. He said he's worked with farmers from Lincolnshire on the crisp advertising campaigns. He even mentioned working near Louth. I bet he'll have come across Brandon Glover.'

Laura promised she would do this before making any further decisions.

'First you must rest your leg,' Frank said. 'I'll drive you home.'

He left her lying on the sofa in her sitting room saying he'd call her that evening.

A short while later she hobbled round to Venetia's room. They decided to have supper together in Laura's rooms.

'Good for you,' Venetia said, when Laura told her of her plan. 'Take plenty of treats with you. That's what the Dogfather says. If this Bailey character does exist, he could need pacifying.'

Laura thanked her for the advice and went to ring Jensen Darby's owner. She asked him if he remembered the farmer from the crisps adverts they'd done in Lincolnshire.

'Brandon Glover was one of the first farmers the company featured in their campaign,' the actor said. 'That must have been six months ago. Then we did a follow up just recently. I think I told you we were going up there last time we spoke.'

'At his farm?' Laura asked.

'No, it was at a farmers' market. They got Brandon to pretend he was selling Jensen bunches of herbs for a new crisp flavor. He seems a nice enough chap. Huge fan of Jensen's; knew all about his parentage. I think he breeds dogs himself. Not sure what kind. Funnily enough, it was him that told me about the Japanese loving rare cross breeds. Jensen and I are off to Tokyo any day. We've signed a contract with a pet food manufacturer. My agent was onto that one faster than you could say kibbled dog pellets.'

Chapter 30

The morning sun blazed through the windscreen as Laura glared at the road ahead. She had forgotten how tiring motorway driving could be, but at least Frank was proving a helpful navigator. He'd got Jervis to print out directions for them. There was no way he was going to let her go on her own.

If only he would stop putting doubts into her mind. It was his idea they might be better off ringing Brandon Glover when they got nearer and suggesting they'd heard he had some puppies for sale. Laura said she couldn't see how that would help as they didn't even know what kind of dogs he was breeding.

She thought of Venetia's conversation about puppy prices. Is that what his "other business" was? Maybe even selling puppies overseas? A Japanese connection? But surely he would need some sort of go-between? The man in Leicester? Had she been too hasty yet again? It was just the sort of thing Ronnie might have had an idea about.

They reached the Lincoln ring road. Frank suggested she clean the bug-splattered windscreen.

'It will only make a smeared mess if I squirt water at it,' she said, as they hit a queue of traffic. 'Anyway, please don't put me off. I'm trying to concentrate.'

They crawled along nose to tail. She could see Frank was hurt.

He asked if she had a plan if they did find Parker.

'When I find him,' she snapped. The endless identical roundabouts were disorientating her. It was a perfectly reasonable question, but he wouldn't like the answer. 'Some things are better left to chance,' she said. She'd act in any way she thought necessary, even if it meant making more trouble.

They turned east passing through flat straggling villages. Then, as they reached the Lincolnshire Wolds the land began to resemble the undulating landscape Laura was familiar with. She felt more at home bowling up and down the steeply curved route surrounded by woods and fields on either side. She suggested they stop and eat the picnic Alfredo had prepared for them. They took a turning off the main road and meandered along some lanes before stopping at a field full of ripening pumpkins that sat in the plough like a convention of miniature spacecraft. It was bordered by a hedge and wide grass headland that offered some protection from the wind.

Frank threw down the rug they had brought with them. As Laura opened the cool box, she noticed Alfredo had included two packets of crisps. They weren't the same variety that Jensen Darby endorsed, but it reminded her of what lay ahead.

'We're not that far away now. We should be at the farm by mid-afternoon,' she said, as they huddled close to one another on the ground. They had agreed to pretend to be man and wife; she thought it an unnecessary complication, but Frank insisted it looked more authentic.

Finishing her sandwich Laura persuaded him that she should do the talking.

'It'll sound more convincing coming from me.'

'But men want to buy puppies,' Frank said.

'Gun dog puppies mostly,' she generalized. 'And anyway, it's invariably the women who look after them.' It was a weak attempt to remedy the situation but seemed to satisfy him.

Leaning back on her elbows beside him she felt tired by the amount of detail he was insisting on. She felt her eyes grow weary. Her head fell back against his shoulder. He was talking about puppy inoculations. Still, it felt warm and comfortable as the wind blowing in from the coast buffeted them.

She woke with a start. How could they have fallen asleep? Another hindrance of old age. She checked the time. It was nearly three 'o clock.

'Wake up.' She nudged Frank with her elbow. There was no way they'd make it back to Wellworth Lawns that evening. They'd have to find a hotel. At least she'd taken his advice and packed a bag.

They set off again, following the road to the outskirts of Louth where they took the bypass in the direction of the coast. The land flattened off again. The road straightened. They knew they were nearing their destination.

'There it is,' Frank pointed to the caravan park Jervis had told them to watch out for.

'The farm turning is on a corner shortly after,' he had said, scrolling Google Earth.

They saw a sign to Merrifield Farm on one of a pair of open galvanized metal gates. Below was the same logo of a potato and crown that Laura had seen on the side of the cab door of the lorry in the yard at The Blue Dolphin.

They clanked over a cattle grid. A pot-holed tarmac drive stretched into the distance with vast open fields of plough on either side. Half a mile or so away stood a series of low concrete storage sheds with corrugated roofs.

They saw a van coming out of a gap between two of them. It turned and headed down the drive in their direction. As it drew closer it maintained momentum. When it didn't look like it was going to move over, Laura turned onto the verge and waited until it had passed.

'Not very friendly,' Frank said, as they rejoined the tarmac.

They reached the buildings and drove into a large, concreted area surrounded on all sides.

In the middle of the open space a vortex of dust and straw was swirling around a vehicle weighbridge denoted by black and yellow striped metal posts. In front of one of the barns a Portacabin looked like it served as an office. Beside it were three parked cars. Laura drew up next to a dirty grey long-wheelbase SUV. They got out and knocked on the door of the Portacabin. Inside a phone was ringing. No one answered.

They wandered round looking for signs of life, but everything was shut up. They peered through a gap in one of the vast barn doors and could make out some large pieces of machinery that looked like they were part of the potato sorting and bagging process.

Then at the far end of the yard they came to an alley through which they could see a much smaller courtyard of broken and uneven concrete slabs that sloped down to the rear aspect of what must have been the original red brick farmhouse. It might once have been attractive were it not for the addition of an ugly glass extension, the view from which was now obliterated by the modern barns.

A pane was missing from the open door that creaked as it swung back and forth in the breeze.

'Is anybody there?' Laura called out, as they walked forward.

There was no answer. She looked around. Within the courtyard, dwarfed below the back of one of the barns were a series of small red brick sheds and outhouses. Dating from the same period as the house, they had fallen into disrepair. A washing line was slung from one corner of the glass structure, attached at the other end to the side of what might have been a stable, except that a wire mesh frame held in place with metal hinges had replaced the top half of the door. From within it a lone bark was cut short, falling away into a hesitant whimper. Laura's heart missed a beat. She knew what had caused it. She turned to Frank who nodded in recognition.

They took a few steps towards the stable when a voice called out behind them. A middle-aged woman with short brown curly hair held back by an off-white knitted band was coming towards them from the sunroom, a lit cigarette in her hand. She had on an old grey sweatshirt, rolled up khaki cargo trousers and a pair of grubby trainers.

'You after someone?' she asked, flicking cigarette ash onto the ground.

'Is it Mrs. Glover?' Laura asked. 'We heard you had some puppies for sale.'

'You what?'

'We've come a long way…'

'From where?' The woman frowned and took a drag from the cigarette. Her lips puckered; a myriad of lines fanning out like a miniature sunburst.

'Woldham.' It slipped out; Laura tried to cover her mistake. 'You've probably never heard of it.'

'As it happens, I have. My sister-in-law lives there. But I dunno where you got the idea we had puppies. The collie's way past it.' She nodded her head in the direction of the stable and laughed. Her open mouth revealed a set of even yellow teeth that Laura took to be dentures.

'Dachshund crosses, we were told,' Laura said.

The woman laughed again, a deep throaty cackle. 'Someone's been telling you porkies. Who was it?'

'A friend.' Laura breathed a silent sigh of relief. The Woldham connection seemed to have been passed over. 'He knows Jensen Darby's owner. You know, the dog that advertises the crisps. They're made with your potatoes, aren't they? Absolutely delicious.'

The woman frowned again. 'What's that got to do with it?' She turned towards the house and shouted, 'Brandon.'

They heard a door slam somewhere inside.

'Brandon,' the woman called again.

A man in green overalls appeared in the doorway. He didn't have any shoes on and stood legs apart, taking up most of the space of the doorframe. 'What's going on Pam?'

Laura recognized the gravelly voice from The Blue Dolphin.

The dog in the stable tried barking again.

'Shut up Bailey,' the man shouted.

So Bailey did exist. Laura had a moment of panic. Had she made a terrible error? But no, the crate in the front of the lorry Eva had described was for a small dog, it would never have fitted a collie.

Brandon turned to the woman and nodded his head in Laura and Frank's direction. 'Who's this?'

'Lady's on about some puppies.'

Laura took a few paces forward leaving Frank behind her. 'It's Mr. Glover isn't it?' she ventured. 'I was saying to your wife, we heard that you had some puppies for sale.'

Brandon stared at her. Was there a family resemblance between him and his sisters, Sally and Val? Not as far as Laura could see; his greasy brown hair receded from a wide sun damaged forehead. A big pink nose made his eyes look insignificant. The girls had pretty noses as far as she remembered, not like his, but where had she seen that protrusion before?

'Dachshund pug crosses,' she carried on hopefully. 'Daugs; Like Jensen Darby. Perhaps my friend got it wrong?' She wished she'd let Frank do the talking. 'Perhaps you've sold them all? I know how popular they are…' She carried on with what she hoped was a confident tone. 'I'd like to be put on the waiting list for the next litter if I may?'

Brandon came forward and stood beside his wife.

'I know they're fetching big money.' Laura tried a small giggle as her heart pumped faster. 'I'd be prepared to put down a deposit. Perhaps we could see the bitch?' She steadied herself with a deep breath. Oh, for a pacemaker... 'Or should we go through your dealer?' This was a big gamble. 'He's in Leicester, isn't he?'

'Dealer?' Brandon Glover crossed his arms. His forehead turned into a tangle of lines. A vein throbbed at his left temple. 'I think you've mistaken me for someone else.' His jaw protruded. 'Now if you don't mind, I'd rather you got off my land.'

Chapter 31

'I knew I'd seen that ugly mug before; it was the fat bulbous nose,' Laura said. 'I was with Alfredo. Brandon Glover was delivering potatoes to Wellworth Lawns.'

She turned to Frank. They had got forty minutes down the road toward home.

'I'm going back,' she said. 'I know it's getting late.' She indicated and drew in to the side of the road. 'You can stay in the car if you like. Or I can leave you in that pub we just passed.'

Frank sighed. 'Don't be a fool, Laura. I wouldn't dream of letting you go alone, and I can see there is nothing I can do to stop you. Let's book into that pub to be on the safe side. Then we can get something to eat.'

Laura could only thank him. She turned the car round and drove back to the village where she'd seen an old coaching inn.

The Dark Horse was dreary but serviceable. They took their bags up a creaking staircase to a twin room on the first floor, then went down to the bar and ordered from the menu.

'I'm not sure what the Michelin inspector would say about this steak pie,' Frank whispered, prying into the steaming grey suet case and sloppy dark brown gravy in search of meat. 'Still, mustn't complain, at least it's hot.'

Laura laughed, 'Good stodgy food will keep us going and this place isn't too far for us to get back to later.' She sliced into her own pie. 'It does smell rather odd…'

'You're right,' Frank sniffed the air. 'And that reminds me, there was something about Brandon and Pam Glover that was distinctly malodourous. They were hiding something, I'm sure.'

'Exactly what I thought. Why weren't they more open in their appreciation of Jensen Darby? They didn't even smile when I mentioned his name.'

'But it's hard to know if there were any other dogs there apart from Bailey. Don't you think we would have heard something.'

'Not necessarily, we know he's using some sort of bark deterrent device, and he could be keeping other dogs in one of the other the barns, maybe insulated with straw. Remember we saw how it was blowing about in the yard. That aside we've no idea what was in the house.'

'You're not suggesting…' Frank raised his eyebrows at her.

'Would I? Of course there's no knowing what one can see when one's hiding in the dark and lights are on indoors.'

Laura felt strange mix of unease and excitement as she turned the headlights off and drove back up the drive to Merrifield Farm. It was as if she could hear every loose chipping the tyres crushed as they inched along.

'Should we be getting so close?' Frank asked.

'There'd be nowhere to hide out here if we had to retreat in a hurry,' she said. 'Not that we're going to need to.'

Her courage gaining, she felt her previous nocturnal forays, first in Sack Lane with Frank and then Cheltenham had just been a testing ground in covert operations. Everything those important failures had taught her would come into play now. She had to be confident they wouldn't be caught. Anyway, what were the laws of trespass? A fine? So what, if it meant finding Parker.

She stopped at the back of the nearest barn and felt for the torch she'd put in the side pocket of the car door. Getting out, they left the doors an inch ajar. The moon was obscured by cloud, and it was a lot darker with no urban light pollution in the middle of the countryside. It meant they had to tiptoe close to the sides of the barn without falling into the narrow drainage ditch that surrounded it.

Laura's eyes were becoming accustomed to the dark, so when she turned the corner, a small green light attached to the side of the building came as a shock. The pulse in her temples throbbed. She nudged Frank and pointed up at it. They hadn't noticed the camera that afternoon.

'If we keep down, we'll stay out of range,' Frank whispered.

Crouching, they edged along until they were in the main yard. The cars had gone, but there were now three lorries parked up in a neat row close to the front of the barn nearest the alley that led to the house. They squeezed in front of them feeling the residual heat from the engines. As they reached the corner of the alley, Laura peered round. The sunroom was in darkness, but she could see light coming from a window to one side and she could hear the sound of a TV blaring.

They crept into the courtyard. Laura tried the door of the nearest shed. The latch lifted easily but opened with a creak that sounded deafening. She took the torch from her pocket. Its beam cast light on a lawn mower and a jumble of gardening equipment. They carried on along the row until they got to the stable. A warm acrid smell in the chill night air made Laura wince as she shone the torch through the wire netting. Asleep in one corner on a raised wooden pallet was an elderly sheepdog.

'Bailey,' she whispered. The dog lifted his head, looked up at her and then lowered it, tucking his muzzle between his front paws with an air of resignation.

'Come on,' Frank whispered.

Laura pointed towards the house.

'No,' Frank said, but Laura set off.

She went round the sunroom to the side of the house. There was one small crackle glazed window followed by a bulge where the chimneybreast protruded. As she carried on to the front she could hear Frank's footsteps behind her. She stopped to look into a bay window. Paint was peeling off the sill and frame. She turned off the torch. Dim light from further within allowed them to identify it as a sitting room. It looked unused – the relic of a more genteel era; the "best room." They crossed under the porch of the front door to a matching bay window the other side across which a pair of thin curtains was drawn. There was no chink through which to see further. Laura turned the torch back on. The broken cord of a sash lay looped on the ledge of the central window. She beckoned to Frank, pointed to the top of the window and gestured for him to give it a push.

The window opened slightly. Frank let go. It fell back down with a thud.

They froze. Laura flicked the torch off; waited in the darkness.

After a few minutes, Frank whispered, 'Let's go.'

They crept round the fourth side of the house. Heard the slam of the sunroom door; clung to the wall of the house and waited again. Laura could feel Frank's warm breath at the back of her neck. She took a few steps forward to the corner and saw the beam of a torch heading towards the storage barns. Again, they waited. The beam changed direction. They heard the rasp of a metal bolt being drawn. As the door opened a reddish aura illuminated the figure of Brandon Glover.

In the glow Laura saw he was balancing a tray on his hip that was laden with plastic containers. Then he went into the barn. He slid the door shut behind him, throwing Laura and Frank into darkness once more.

The air had chilled further and to Laura's horror the moon appeared, bright and sickle in the night sky. The light gave Frank's white hair a ghostly blue sheen.

'We'll have to try the other way. Round the outside of the barns,' Frank said.

They returned to the front corner of the house, but a tall paling fence precluded any way round.

'He could be some time in there,' Laura said.

'We'll have to chance it. I'll go first,' Frank said.

They retraced their steps.

She held onto the sleeve of his jacket, fear ready to engulf her. It was about ten yards to the door into the barn and then another ten before they would reach the corner and some cover from the lorries. Every step they inched seemed to ricochet noise as they crossed the open ground and down the alley.

Laura had an overwhelming desire to run.

And then they were thrown into darkness as the moon disappeared. All they could see was a razor thin red line of light from under the doorway and a large padlock hanging from the open bolt.

They passed the door. The light was behind them.

They reached the corner. Turned. Took a few paces forwards. They knew where the lorries were. They weren't in range of the camera until they reached the outer edge of the yard. They were safe.

'I'm putting the torch on,' Laura whispered.

In front of her Frank tripped in the drain. He was losing his balance. She let go his arm. He tried to right himself and fell onto the bumper of the first lorry.

An ear-splitting siren sounded. Laura's head pounded. She almost fell into him as a light at waist height started flashing. Frank was almost on top of it.

They had set off a movement sensor.

Frank grabbed Laura's hand as she grappled for the keys in her pocket. They ran straight past the camera. She bleeped the key in the direction of the car and saw the interior light come on. She ran forward, pulled the door open and slid in, turning the ignition before Frank had even closed his door. The tyres crunched as she accelerated. With no attempt at secrecy, she headed down the drive.

Frank turned to look behind them. 'I can't see any lights, but whatever you do keep going.'

Anxiety fuelled adrenalin, as Laura hurtled on and slewed into the main road.

'Never again,' Frank said. 'You must promise me this is the end of it.'

Her heart pumped with a new ferocity. 'I know what that red light was,' she said. 'Heat lamps; for puppies.' It was the evidence she needed.

Chapter 32

Jervis eased back from his computer putting his hands behind his head. 'So, Brandon Glover's behind some sort of puppy farm racket for the foreign market; he's breeding puppies like Jensen Darby that he knows will be worth thousands.'

'And that's why I know he's got Parker,' Laura said.

'I'm sorry Laura,' Jervis continued. 'If you are right, it's far too dangerous to go back there. And what if he's gone through the CCTV footage. He'll know it was you.'

'You must call Inspector Sandfield. He can be liaising with colleagues in Lincolnshire,' Strudel said.

'They'll be too slow. All I need is a little help,' Laura said.

Jervis held his hand up. 'Me you mean?'

'And Strudel,' Frank said. 'Laura's right, what we need is more boots on the ground, and some military planning.'

'What do you know about military planning?' Laura asked.

'Well actually…' Jervis put his hand up again.

'It's true I'm no Leonidas,' Frank said. 'Perhaps Ronnie would be a better bet. Do you think he could help us?'

'Yes, where is he?' Laura asked.

'My poor Ronnie.' Strudel fanned herself. 'He is in Romford.'

'Net's closing in on him I'm afraid.' Jervis shook his head. 'He knows he will have to face justice.'

'For what?' Laura asked.

'He's been in receipt of some stolen funds, as far as we can tell.' Jervis sighed.

Frank raised his eyebrows; ravens flying skywards. 'Bad business, that's for sure.'

'He is thinking he may be nearer eighty by the time he is released. This is such an age…' Strudel sobbed.

'Prison?' As Laura had no idea how old Ronnie was, it was hard to gauge the ramifications of this. 'Oh dear, that is a very bad business,' she commiserated.

'A spot of intimidation?' Ronnie said. 'I think I could fit that in quite nicely. Give me a few days to put something together.'

They were on a zoom call from Jervis's computer. In the background, light percolated through the grimy windows of the empty flat where Ronnie had taken up residence. He was seated on a solitary chair in the middle of the room, a newly sprouted beard glinting a curious shade of brown. He had also shaved his head.

Not knowing how long he would take to get back to them was agonizing for Laura, but it was only two days later that he face-timed them from his phone. He was sitting in a caravan on the site down the road from Brandon Glover's farm.

'Perfect for a spot of recceing, plus I had to make a bit of a fast exit from the smoke last night. So, what I suggest is you meet me here. I'd ask you to stay but it's a bit cramped and before you ask Strue, I don't think you'd be too happy with the facilities.' Ronnie got up and coughed. 'Excuse me; damp's getting to my lungs.'

As he coughed again the mobile's camera swung round revealing the spartan interior of the caravan. They could see a pile of rumpled clothes lying on a melamine tabletop. Behind, pieces of tattered red gingham hung from the window.

'Frank's right about troop numbers,' he said. 'I'm thinking with me, Strue and Jarvie, we can keep Laura and the Canon in the background if necessary.'

Laura wasn't happy about this, but was persuaded it was better to follow Ronnie's instructions, even though Jervis had some reservations about putting Strudel in the line of fire.

'Don't be silly,' Strudel said. 'You have no idea what I have seen. Life with Ronnie was always unexpected.'

'Nicely put.' Ronnie said.

They had a view of a tatty piece of brown carpet on the floor as he sat back down.

'I think the best plan is if we all go together,' Jervis said. 'I'll drive us in the Merc.'

Laura wasn't happy about this either, but they'd have been too squashed in either her or Frank's car. She would have to put up with Jervis's erratic driving style.

'We could stay in The Dark Horse afterwards,' Frank suggested. 'It wasn't that bad, and they offered me a discount if I was ever in the area again.'

'Why don't you join us there,' Laura said, to the blank screen. 'It would be much more comfortable for you. I'll pay of course.'

'I'd prefer to keep a low profile.' Ronnie came into view again. 'I wouldn't want to get carted off to Her Majesty's prematurely, if you get my drift.'

'Understood.' Jervis held up his hand, fingers crossed.

'I think that's all,' Ronnie said. 'I'll send Jarvie a map of where I'm parked. All these caravans look alike, but you'll see a dark blue Ford Transit parked outside. I've borrowed it off an associate of mine. Now if you don't mind, I've still got a few loose ends to tie up. I'll see you mid-afternoon the day after tomorrow.'

Desperate to get going and with a day to kill Laura had to keep busy. She dropped in on Venetia. Sitting in a chair beside her was a small round woman with a grey pudding bowl haircut. She was dressed in black with a white collar round her neck.

'You've met Vicar Rachel, haven't you?' Venetia said.

The dumpling elevated herself from the chair and held out a hand, a wide smile on her rosy face. 'I've heard so much about you,' she said. 'Your kindness in helping Venetia sort out her charitable donations and all when you have so much on your mind.'

'Vicar Rachel has been to see Angel in prison for me,' Venetia said.

'Mrs. Hobbs's daughter has assured me she won't be divulging any more information about her mother.'

'I'm giving my spare cash to the church instead,' Venetia said.

'Is that right?' Laura looked at the vicar. This woman was a leech of the first order.

'Obviously I've declined the kind offer,' Vicar Rachel sat back down and stroked Venetia's hand.

'We can discuss it in the car,' Venetia said. 'We're going out with Gladys Freemantle and Lulu Vandermoss to Oxford. Lulu wants our opinion on a dress she's seen. It has to have a certain amount of gravitas as she say's she's possibly going to be a witness in a murder trial. We're going to have lunch at The Randolph. She's paying.'

In equal measures piqued, disbelieving and intrigued, Laura pestered Frank. He took her out to lunch at the pub in the next-door village to Chipping Wellworth.

'Rachel's got a heart of gold,' Frank was saying as they returned to his car. Thinking that as usual he was probably right, Laura was about to get in, when they heard a familiar voice.

'Come along Wellington.'

From the lane at the side of the pub Gwendoline Shackleton marched round the corner, her tweed skirt flicking from side to side in time with her military step. Beside her on a lead was a jaunty chestnut long-haired Dachshund.

The sight of the dog threw Laura. She gripped the door handle.

'Afternoon Ms. Shackleton,' Frank said. 'Have you walked here? Quite a long way for a little dog like that.'

'Canon Frank… And Lady Boxford too.' Gwendoline's eyes narrowed. 'Yes, he's my latest charge. A tad overweight; I have him on a programme involving plenty of exercise.'

'Did you manage to re-train Prendy?'

'Oh Canon, what a good memory you have for names. Yes. That recalcitrant creature took an eternity to get the message.' She let out a high-pitched titter.

'What a palaver though; all Harry's fault for entrusting him to his wayward son to look after.
'Ludo Constantine?' Laura asked.

'Yes.' Gwendoline gave her a fleeting glance before returning her attention to Frank. 'To be fair to Prendy, the vet did say he had ingested marijuana and it took him some days to recover. It's a good thing that boy's being sent to South America. They're calling it a gap year even though he'll never get to university in his wildest dreams.'

'No wonder the dog forgot all the basics with a layabout like that,' Frank said, with a degree of confidence in canine habits Laura had not heard before.

'Quite,' Gwendoline agreed. 'Even so, I've changed my terms and conditions with regard to working with Harry's charity. We are getting on much better now. Wellington here had been living under a much too lax regime. Not his fault his owner had been dead for over a week I suppose, but time enough for him to pick up some very dirty habits. Not that the Dachshund as a breed is ever truly trustworthy in matters of a scatological nature.'

'Hard to housetrain?' Laura asked.

'As I said. And now what with this perfectly disgusting habit of interbreeding, it can only get worse. Churning mongrel puppies out; it's as bad as battery hens.'

'Terrible,' Frank agreed.

Gwendoline smiled at him and continued to prattle on. 'Only the other day I met a young man with a Dachshund pug cross. Can you imagine anything more vile. I guarantee the chances of that particular combination ever being capable of bowel constraint would be extremely low.'

Laura felt a certain rage, even though Gwendoline was only echoing Ned's thoughts on the subject.

Gwendoline turned to Laura. 'Didn't you lose a pug once?'

Laura felt a cold sweat break out.

'We still have high hopes of finding Parker,' Frank said. 'Come on Laura, or we will be late.'

'Yes,' Gwendoline said. 'And I certainly don't have time to stand around in idle chatter.'

Frank waited until she was out of earshot. 'Well, at least that clears a few things up.' he said.

Watching Jervis and Frank load the boot of the car the next morning, Laura found herself struggling to remain patient. Frank had decided to wear dark blue military-style overalls that he had tucked in to a pair of boots. None of this attire had Laura ever seen before. When she asked him what its provenance was, he told her it was from his time as an army chaplain.

'Didn't you know Frank was in the SAS?' Jervis said.

It was another area of Frank's life that Laura had no idea about. She felt guilty as she handed Jervis her shepherd's crook and waited in agonized silence while he decided where to place it.

Finally, they were ready and headed off down the drive.

Jervis stalled the aged Mercedes, turning onto the main road. 'Whoops,' he said. 'Must have put her into third.'

A car coming towards them honked its horn as Jervis shuddered forward veering across the double white lines while at the same time adjusting his seatbelt.

Even though Laura was sitting in the back with Strudel, she put on a pair of sunglasses.

They made it to the dual carriageway junction without further incident. Then Jervis hit the fast lane. After twenty minutes of his eighty-mile an hour tailgating, Laura kept her eyes closed until they took a break to pick up sandwiches at a service station outside Lincoln.

Heading off again Jervis took a roundabout at speed, causing Laura to drop her sandwich.

'Plenty of time,' Frank said, as she tried to brush the crumbs from her lap.

Laura closed her eyes again.

After a while Frank said, 'We're almost there. Should you call Ronnie, Strudel?'

He was waiting outside for them, leaning cross-legged against the side of the blue van. It looked very much like the ones Laura had seen being used to pick up bank cash deposits and Ronnie, dressed in a dark blue hoodie, faded black skinny jeans and a pair of white trainers, looked not dissimilar to someone who might be involved in holding the van up.

As Jervis drew up beside him, Ronnie came forward to open Laura's door.

'Jervie's driving up to scratch?' he asked.

'Just about.' Frank offered when Laura didn't answer. He stretched and rubbed his neck as he got out.

'Very relaxing in the back,' Strudel said.

'Nice combats Canon,' Ronnie observed, as from behind him Laura heard a deep howl. It appeared to be coming from inside the van.

'What's that?' she asked.

'Bait.' Ronnie walked back. He opened the driver's door and a huge Bassett hound sitting behind the steering wheel greeted him with a friendly guttural bark, its tail smacking like a drumstick into the back of the passenger seat.

'Meet Pancake.' Ronnie lifted the dog down and placed her on the ground. 'An interesting fact about her is that she weighs about the same as a sack of potatoes.' He rubbed his back. 'I can see why there's vacancies in the haulage industry.'

Pancake began sniffing at the front wheel of the Mercedes. Ronnie clapped his hands, and the Bassett lumbered back to stand obediently at his feet, tail wagging.

'Don't tell me,' Jervis said. 'You borrowed her from an associate of yours.'

'Most fortuitous she was available.' Ronnie walked round the van to where the caravan was parked.

'Do come in,' he said, opening the door. 'Pancake's a greedy bitch. I must feed her before we go.' He lifted her in.

Following him up the steps, Laura and Strudel sat down on the bench bed at the far end. Jervis squeezed in between them leaving Frank to take the only chair where Pancake sat panting at his feet. Beside Frank, perching on the table next to a small primus stove, Ronnie stretched over to the single wall mounted cupboard and took out a can of dog food.

He twisted the lid off, shook the contents into a bowl, then took a handful of dog biscuit from a bag and scattered some on top. He put it on the floor.

The smell was so familiar to Laura. She felt near to tears as she watched Pancake lurch at the food, taking great slobbering mouthfuls. Moments later, when the dog had finished, she sat back down on Frank's feet, leant against his legs and let out a series of contented burps.

Meanwhile, Ronnie lit a match under the stove and boiled some water in a pan.

'You'll have to share tea bags,' he said. 'And cups.'

'Wait a sec,' Jervis said. 'I brought some with us.' He jumped up causing Laura and Strudel to fall into one another.

'We can't be long,' Ronnie said. 'The lorries get back from deliveries around six thirty. We want to be out before that.'

Jervis dashed out down the steps. He returned with a thermos and cups and as they drank the tea, Ronnie outlined his plan.

'We'll park in the yard. Pancake's key to this part of the operation; I've got a fake pedigree for her and I'm going to sell Brandon a story he'll find hard to resist.'

'What's that?' Jervis asked.

'Bassuggs. Bassett pug crosses to you and me. I'm going to tell him I've got a client willing to pay top dollar for a litter. If he's got Parker there, I guarantee he'll fall for it.'

'Christ,' Jervis said. 'How the hell does that work?'

'Stairs. Plenty of tricks these breeders use. I'll make him a deal he's unlikely to refuse.'

Laura frowned. 'But why would he jeopardize his business for you and Pancake?'

'Hard work stealing a Bassett hound,' Ronnie said. 'I'm pinning my hopes on his experimental nature and greed.'

'But you'll have to tell him you know about the pug crosses won't you? The Daugs I mean,' Laura said.

'He'll get the picture the way I tell it.'

Laura hoped Ronnie's bravado wasn't misplaced.

'Either way, if Pancake fails, I've got something else on Brandon,' Ronnie continued. 'You see this park and the caravans on it,' He waved an arm at the window. 'It's all owned by Brandon.'

'Good investment,' Jervis said.

'Only most of the caravans are stolen. He mainly uses them to house seasonal labour. They work on another lot of land he's got the other side of the main road. As it happens there aren't that many here since Brexit. That's how I managed to avail myself of one.' Ronnie poured water into Pancake's empty food bowl. She heaved herself up from Frank's feet and took half a dozen noisy slurps.

'How do you know they're stolen?' Laura asked.

'Obvious signs; tow hitch damage; some have wheels that don't match. They're old, but even so they should have identification on the windows.' Ronnie pulled back a gingham curtain. Laura could see scratch marks covering one corner of the glass.

'Then the chassis number's been removed; I've checked underneath quite a few of them.'

'My Ronnie is so thorough,' Strudel said.

'He may be so.' Jervis gave a short nasal exhalation. 'But the trick is, how do we know Brandon will even be there?'

'He only does one run a week. That's as we know to the Midlands on a Thursday. The rest of the time he employs local drivers. I met one of them in the pub. He's laid off with guess what, a bad back. Told me a bit about the layout of the yard and I've checked it over myself.' Ronnie picked up the dog bowl, opened the caravan door and threw the water out.

'There's three locked storage barns,' he continued. 'Most of the space is for potatoes and machinery, but Laura and Frank know all that. The keys are kept in the Portacabin. They're labeled one two and three. Number three's the one Laura and Frank saw the lights in. Its main access is from outside the yard itself. I had a brief gander; stacks of spuds, but then there's like a wall of straw bales at the end nearest his house. I reckon that's how Brandon keeps the dogs a secret. He's blocked off the area. It's got a separate entrance; the one Laura and Frank saw him using.'

'Will you go to the back of the house like we did?' Laura asked.

'That's it. I'll take Strudel and Jervie. They'll pretend to be Pancake's owners with me acting as their agent. Jim and Doreen…what shall we say…Foxtrot? No that's a bit obvious. Jim and Doreen Charleston. How's that?'

Strudel took offense. 'So, this is what you think of our ballroom, some sort of joke? And just when I was thinking how improved in nature you were.'

'You've got the leading role, Strue.' Ronnie winked at her. 'You're going to charm his missus. Tell her what a wonderful dog Pancake is and get a cuppa out of her if you can. Be good to sniff around the house. Meanwhile I'll do the business with Brandon. Laura and Frank; you'll wait in the car. Then of course we face the million-dollar question…the actual whereabouts of Parker…' Ronnie ruffled his beard. 'I'll work that out as we go along, don't you worry.' He stretched his arms, yawned and said he'd better take Pancake out for a quick constitutional.

It was all a bit too relaxed for Laura and as they waited for him her heart was beating fast. She couldn't countenance the idea of failure. Parker had to be there.

The light was already fading as they piled into the Mercedes, Ronnie in the front with Jervis. Frank sat between Strudel and Laura in the back as Pancake panted down their necks from where she was sitting on top of the cases in the boot.

Jervis had the key in the ignition when Ronnie said he had to go and get something. He limped back to the caravan and returned having swapped his blue hoodie for a black leather bomber jacket.

'OK Jervie, let's hit it,' he said, zipping it up.

They headed out of the park onto the road. It was less than half a mile before the turning to the farm. They drove up to the barns. Ronnie told Jervis to pull up as they reached the outside of the yard. He jumped out and ran round the corner.

'All clear,' he said, reappearing moments later.

They drove into the deserted yard. Ronnie told Jervis to back up beside the Portacabin, next to the truck driver's cars. He got Pancake out of the boot and called for Strudel and Jervis.

'Much as it pains me not to have you up front with me Canon,' Ronnie said to Frank. 'But you and Lady B stay put. I reckon we'll be half an hour. Forty-five tops.'

Laura watched them cross the yard. They turned down the alley that led to the back of the house and were out of sight.

As she waited in silence on the back seat, Laura looked at the Portacabin. She was never much good at taking orders. She couldn't just sit there. 'I'm going to find the key to the barn,' she said, reaching over into the boot where she could see her crook. 'We might be able to get in from the other end.'

'Ronnie told us to stay in the car,' Frank said, ducking as Laura brought the stick to rest beside her.

'What if he fails with Pancake?' she said. 'We'll have wasted all that time.'

Frank followed her as she opened the door to the Portacabin. She saw the bunch of keys hanging on a hook above the desk and leant over to grab them. Turning them in her hands, she found the one with the number three written on the tag.

'Let's go,' she said.

'Steady,' Frank implored, as he ran after her out of the yard to the huge sliding metal door of the barn.

Laura put the key in. Opened the padlock and put it on the floor.

'It's going to make an infernal racket.' Frank was whispering now. 'Let me do it.'

He pulled the lever handle. They heard the great roller overhead start to revolve. 'Slowly does it,' Frank whispered, as inch by inch he opened it enough for them to slip through.

The light from outside was enough for them to see where they were going. On either side they passed potatoes piled high like knobbly brown hills. Beyond they could see the huge circular bales of golden straw stacked neatly to create a barrier across the whole of what appeared to be the end of the barn. It was only when Laura pointed upwards that they could see the metal rafters continued above the bales to the roof.

Silently they continued to explore from one side to the other, searching for a way through. As Laura was poking at the impenetrable barrier with her crook,

Frank tapped her on the shoulder. He shook his head and gestured with his thumb that they should leave.

It was then they heard a voice. It was coming from the other side of the bales. Laura's eyes widened as she stared at Frank.

'It's Ronnie,' she whispered. He must be in there.'

They squeezed back out of the barn door, retraced their steps into the yard, then edged along the side of the building until they reached the corner.

They stopped. Ronnie was speaking again.

'Jim, take Doreen and Pancake back to the car. I've got this under control,' he said.

A few seconds later, Pancake rounded the corner towing Strudel behind her. 'My Ronnie,' Strudel cried out. 'He has a gun.'

Chapter 33

'What shall we do?' Strudel pleaded, as Pancake lurched to a halt at Frank's feet.

Jervis caught his breath as they all cowered out of sight around the corner of the barn. 'There must be half a dozen bitches and litters in there,' he said.

They could hear Ronnie inside. 'I've got the evidence I need, so before I call the cozzers, where's the pug?'

'I think it's time you stopped pointing that thing at me and my wife.' It was Brandon Glover. 'Since when's having a few litters of puppies been against the law?'

'Take one step closer,' Ronnie shouted. 'And I'll be left with no choice.'

A moment's silence, then they heard a shot.

A thud.

'Run Pam. Get back to the house.' It was Brandon Glover again.

'My Ronnie,' Strudel screamed. She let go of Pancake and ran round the corner.

Frank grabbed the lead as Laura ran after her. Another scream.

Laura rounded the corner. Strudel was lying in the alley clutching her head as Brandon Glover and his wife ran towards the house.

'Are you alright?' Laura knelt on the stony ground next to Strudel.

'What?' Strudel looked up as Laura repeated the question.

'He punched my earhole. I can see a firmament. Many colours are circling my head.' Strudel heaved herself into a sitting position. 'But where is Ronnie?'

'I'll find him. You wait there. Gather your senses.' Laura got up and ran into the barn.

A strange quietness filled the space. Heat lamps slung from cable hung low, looped untidily from makeshift beams overhead. The whole area emanated a warm red glow.

Four yards in, Laura could see the wall of round bales. In front of them sections were divided by small oblong bales, an entrance to each made of a wooden pallet kept in place with bricks on the floor.

To the side of the doorway Jervis and Frank, entangled in Pancake's lead, were pulling Ronnie to his feet.

'What happened?' Laura asked. 'Are you hurt?'

'The bastard overpowered me,' Ronnie said. 'Whacked me on the chin. Then he had my arm in the air and the gun went off.' He looked down at the pistol in his hand. 'I dropped to the floor like a bleeding amateur.'

'Thank the Lord,' Frank said.

'Not much to thank him for.' Ronnie spat some blood on the floor and wiped his mouth. 'So now the pair of them are holed up in the house, I bet.' He put the pistol back in an inside pocket of his bomber jacket and zipped it up.

'It's too damn hot in here,' Jervis mopped his brow. 'What say we take some photos of the dogs for evidence and vamoose.'

Strudel staggered in. 'Leave?' She fell into Jervis's' arms.

'Not a chance,' Laura said. 'I'm going into that house. Three men and a pistol should be enough to keep Brandon Glover quiet. Strudel, you better stay in the car with Pancake. I'll deal with the wife.'

'I've always liked your spirit,' Ronnie said. 'We've not much time before the trucks get back and it's getting dark. We need a strategy.' He sat down on a sack of dog biscuits that Pancake was sniffing.

'But I thought…'

'Leave it Strue. Let me think.'

'Come and sit in the car,' Jervis said, taking Strudel by the arm and pulling Pancake behind him.

Laura got her mobile from her pocket. 'I'll get some photos.'

Setting off into the maze of straw bales, Frank behind her, she clicked the camera on the first Dachshund mother who lay surrounded by tiny mole like offspring. The bitch stared up from the bare concrete floor. A flea jumped from her coat. She lowered her head to nuzzle a puppy. Baffled, Laura saw that she was pushing it away from her.

Then she realized it was natural instinct; the puppy was dead.

Abandoning the task, the bitch got up, turned around and lay down again. The puppies made tiny mewling noises as they repositioned themselves around her belly.

Laura and Frank moved on to similar scenes.

A couple of the litters were in bigger pens. The puppies were older; still too young to be weaned. It was impossible to tell what their breeding was at that age. All puppies looked much the same. Laura covered her nose; the floor of their pens was wet and dirty. A single pen contained three heavily pregnant bitches huddled silently together. Fighting back her disgust, Laura felt a renewed sense of urgency. Could Parker be the father?

'He must have a serious sales network,' Frank said.

'That's why we have to stop him.' Laura was hot, claustrophobic. She had to get out. 'I know what we must do.'

She waited until Jervis had returned, before outlining her plan.

'We'll split up. They don't know I'm here, so I'm going to get to the front of the house. Give me ten minutes. Then you lot go to the back door. They'll be expecting you that side. Start making a racket.'

'You're not going alone,' Frank said. 'They don't know I'm here either.'

Laura and Frank retraced their steps out of the yard. They passed the barn they had entered, its door still ajar. Ronnie had recce'd this way, so they knew the first obstacle was an orchard. Laura wound her way through the rows of trees. She smelled the rot of fallen apples as they squashed softly underfoot. She stumbled on thick tufts of grass, saving herself from falling with the aid of her crook.

At the end of the trees was a loose barbed wire fence. Frank put one foot on the top strand and lowered it for Laura to climb over. Now they were on the old driveway. They could see the house in the gloaming ahead. Their feet crunched on mossy gravel as the drive passed between a privet hedge – now so overgrown it was too narrow for a car.

It opened into a semi-circular parking area leading to the front door of the farmhouse. They waited. How long would Ronnie be? Laura could hear her heart thump as they stood in silence staring at the gloomy edifice.

Then they heard him.

'Come on out Brandon,' he shouted from round the other side of the building.

They ran towards the house making for the bay window to the left of the front door.

The curtains were drawn as they had been before. Laura pressed her face to the window, her hands cupped either side of her eyes the better to see into the darkness. She focused.

Yes. The slack cord was still lying on the window ledge.

Frank pushed on the top of the frame.

It opened a few inches, creaking like the timbers of a storm torn galleon. It seemed deafening, but it was nothing compared to the noise that started in the yard.

'I've got a shotgun,' Brandon Glover shouted.

A loud clatter of smashing glass from the direction of the sunroom covered the creaking as Frank opened the window higher.

'Fancy a spot of pheasant shooting?' Ronnie's bellow hid the screech of rusty metal rings on a metal pole as Laura pulled one curtain aside.

She clambered in. Wooden floorboards groaned as Frank followed. At the far end of the room was a closed door under which a small amount of light filtered. They got their bearings. A musty dining room filled with heavy oak furniture.

'Keep in to the side of the house Jim.' They heard Ronnie shout to Jervis. 'I've got him in my sights.'

Laura felt sure Ronnie was saying it for her benefit. She tried to picture where he might be hiding. Could he see Brandon? Was he in the sunroom…Or in the kitchen next to it? It was guesswork, but all she knew was that now was their chance to search upstairs. She pointed at the ceiling. Frank nodded and they crept past the table to the door.

It led to a narrow hallway. Directly ahead was a steep flight of stairs carpeted in aged dark red Axminster. Laura mounted the first step. It sagged under the weight of her tread. Did anything in this house not creak?

Brandon was shouting at Ronnie, threatening to call the police. Ronnie answered back.

'You know you wouldn't. D'you think they'd fall for that lot in the barn being family pets? Come off it Brandon. They'd have you and your missus banged up before you could say Lincolnshire Poacher.' Ronnie let out a raucous cackle.

Laura wondered how he knew the cheese. Either way he was doing his best to cover for them.

They reached the landing undetected. Light from outside illuminated a window in front of them. They looked out onto the yard. Directly below, the sunroom was in darkness. Ronnie and Brandon's voices were close now.

'Breaking and entering. Threatening me and my wife with a firearm? D'you think they're going to bother with a few puppies?' Brandon countered.

'Talking of dogs, where's my secret weapon Jim? Where's Pancake. Send her in. Watch your ankles Brandon, she's got teeth like razors.' Ronnie couldn't keep this up indefinitely.

Laura opened a door to her right. It was a child's bedroom. She lifted the valance on the single bed. Behind her Frank threw open a cupboard. Ronnie had temporarily ceased his banter. The house was deathly quiet.

They crept to the room opposite. A bathroom. Lino on the floor. Nowhere to hide.

They carried on down the landing to another closed door. It was another single bedroom. A cat sidled off the bed and ran out.

'I'm in position now Jim,' they heard Ronnie shout. 'You stay where you are. Wait for my signal.'

'A-OK,' Jervis shouted back. 'I've got the flares.'

Back on the landing there was only one more door. It was at the end. Laura turned the knob. Pushed the door open. It hit something and bounced back at her. She put a hand out to stop it and ran in with Frank behind her.

A double brass bed took up most of the space in the middle of the room. Laura was halfway round it heading towards a cupboard and a chest of drawers that she could see in the gloom on the far side, when Frank let out a long low moan.

Laura turned. Pam Glover had come out from behind the door. She was hitting Frank with a poker. She held it above her head with one hand, about to strike again.

'Oh no you don't,' Laura threw her crook to one side, climbed on the bed and launched herself at the woman. As she gripped her round the neck with both hands, Laura heard whining. Then Pam began to choke. Trying to pull Laura off using only one hand, she dropped the poker. It clanged to the floor.

'Shut the door Frank,' Laura said.

The door clicked. Frank got hold of Pam around the waist.

'Push her down,' Laura urged.

'Just trying to recall the move,' he said. As he tussled with her, Pam toppled sideways. She let go of the thing she was holding under her other arm. It fell to the floor.

Laura heard more whining. She let go her grip of Pam's neck. Pam yelled. Frank put his hand over her mouth, wrestling her to the floor. Laura picked up a pillow. She threw it to Frank who held it over Pam's head.

Between Pam's muffled moans Laura heard scratching. There was something by the door. She strained her eyes.

It was a pug; a fawn pug. She heard more whining. The sound was so familiar…

'Parker,' she called out, jumping off the bed.

But the pug carried on scratching.

'It's not him,' she said.' But he's here somewhere, I know it.'

'Help me tie this woman up,' Frank said, still grappling with Pam. 'And I need a proper gag.'

Laura took another pillow. Removed the case. Pam tried to cry out as Frank stuffed part of it in her mouth.

'Jesus,' he moaned. 'She's bitten my hand. Get that dressing gown.' He nodded in the direction of the door.

Laura lifted the dressing gown and a pair of striped pyjamas off the peg.

She took the cord from the dressing gown and handed it to Frank who tied the gag in place.

After securing Pam's legs with the pyjama bottoms, they bound her hands behind her back with the top. Then Laura knelt down beside Frank. She helped him roll Pam under the bed. As she tossed another pillow in the direction of Pam's head, Laura noticed the pug. It had given up scratching and was sitting by the door.

'We need to let Ronnie know what's going on.' Laura blocked her senses from the sound of its whining.

'We can't,' Frank said. 'Not while Brandon's in the house.'

'Unless we disarm him...' Laura picked up her crook. 'My guess is he's in the kitchen,' she continued. 'I'm sure there was one window that faced into the yard but wasn't part of the sunroom.'

They shut the pug in the bedroom with Pam and crept to the top of the stairs, from where they could hear Ronnie.

'OK Brandon, we've got back-up,' he shouted. 'Boys, in positions; wait for my command.'

Whatever Ronnie had in mind, it was now or never.

Gripping the banister rail in one hand, her crook in the other, Laura followed Frank down the stairs. They were about to head towards what they thought was the kitchen, when they heard Brandon call out in a harsh whisper.

'Pam, is that you? Get me a cushion.'

They turned. Peered round the corner down the passage.

Visible in the light emanating from outside, Brandon was lying in the opening of the back door, legs splayed, a shotgun pointing into the sunroom.

From outside Ronnie shouted, 'Right boys, we're going in.'

Brandon cocked the gun.

The click of the safety catch set something off in Laura's brain. Adrenalin coursed through her veins. She turned the stick round in her hands and with the deer antler handle facing forwards, rushed at Brandon raining blows down on his prone figure.

He raised himself to his knees. The gun was swinging in her direction. She hit him on the back of the neck. He fell back, the gun still in his hands pointing back in the direction of the sunroom. He was trying to inch forward when Frank landed on his legs.

'Now I remember, that's how you do it,' Frank said, as Laura hurled herself on top of Brandon's upper body, flattening him to the floor.

'Ronnie,' she shouted. 'We've got him.'

Pinned down, he struggled and managed to free his arm. A shot fired out. The smell of cordite filled the room.

Laura picked up the crook at her side. She hit him again. His head fell forward, but his finger still on the trigger, loosed the second barrel as Ronnie burst through the sunroom door.

Ronnie cried out, he's got me in the foot,' and fell to the floor swearing.

Brandon managed to raise his head. 'I'll finish you off later,' he said.

'Oh no you won't.' Laura dug her nails into the back of his neck and pressed his head into the ground.

He yelled out in agony.

'My Ronnie,' Strudel screeched, running in with Pancake. Jervis followed her with three men close behind him. One of them turned on the light.

'Who are they?' Laura asked.

'His truck drivers,' Jervis said. 'When they came back to the yard, Ronnie showed them what was in the barn. He persuaded them to join us.'

'Get me some cloths,' Strudel cried out, bending over Ronnie's blood-spattered trainer.

'I'll call an ambulance,' one of the drivers said.

Ronnie grunted. 'Hold off on that, I'm only peppered. It's my bad leg anyway. Help Lady Boxford and the Canon.'

The other two drivers edged Laura and Frank out of the way, as they took up positions on top of their boss. Brandon grunted and let go of the gun.

'We need rope,' Frank said, pulling it to one side.

'Dog lead any help?' Jervis offered, undoing it from Pancake's collar.

'It's a start,' one of the drivers said. 'But we need more.'

Laura ran into the kitchen. She threw open the drawers of an oak dresser standing adjacent to the sink and found a pair of scissors and a selection of tea towels. She ran back, gave the towels to Strudel before heading into the yard where she cut down the washing line.

Frank and the drivers started binding Brandon, as Jervis stuffed his mouth with a tea towel Strudel wasn't using on Ronnie's foot.

Leaving them to the task, Laura headed back to the kitchen. There was something she'd seen on the shelf of the dresser.

In between a wooden tea caddy and a cream jug lay a dog's collar. Laura picked it up. She felt the supple leather; ran her fingers over the brightly coloured Masai beadwork. Held it to her nose; inhaled the scent.

'Parker,' she yelled, running out of the kitchen. She checked the downstairs rooms again. She shone her torch into the under-stair cupboard. In the far corner, a pair of eyes gleamed in the darkness. She bent down. It was a black pug, frightened and shaking, curled up behind the hoover. She left the door open, ran upstairs taking steps two at a time and reached the landing. Now she knew where he must be.

Opening the door of the main bedroom she flicked on the light. The pug scampered out and ran down the passage. She could hear Pam Glover moaning under the bed.

'Parker,' she called.

From the far side of the bed she heard a short plaintive whimper. She ran round. Beside her was a chest of drawers. She got down on her knees and pulled out the bottom drawer.

Chapter 34

Parker looked up at her with his big black saucer eyes and his tail gave a little flap as he tried to move, but his feet were tied together, and he had a muzzle on.

Laura picked him up and cradled him in her arms. She kissed his head as she removed the muzzle. Instantly his whine grew stronger. That whine she knew so well. She had been right all along; she'd heard it in the chip shop.

'Oh Parker,' She threw the muzzle to one side and stroked his head as he licked her face.

Then she put him on the floor and untied his legs. He jumped up at her.

He was safe, unharmed. Picking him up again, she got up. She walked back towards the door and was about to leave when she had a second thought. She turned to the bed, lifting the valance. As Pam let out a faint groan, Laura put Parker down. She pulled away the pillow hiding Pam's head and removed the gag.

'Parker,' Pam croaked.

To Laura's utter consternation Parker trotted forward and licked the woman's face.

Laura called him. He gave Pam a second look and returned to her.

'He likes me, honest he does,' Pam said.

Laura picked him up, holding him close. 'Why did you do it?' she asked.

'It was Brandon.' Pam tried to edge herself out. 'When Jensen Darby first came here for the crisps adverts, Brandon saw money written all over him.'

With her free hand Laura took Pam's nearest trouser leg and pulled. When she was clear of the bed, Laura untied the pyjamas still binding her and helped her sit up. 'Go on,' she said.

Pam rubbed her wrists. 'Brandon found a man in Leicester who sold stolen dogs. They did a deal. Said between them they'd make thousands. He got us various Dachshund bitches and the two pug dogs.' Pam arched her shoulders. 'Then Brandon found out who Jensen's dad was and where he came from.' She made a choking cough. 'He became obsessed with getting Parker.'

'So he got his sister Sally to steal him?'

'Sally didn't steal him, although she knew Brandon was planning it. He was promising them all sorts, new fryers and the like, to keep them on board. No, it was Brandon that went to Wellworth Lawns. He knew the layout from delivering there. He found out your movements from his other sister Val, who was in with your best friend.'

'Venetia?'

'Val didn't mean any harm. When Brandon was getting information out of her, I don't think she realized what she was saying until it was too late.'

'So he knew where to wait for Parker?'

'It didn't all go to plan the night it happened. Brandon had dropped in at The Blue Dolphin to pick up some scampi – Sally had told him about Parker's love of seafood. It was pure chance you'd been there earlier. But the fact that Parker had probably already had plenty of scampi meant Brandon needed something extra to lure him with. He got a tub of crabmeat from the supermarket, said it smelled stronger than Bryan's crabsticks. Then he went and hid in the bushes. Parker fell for it good and proper. Brandon caught him, put a canvas bag over his dear little head…' Pam looked at Laura, tears in her eyes. 'But I loved Parker,' she said. 'You can see he's not frightened of me. None of them are. They're frightened of Brandon. I only tied Parker up earlier 'cos Brandon made me. He said Parker's not like the others; he's got attitude; barks all the time.'

'Maybe it is all your husband's fault,' Laura said. 'But you have no idea of the grief you have caused.'

Pam began to cry as in the distance they heard a police siren. 'I'm so sorry, please forgive me,' she said.

With Parker in her arms, Laura stepped over Brandon's legs. He was propped up in the doorway to the sunroom, hands behind his back, scowling at Jervis who was applying an ice compress to Frank's head. Seated thus, his arm outstretched as Strudel applied ice to his hand, Frank looked up.

'Parker!' He leapt to his feet, rushed forward and embraced Laura.

'I'm sorry, I didn't mean to bite you,' Pam said to him as she sat down on the floor next to her husband.

Brandon grunted at her.

'Oh shut up,' she said.

Laura looked around. 'Where is everyone?' she asked.

'I've sent the truckers home,' Jervis said. 'We've got their details.'

'What about Ronnie?'

'He's gone,' Jervis said. 'He had to return Pancake and the van.'

'You mean he's walked back to the caravan site?'

'I told him, you will have to see a doctor,' Strudel said. 'But he said it is a few pieces of shot that's all.

The police interviews turned into a protracted affair even though Brandon's lies were thin. He said he'd been gifted Parker to aid him in the scientific research he was conducting into the cause of safe canine interbreeding to eliminate current defects in certain breeds. It sounded like he'd been talking to Gwendoline Shackleton, until Jervis pointed out there'd been an article about just such a programme in the Sunday papers. Brandon threw Ronnie in the mix and said he was the one the police should be after.

'I shot him in the leg,' he said. 'He shouldn't be hard to find.'

Jervis and Frank then prevaricated on the nature of the wound until Strudel started to get cross and Laura took her to one side to explain it was a ruse, giving Ronnie more time to get away.

They were allowed to go after Brandon and Pam were taken away for further questioning. But then Laura refused to leave until the RSPCA arrived and she was sure all the dogs and puppies were taken care of.

'I think we've missed supper at The Dark Horse,' Frank said.

'There's a 24-hour MacDonald's just off the ring road, a policeman offered.

Chapter 35

It had come as a bit of a revelation some weeks later when Venetia had recognized a photograph of Brandon Glover with Jensen Darby that Laura had inadvertently left on her desk. It was a promotional shot for the crisp company that she had found in Brandon's kitchen and taken in case it was needed for evidence.

'I know this man,' Venetia said, turning to Laura and Frank who were sitting on the sofa with Parker asleep between them. 'Who is he?' she continued. 'I met him one afternoon here in the gardens at Wellworth Lawns. We got into conversation. He asked me about you and Parker. I presumed he was a friend of yours.' She picked up the photograph. 'Then I saw him again that day in Woldham when I had the accident. Goodness, I'd forgotten all about that. I waved at him. I'm sure he recognized me.'

Laura felt the blood drain from her face.

'That's quite a coincidence,' Frank said. 'He's only the man who stole Parker.'

Venetia stood in silence for what seemed an age to Laura.

'So perhaps I was pushed after all,' she eventually said. 'Quite a lucky escape wouldn't you say?' She turned to them.

Another silence ensued, but before Laura had time to formulate a reply Venetia put the photo down. 'That's as good a mystery as you'll see on Midsomer Murders,' she said with a laugh looking over to the clock on Laura's mantlepiece. 'Talking of which I must love you and leave you or I'll miss the next episode of House of the Dragon.'

It was almost as if Venetia's disclosure was too much for them to take in and both Laura and Frank were keen to change the topic of conversation after Venetia had gone.

'Let's discuss the merits of the burger versus fish and chips,' Laura suggested.

Their visit to the well-known fast-food chain had also been a revelation, but of a very different kind. Frank had professed a Damascene conversion to the chicken nugget.'They were divine,' he said, closing his eyes as he remembered.

To please him, Laura agreed. 'Although I could never tell Alfredo that,' she said. The piece de la resistance for her had been the little carton of sweet and sour sauce.

'But then again you can't beat a nice piece of battered cod and more importantly,' she continued. 'It was not a success with Parker.'

'I think he was overcome by events. He simply lost his appetite,' Frank said.

'Even so, I'm pleased we've discovered "The Fish Shack." Their scampi are every bit as good as...'

'Don't let's be reminded,' Frank said.

Brian and Sally Bowman and Sally's sister Val were under investigation for their part in Parker's abduction. In the meantime, The Blue Dolphin remained closed.

'To change the subject,' Frank said.

'Something we are getting good at…'

'I've a proposition for you,' Frank continued ignoring her sarcasm.

'Not that again?'

'I'm not suggesting marriage, but life's short and Jervis and Strudel have convinced me that co-habiting is just as much of a commitment. I'm sure I can make amends with the big man.' Frank raised his hand, one finger pointing to the ceiling.

Join forces with him on a permanent basis? Put up with all those Biblical quotes and pompous Classical references… Laura smiled. These were small considerations when weighed against his generous nature and compassion, to say nothing of his bravery. The eyebrows were another matter, but a quiet word with his barber should do the trick.

She was about to take his hand when the phone rang.

It was Jervis.

'We've heard from Ronnie,' he said.

Laura put the phone on speaker.

'He says he's sorry he hasn't called earlier, but he's been a bit tied up,' Jervis paused. 'Well, they haven't actually tied him up in the prison hospital. He's on remand.'

'Where?' Laura asked.

'Long Lartin.'

'That's down the road from here. We must visit him.'

'It's category A,' Frank said.

Laura grasped Frank's hand. 'Why's he there?'

'Surely not the stolen funds?' Frank said. 'It must be a mistake. Is he there with his business associates?'

'Those who joined him in the heist of a financial institution?' Jervis said.

'Bank robbers?' Laura and Frank said in unison.

'It was some years ago.' Jervis said. 'Unfortunately, Ronnie had a gun.'

'Armed robbery?' Laura gasped.

''Fraid so. That's why he did the bunk to Spain. But he was lured back, a one off they said, but the police got wind of their activities. The sad thing is he was going to give his share of the money to an orphanage he's been supporting recently. He said meeting Frank had changed his life.'

'He truly is a saint, and the sole reason I have Parker back.' Laura knew it was over the top. She wondered about her moral compass.

Thinking Frank would take a different approach, she glanced in his direction.

'Good for Ronnie,' he said and winked at her.

'Oh Frank!'

Her exuberance was infectious. It woke Parker. He leapt at Frank, licking his face.

'Steady,' Frank said.

Laura wiped the saliva off with a handkerchief. She kissed his cheek then patted Parker. What could be better than to have him and this good man beside her?

Printed in Great Britain
by Amazon